"Unusual and absorbing... Regency readers looking for something new and fantasy fans looking for a light romance will find this splendid crossover beguiling."

—*Publishers Weekly* Starred Review

"Mystical and highly amusing... I was completely enthralled."

—*Fresh Fiction*

"Full of spirit, emotion, and love for the two main characters... Falkner writes a good story."

—*Long and Short Reviews*

"Magical, humorous, sexy... touches your heart and makes your skin heat up."

—*BookLoons*

"The story is ripe with magic, hot with steamy scenes, and paced beautifully with its smooth writing style."

—*Yankee Romance Reviewers*

"I laughed, I cried, I fell in love with the characters. *A Lady and Her Magic* took all of the elements I love in the historical romance genre, splashed it with a huge dose of magic, and left me wanting more!"

—*Bitten by Paranormal Romance*

The Magic of "I Do"

TAMMY FALKNER

sourcebooks
casablanca

Copyright © 2013 by Tammy Falkner
Cover and internal design © 2013 by Sourcebooks, Inc.
Cover design by Aleta Rafton
Photography by Jon Zychowski
Typeset by Joanna Metzger
Models: Danielle Day and Dylan Solon/Agency Galatea

Published by Sourcebooks Casablanca, an imprint of Sourcebooks, Inc.
P.O. Box 4410, Naperville, Illinois 60567-4410
(630) 961-3900
FAX: (630) 961-2168
www.sourcebooks.com

Printed and bound in the United States of America
VG 10 9 8 7 6 5 4 3 2 1

For Jane Charles—this book wouldn't exist without you. And for my parents, Glenn and Rebecca Switzer, who are at the root of every love story I've ever written.

Unpardonable Errors

1. Never let a human adult see you in faerie form.
2. Never let your dust fall into the hands of the untrained.
3. Never share the existence of the fae.
4. Never use your magic to cause harm.
5. ~~Never, ever fall in love with a human.~~

One

A FAERIE WITHOUT MAGIC WAS ABOUT AS USELESS AS A carriage without a horse. If Claire Thorne had known that this would be her reward for trying to save her sister from the dangerous Duke of Robinsworth, she never would have gotten involved in her sister's mission. She would have stayed at home. The land of the fae was so much more comfortable than the land where others resided.

Claire refused to look at her abductor. She refused to acknowledge his presence, although he did have her magic dust. It was in his pocket at that very moment. Despite the fact that she'd warned him it could explode in untrained hands, he'd taken it with no hint of hesitation. And now he refused to give it back. Claire lifted her chin and stared out the coach window. If anyone had told her a sennight ago that Lord Phineas would take her hostage, she would have laughed in his face. Yet here she was, at his mercy.

"Oh, blissful silence," he said. He must have said

it to himself, because he certainly couldn't be talking to her.

"You really should return my dust to me before it does you harm." She didn't look at him as she talked. She continued to stare at the changing landscape. They'd left behind the bustle of Mayfair and were headed toward... nowhere, it appeared.

"And just what kind of harm might a little bottle of shimmer do to me?" He looked much too composed.

"It could explode and blow off an arm." She finally turned to look toward him and found him grinning at her unrepentantly. That man had a smile that could stop a lady's heart. Though it had no effect on hers. Well, almost no effect. His sparkling blue eyes made him look impertinent enough to annoy her to no end.

He held out his hand and appraised his arm with a critical eye. "I can live without an arm." Lord Phineas swiped a lock of hair from his forehead and lowered his arm back to his side. He arched a golden brow at her as though taunting her to continue her threats. He hadn't seen threats yet. Just wait until she turned him into a toad. Or a pig so that his outside could reflect his inside.

Claire let her gaze roam up and down his body slowly. "It might blow off something you use on occasion." Her eyes stopped at his lap. He fidgeted in his seat. "It's really quite volatile in the hands of the untrained."

That wasn't true. Not in the least little bit. But he didn't need to know that. In his hands, the dust was useless. Just shimmery flecks of shiny things he didn't understand. In her hands, however, it was quite useful.

If she wasn't afraid to commit one of the Unpardonable Errors—never use your magic to do harm—she would take a chance and wrest it from his possession. But if she had the dust in her hands right at that moment, she would use it to harm him. In a most satisfying way.

She forced herself into a casual shrug. "Take a chance. Blow off an appendage. Perhaps you'll be lucky and it'll be the smallest one. One you probably don't get to use much."

His smile vanished. "I can assure you there's nothing small about my appendage."

She grinned. "That's not what *she* said..." She left the taunt dangling in the air. His face flushed. She must have touched a sore spot. But since he was holding her hostage, he deserved to be just as uncomfortable as she was.

❧

How the devil could a faerie be aware of his problems with his mistress? Katherine had only left him a few weeks before. It wasn't his fault that she'd spread a bit of a rumor about his prowess in the bedroom. One that was *completely* unfounded upon reality. He narrowed his eyes at Miss Thorne. "Are your people omniscient?"

She didn't answer. She simply turned to look out the window again. Blast and damn. The woman was already driving him toward Bedlam and he'd only had her in his possession for a few hours. His brother, Robin, would owe him dearly for this. Very dearly.

The carriage hit a rut in the road and she bounced in her seat. She uttered a most unladylike oath as her head bumped the roof of the carriage. "Beg your pardon?" he asked. He cupped a hand around his ear. "I didn't quite hear that."

"If I'd meant for you to hear it, you would have heard it." She adjusted her skirts, settling back more heavily against the squabs. The bounce had left her looking a bit disheveled, with a strawberry blond curl hanging across her forehead. She blew the lock of hair with an upturned breath.

She really was quite pretty if one could get over the shrewish behavior. Her body was tall and willowy, her limbs long and graceful. Her heart-shaped face would probably be beautiful if she ever graced it with a smile.

"Just where are we going?" she asked. She still didn't look at him. She gazed out the window with the countenance of someone who had the weight of the world upon her shoulders.

"My house in Bedfordshire."

Her shoulders stiffened and then she exhaled deeply.

"And just what recommends such a place?"

"It has bars on the windows and heavy locks on the doors." It didn't. But she didn't have to know that.

"It will take more than bars and windows to keep a faerie under lock and key." She sniffed and raised her nose in the air.

"Then thank God there are ropes aplenty. I will tie you to my side if I must. I did promise Robin I'd take care of you." That was a bit of a long and sordid tale, and he still didn't understand the half of it. "Pray tell me how you people came to exist."

She arched a delicate brow at him. "The same way you did." Her face flushed scarlet. "Do you really need me to tell you about reproduction?"

Damn her hide. He didn't need her to explain anything about reproduction. This lady knew how to jab him where it hurt, though. He would have to take great care with her. He grinned slowly and leaned forward. "Please do. If you're lacking anything in the telling of how babes are made, I'll fill in the blanks for you. Certainly, you have questions about it."

"Should any pressing questions arise, I'll be sure to let you know." She looked back out the window. Damn, he hoped that Robin finished up his business soon so he could free the harpy.

"How long do you plan to keep me there?"

"As long as it takes for Robin to finish his business." The sooner, the better.

"I'm certain he's done by now. So we can turn around and go back to the city." She looked quite pleased by that idea. A smile tipped her lips and the beauty of it nearly took Finn's breath away.

"He'll send word when he's done. I'll set you free not a moment before."

She laughed lightly, and the sound raked over his skin like silky fingertips in the night. "Only an idiot would think he can keep a faerie confined." She snorted lightly. It was a most unladylike noise, but he found himself biting back a grin at the sound.

Finn leaned over and looked out the window at the cloud-filled sky. If he couldn't keep her confined, the inclement weather would. Unless he was mistaken, the snow would begin to fall before they reached their destination. Then she would be as confined by the elements as she was by him. Perhaps he wouldn't have to tie her to him. He'd have to wait and see.

Two

ROBIN HAD SENT A MESSENGER TO THE HOUSE TO ready it for company before he'd left for... wherever it was he'd gone. But that didn't help Finn at the moment. Evidently, they'd arrived before the messenger did. None of the staff greeted them at the door. Where the devil were they? Mr. Ross should at least be nearby. He never left his post. And Mrs. Ross, the cook-housekeeper, should have been there to greet them as well. Blast and damn. Finn moved to pull off his gloves but changed his mind. It was damn cold in the house. And dark. And empty.

"Hullo," he called. His voice echoed around the empty foyer.

"Looks like no one is home. Let's head back to London," Miss Thorne chirped. She started back toward the door.

"Something is wrong," Finn murmured to himself. "Wait here," he muttered as he started toward the kitchen. Certainly someone would be in the kitchen. But that room was empty as well. "Where the devil is everyone?"

"It appears as though your house isn't quite ready for company," Miss Thorne said, a satisfied smile on her face. "I believe we should make the trip back before the weather gets any worse."

Just then, the back door opened and a tall man stepped through it. He had an apple clenched between his teeth and bit into it viciously. He stopped short when he saw Finn and Miss Thorne standing there. "Beg your pardon," he said around the mouthful of apple. He held up one finger as he chewed and swallowed so hard that Finn could hear the gulp across the room. "My lord," he finally croaked out. He bent at the waist, and that was when Finn finally recognized him.

"Benny?" Finn asked. That man with shoulders as broad as the doorway couldn't possibly be Benny Ross, the son of Mr. and Mrs. Ross. The last time he'd seen Benny... He couldn't remember the last time.

"Yes, my lord," the young man said. "It's a brisk day, isn't it?"

If brisk meant cold enough to freeze a man in his tracks, yes, it was. "Where are your parents?" Finn asked. "Did you receive the notice that I would be arriving?"

"Yes, my lord. We received it. That's why I'm here. Papa took a fall down a flight of stairs a few days ago." He held up a hand when Finn began to protest. "Don't worry. He's going to recover. Just got a nasty bump on the head and a sprained ankle. He'll be right as rain in no time."

"And Mrs. Ross?" Finn asked. Certainly she was on the premises.

"She has refused to leave Papa's side."

This wasn't good. Not good at all. He had a house

with no servants. An offended faerie and a house with no servants.

"That settles it," Miss Thorne chirped. "We'll be going back to London." She waved at Benny and said, "It was nice meeting you."

Benny looked to Finn for confirmation. "You'll be leaving, then?"

Benny looked much too happy about that. "No," Finn sighed. "We'll be staying."

"I was about to say, you don't want to get caught in this storm." Benny parted the kitchen curtains to look out. "It looks to be a nice one."

"Is there anyone else who can come and take care of the house? One of your sisters, perhaps?" If Finn wasn't mistaken, Benny had five sisters, all of whom were older than he was.

Benny flushed. "Oh no, my lord. Papa suggested that, and Mama said it wasn't a good idea. What with you being a bachelor and all."

Mrs. Ross thought he would defile one of their daughters? He shrugged. One of them was quite attractive.

"But I'll be here for you. Mama sent a cold lunch. And I'll go back and get the evening meal before the storm sets in fully." He looked quite pleased with himself. He pointed toward the front door. "Shall I go and take care of the horses?"

"Build a fire, first, will you?" It was growing colder by the second. Even the kitchen, which was always hot as blazes, was cold enough to make his face numb. "In the sitting room, the library, and the bedchamber."

Benny's brow rose. "One bedchamber, my lord?"

Finn nodded. "Yes, just one."

৩৯

One bedchamber? Was the man daft? There was no possible way Claire was going to share a bedchamber with him. "Have you lost your senses?" she hissed as Benny stalked out of the kitchen toward the front of the house. "I will not share a bedchamber with you."

"I'm afraid you don't have a choice, Miss Thorne," Lord Phineas drawled. "Trust me, the idea of it doesn't settle well with me, either."

He didn't like the idea of sharing a bedchamber? She highly doubted that. A small part of her was momentarily offended by his comment. She'd been told she had striking features. "Why don't you want to share a bedchamber with me?" she asked impulsively. She wanted to bite the words back as soon as they left her mouth.

"I tend to favor a warm bed partner, Miss Thorne. Not a cold one." He stalked past her and into the corridor.

Her offense at his lack of interest was absolutely absurd. But it niggled at her more than a little. She shoved the thought aside and forced her attention back to the facts at hand. "I think we should go elsewhere. At least an inn would have staff."

"They have staff where you come from, Miss Thorne?" He continued down the corridor toward… Where was he going? "In your land, Miss Thorne?" he prompted.

Of course. Her land was structured much like his, except hers was prettier. And in hers, things tended to be a little more fanciful. "My grandfather is one of the Trusted Few, my lord. Do not doubt my origins."

"Trusted Few?" he parroted, his brow quirked at her. A grin tugged at his lips. Why was that amusing?

"The governing body in our world. Much like your aristocracy. The House of Lords."

"Only you have a house with a trusted few?" He chuckled. "Certainly, you do." He finally came to a grand room lined with books, which must have been his library. Claire gazed at the overstuffed shelves. One of her favorite pastimes was reading, and she nearly salivated at the thought of looking through all the books. She forced her attention back to him. "When will we be leaving?"

"When Robin sends words that his business is concluded." He dropped into a chair behind his desk and began to sort through a stack of correspondence. "Is Ramsdale really your father?"

"No." She didn't say more than that. Just the single word.

"Robin says differently."

"We were raised by our grandparents." She turned and pretended to peruse the shelves. Talking of her parents still hurt a little. She had never met them. She'd been raised with the fae, along with her brother Marcus and her sister Sophia. There were never any parents in their lives until Sophia stumbled across the Ramsdales. They'd lived in London all her life, right where she could have found them, if she'd only known they existed. Claire still hadn't met them. Nor did she plan to. Nor did she plan to meet her human brother and sisters. The children her parents had kept.

"Would you prefer that I call you Miss Thorne?

Or shall we throw out all social constraints and call one another by our first names, Claire?" he asked, a crooked grin lifting the corners of his lips.

"Miss Thorne will do nicely." she corrected.

"You may call me, Finn, *Claire*." He was taunting her. She was well aware of it. And he was enjoying it.

Benny bustled into the room with an armful of wood. "My lord?" he asked quickly. Lord Phineas motioned with an impatient hand toward the hearth. Benny began to stack wood in the grate and lit it with a quick flick of his flint.

"There," he said, dusting his hands together. "I'll take care of the bedchamber next." Lord Phineas nodded, obviously distracted by the contents of his correspondence.

"Thank you, Benny," Claire said. The boy flushed at her praise.

"I put your things in his lordship's bedchamber."

"That will be all, Benny," Lord Phineas barked.

Benny bowed to her quickly and fled the room.

"You need to clear up the boy's misconception."

"What misconception would that be?" He looked up at her, his blue eyes flashing.

"The lad is under the impression we'll share a bedchamber."

Lord Phineas stood up slowly. He crossed the room to stand in front of her and bent down by her ear, where he said softly, "My darling, we *are* going to share a bedchamber."

Three

IF MISS THORNE DREW HER BOTTOM LIP BETWEEN HER teeth even once more, Finn would feel led to kiss it. She'd been nibbling on that lip for more than an hour, ever since she'd opened the pages of *Northanger Abbey*. She'd nearly knocked him over in her quest to retrieve it from his library when she saw its shiny, red spine faced out on his overpacked shelves. Mrs. Ross liked to read romantic novels. That was the only reason it was there. He certainly wasn't going to read it. But Claire looked enraptured. About as enraptured as he was with her.

She was a prickly little thing, all backbone and iron. But spending the day with her sharp tongue and that curl that kept falling from the upsweep of her hair was nearly maddening. She had a retort for every comment he made, and it had become something of a sport to antagonize her.

"He dies at the end," Finn said without looking up at her.

Her quickly indrawn breath let him know she'd heard him. "He does not," she cried, her breath catching in her throat. A grin tugged at the corners of his lips. He couldn't help it. She was too much fun to tease. She picked up one of the many books she'd piled beside her and flung it toward his head. Finn ducked and let it hit the wall behind him.

"That wasn't very nice," he replied, making a show of straightening his hair after she'd ruffled it.

"I am not a nice person," she said, ducking her head back into the pages of her book.

"Would you like to play chess?" He didn't know why he asked that. It was a foolish question. But he was her host, after all, and he was bored. Not to mention that if he had to look at her silk-clad toes peeping from beneath the hem of her dress for one more moment, he would go completely mad.

She'd lifted her feet to rest on the settee and laid her open book against her bent knees. Her slippers lay beside her where she'd kicked them off her dainty little feet. It was much too comfortable of a pose. His mistress had never even gotten this comfortable in his presence, and he'd very nearly lived with Katherine, for God's sake.

Miss Thorne made a grunting noise in her throat.

"Was that a yes or a no?" he asked.

"What do you think?" she muttered, not looking up from her book.

"Cards? I could teach you to play vingt-et-un," he suggested. He tried not to sound hopeful.

She grunted in response.

"You're such a scintillating conversationalist."

She snorted. "Don't even pretend you want to talk to me."

"Heaven forbid I should want to interact with you."

"No doubt you'd love to interact with me. You haven't taken your eyes off me the whole night." She grinned down at her book. She turned the page.

He wasn't aware she'd noticed. But she was rather easy on the eyes. And the more comfortable she got, the more he liked looking at her. He could imagine her sitting there in her dressing gown. Or better yet—he could imagine her without her dressing gown. He'd done so more than once that night. He shifted in his chair.

She looked up and arched a brow at him. "Problem?" she asked.

He was getting hard and she chose that moment to look up? Of course, she did. Damn contrary female.

"Aside from the fact that you're a terrible conversationalist, no."

She went back to her book.

"How long do you plan to keep me here?" she finally asked, breaking the silence that hung about the room like a heavy blanket.

"Didn't we already discuss this?"

"I'd like to solidify my plans."

He'd like to solidify the palm of his hand across her arse. Preferably when it was bare. Finn crossed to the window and drew apart the curtains. The gardens behind the house were coated with a fine dusting of snow. "The snow has already started to cover the ground. So, even if Robin sent word, we'd probably not be ready to leave here for a few days. Benny said his mother thinks it's going to snow heavily."

"How would she know?" Claire's dark little brows drew together.

"She's older and wiser than you."

"Someone's growing surly." She shrugged and went back to her book. But then her head darted up. "If you're bored, you could give me my magic dust, and I could do some tricks to entertain you." She looked almost giddy at the idea.

"No."

"Why not?"

He patted his pocket, where the vial of dust was still safely hidden. "Do I look like an idiot?"

She tilted her head at him. "Well, as a matter of fact..." She blinked those innocent green eyes at him.

He wanted to strangle her and they had only been there for a few hours. What would it be like after a few days? He'd be ready to brave the weather just to hand her over to someone else to take care of her.

⁂

Claire watched closely as he poured himself another drink. He'd already had two glasses. And was pouring a third. Perhaps there was a chance she could get her dust back after all. He might lower his guard if he were foxed. She could only hope.

She looked back down at her book and forced herself to turn the page. She hadn't read a single word all afternoon. She'd been too busy studying his actions. He was a fidgety man who obviously had a hard time sitting still. He was also almost as observant as she was, if his keen gaze was any indication. More than once she'd felt the scorch of his hot glance.

"What would you be doing if you were at home?" A better question was probably *who* he would be entertaining. But she didn't dare ask that question.

He shrugged.

She closed her book and regarded him over her bent knees. "What are you drinking?"

He gazed into his glass for a moment. "Whiskey."

"Would you pour a glass for me?" She dropped her feet to the floor.

"Absolutely not."

She startled. "Well, that was rude."

"The last thing I need is an inebriated faerie on my hands."

She raised her feet back up onto the settee. "Well, the last thing you'd need is a personality," she murmured to herself.

He set his glass down with a clunk and glared at her.

"I didn't ask to be here," she reminded him.

"Nor did I." He continued to glare.

❧

She really was startlingly beautiful. When she kept her mouth shut. Unfortunately, she'd done that most of the afternoon, and now that the sun was setting, Finn realized how much of a predicament he was in. He had an irritated faerie, a pocketful of magic dust, and orders to keep her out of sight until Robin returned with Sophia from the land of the fae. It would be so much easier if Claire wasn't quite so comely. He could get used to looking at her.

Until she spoke, that is. The chit had a rapier-sharp tongue. "Can I have my dust? Please?"

She tried a smile that would melt a normal man's heart. Good thing he wasn't a normal man. "No."

"Fine," she murmured to herself as she looked

back down at her book. She began to twirl a lock of her hair around her finger. He wondered what it would feel like sliding across his own finger. He shook the thought away. It would get him nowhere. The lady was his brother's sister-in-law. A part of his brother's family. Robin would cut off Finn's stones and feed them to him if he even dared to think lascivious thoughts about her. But it was hard to think anything else.

The quick clip of footsteps in the corridor made Claire's head tilt to the side as she waited. Finn was somewhat startled when the round face of Mrs. Ross popped around the corner. "Just wanted to come by and be sure you don't need anything, my lord," she said as she brushed a hand over her hair to shake away the snowflakes that clung to her graying coiffure. "Did Benny get you settled in properly?"

"Mrs. Ross," Finn began smoothly. He was actually overjoyed to see her. The house felt a bit like a prison with its quiet corridors and cold kitchen. "How is Mr. Ross? Better, I hope?"

Mrs. Ross shook her head, her lips turning down in a grimace. "No better yet. I fear he has done more damage to his leg than he wants to admit." She looked at Claire and grinned. "Some men refuse to age gracefully."

Claire grunted and continued to read.

"Are you here to stay?" Finn asked, trying not to sound too hopeful.

"Unfortunately not. I just came to bring you a warm dinner and be sure you're all right." She eyed Claire inquisitively as she held up a basket of food.

The smell that emanated from it was enough to make Finn's mouth water. They'd had a lunch of fruit and cheese. "It's just some shepherd's pie and an apple tart for dessert."

Finn loved shepherd's pie. His stomach growled loudly. Mrs. Ross's laugh bounced around the room as she set the basket on a nearby table.

"I left Benny to bring in more wood for the fire. I don't want the two of you to freeze." Finn couldn't help but think he might freeze from the icy glare that emanated from Claire.

"Thank you, Mrs. Ross, for braving the weather," Claire said suddenly. Her voice was kind and smooth as warm honey on a summer day. Why didn't she ever talk to him like that?

"You're quite welcome, miss." Mrs. Ross nodded her head toward Claire. Claire dipped her head back into her book. "I hate that the two of you will be stuck here for so long."

"So long?" Claire croaked.

"I'm suspecting it'll be about a week before the snow clears enough to travel. By tomorrow, we'll be buried pretty deep." At least then he wouldn't have to worry about keeping Claire prisoner by any extraordinary means. The weather would do it for him. Even she wouldn't be stubborn enough to try to escape in the frightful weather.

Claire looked like she wished with all her heart that she could call out to Mrs. Ross and beg her to take her along with her when she left. But that would do her no good whatsoever. Benny stomped into the corridor and filled the hearth with more wood, causing it to crackle and pop as he tossed on more split logs. "That should hold you for the night."

"Did you stoke the fire in the bedchamber?" Finn asked.

"Yes, my lord. It should be nice and toasty by the time you're ready to retire."

Mrs. Ross looked as though she wanted to scold Finn for his choice in ladies. But she thankfully bit her tongue. The cook-housekeeper would never have to see Claire again. Let her think whatever she wanted. He was a libertine on the best of days. And on his worst.

She patted her son on the shoulder with a look of pride. "I'll send my Benny over tomorrow with some food." She clucked her tongue and looked around like she was forgetting something. "Have a good rest, then," she finally said, and she left without looking either of them in the eye. Benny trotted out behind her.

⚜

As Lord Phineas peeled back the cloth that covered the shepherd's pie, his stomach made a loud protest about all the time he was taking to smell the concoction. Claire had to admit that it smelled divine. And she was suddenly as hungry as he was. He cut a small wedge of the pie and placed it on a piece of china that Mrs. Ross had conveniently put in the basket. Then he pulled the rest of the pie over to his side of the table and sat down heavily.

"Wait a minute," she protested. "That pie is big enough to feed a family of eight. And you gave me one little sliver?"

"A lady who likes to eat?" he drawled, a grin tipping

the corners of his lips. "What a novel idea. Most women pick at their food." He cut a larger piece and put it on her plate.

"Thank you," she said begrudgingly as she sat down across from him at the small table in the corner of the library. He poured himself more of the amber liquid in his glass and raised it to his lips. He set it down and turned to pick up his napkin, which he'd dropped on the floor. Claire raised his glass to smell it. It smelled fairly harmless. By the way he was acting, she'd have to get him to drink a lot more of it before the night was over if she wanted to slip away. She brought his glass to her lips and took a sip, simply out of curiosity.

The liquor slid in a fiery trail down her throat, numbing her tongue and stealing her breath. Lord Phineas glared at her and took the glass out of her hand. "Do you listen to anything anyone tells you?"

"I asked you very nicely to pour one for me."

"And I said no." He spoke around a mouthful of shepherd's pie. He jabbed his fork toward her plate. "Eat."

Claire heaved a sigh as she took a bite of the meat and potato pie. It was nearly flavorless after the fiery burn of the liquor. She laid her fork to the side and picked his glass back up. If her dinner was going to be ruined, she might as well enjoy it.

He held out his hand and glared at her the way a governess might glare at a girl taking an extra biscuit from the tray during tea. That was immensely amusing and she laughed out loud. She wasn't quite certain why it was so hilarious, but it was. She just knew it was by the way she was laughing at herself.

"Give it to me." He clasped and unclasped his hand in her direction in a grasping motion.

"I bet you say that to all the girls." The corners of his mouth tipped in a grin.

"You are foxed." He sat back in his chair and ran a hand through his hair.

"Oh, I only had a little."

"It only takes a little."

"That's not what she said."

His face flushed. She offered his empty glass to him. "Did I drink all that?" A bubble rose from her belly and she made an unladylike sound. "Pardon," she said quickly, suddenly mortified. But the feeling only lasted for a moment. She put the glass in his hand. "I want my magic. What would you like in exchange?"

Four

CLAIRE ARCHED A PLAYFUL BROW AT HIM, HER GREEN eyes darker in the waning light of the room. They were rimmed in brown, flecked with gold, and green around the center. They were striking. Like limpid pools he could drown in if Finn wasn't careful of his footing. He poured himself a drink to replace the one she'd just downed. She looked longingly toward the glass. "Don't even think about it," he warned.

She lifted her elbow to the tabletop and rested her chin in the palm of her hand. A smile hovered around that pretty mouth. "You have no idea what I'm thinking about."

Her gaze traveled down his body. He suddenly knew what the courtesans felt like when men leered at them. It wasn't entirely unpleasant. "I would dare to wager on what you're thinking about."

She held her hands out to the side in a motion of surrender. "No need to wager. I'll just tell you. I was thinking about how handsome your arse is in those breeches. Why don't you stand up and spin around so I can take another look?"

Finn jumped to his feet. He had a sudden and confounded urge to cover his arse with his hands to keep her from looking at it. How had he gotten into this mess? A mere mention of his arse and how much she liked looking at it, and he was getting as hard as the tabletop. He would have to take drastic measures. He pushed his glass in her direction. "Here. Drink this." Soon she would pass out and then he could tuck her into bed and stand guard over her all night.

She drank the contents of the glass in one large swallow that was loud enough for him to hear. "That gets smoother and smoother the more I drink."

He filled one for himself and did the same. He could do no more than nod in response to her comment. His lack of the ability to speak wasn't a big problem. The chances of her remembering anything that she said tonight would be slim to none.

"Is it safe for the both of us to be foxed?" she whispered dramatically, her hand curved around her mouth as though she wanted to impart a secret.

He couldn't keep from smiling. He tried to be stoic and proper. And failed. Miserably. "Only one of us is drunk." *Thank God.*

She lurched to her feet in a quick motion that had her grabbing for the back of her chair. "Goodness," she breathed.

"You should sit."

"*You should sit.*" She mocked his tone. Poorly. But she didn't sit. She began to wander around instead. She ran her finger down a row of books on his bookshelf. Then she spun the globe on its stand beside his desk. She hitched her little bottom up to sit on the edge of his desk.

"Have you lost your mind?" He shot to his feet.

⤳

She would get to him. She was certain of it. But she wasn't at all certain how. He thought she was inebriated. And she had drunk a little bit much, but not as much as she pretended.

She forced herself to slur her words. "What? You told me to sit."

"I didn't mean on my desk."

She lifted one side of her bottom and looked down. "I don't think I'm hurting it."

He scrubbed at his forehead. Then he pointed toward the settee. "Go sit over there."

"Don't want to." She forced herself to hiccup. "I'm fine right here."

"You are going to regret this tomorrow."

"You're probably regretting having brought me here already."

"I certainly am." He glared at her a moment. Then he scooped her up in his arms and carried her to the settee. He tried to drop her onto the velvet surface, but she clung tightly to his neck when he would have dropped her. The result was that she tugged him down on top of her. He stilled. Completely.

His breath blew across the shell of her ear as he held himself suspended above her, one hand on the back of the settee and one stiff beside her. "You're playing with fire," he growled. Then he unlaced her arms from around his neck, shoved himself back, and sat down on the opposite end of the settee. "You certainly know how to ruin a good meal."

She turned into the corner of the settee and nuzzled her body into the edge. She was more foxed than she'd planned. She should probably go to bed and try a different tack tomorrow. That would be the safest thing to do.

"Such a spoilsport," she whispered. She closed her eyes and nuzzled farther into the settee.

He got up with a groan and went to pour himself another drink. She heard the clink of the glass against the edge of the decanter. Perhaps she would get her wish after all and would disarm him long enough to get her magic back.

❧

Finn set his glass to the side and glared across the room where she slept on the settee. He supposed he should do the gentlemanly thing and wake her so they could go to bed. He had no intention of sharing a bed with her. He planned to put her safely beneath the counterpane and settle himself in an oversized chair in front of the doorway. He could sleep that way. He'd spent many a night in that chair. One more wouldn't hurt him.

He walked across the room and looked down at her sleeping face. Damn, but she was pretty. Gorgeous, in fact. Her strawberry blond hair fell in loose ringlets around her neck. And her lightly colored lashes lay heavily against her cheeks. He was almost afraid to wake her. When he did, he would have to deal with that sharp tongue again. He sighed heavily and nudged her shoulder. "Claire," he said softly. She didn't budge. He held a finger beneath her nose, just to be certain she was still breathing. "Claire," he said a little more loudly. She still didn't move.

He groaned as he lifted her in his arms. "What are you doing?" she asked, her voice drowsy from sleep.

"Taking you to bed," he said softly. "Go back to sleep."

"All right," she sighed. She wrapped her arms tightly around his neck and snuggled deeper into his chest. He resisted the thought that she felt good in his arms. She was trouble. Trouble. Problems. Neither of which he needed.

Her breath blew across the sensitive skin of his neck and he held back an oath as he took the stairs carefully, turning sideways to avoid hitting her feet against the wall and into the doorway to the master chamber. A fire crackled in the hearth, but the room was dark. Soft shadows played across the walls from the flicker of the flames. Finn crossed to the side of the bed and was about to lower her to the feather ticking, but she suddenly moved in his arms and he lowered her to her feet instead. "Are you all right?" he asked as he steadied her.

"Fine," she said quickly. She yawned into her open palm, and Finn couldn't help but think of how endearing a sound that was. She was completely unreserved, and that was a rarity. She turned her back to him. "Can you help me with the fastenings?"

"Pardon?" he squeaked. She regarded him over her shoulder as a governess might an unruly child.

"Please?"

She didn't make any quips about the number of

women he'd undressed in his lifetime. Or say a word about the accommodations. She just held her hair to the side and presented her back to him. He steeled himself for a moment and then began to unfasten her dress. She couldn't sleep in it, could she? And he hadn't let her bring a maid. He supposed he had no choice.

The delicate skin of her shoulders was the first to appear. And he had to hold himself back from placing his lips on her freckles, one by one. He groaned low in his throat, a noise he didn't even know he could make. She looked over her shoulder at him, her eyes dark as night in the low light of the room. As he revealed the back of her chemise, his trousers became unbearably tight, and if she chanced to look at him now, she would get the surprise of her lifetime.

He wanted her unlike he'd ever wanted anyone. "Are you still foxed?" he asked as she spun around in his arms and began to shove her gown down over her hips.

"No." She looked him in the eye as she tugged the string at the neck of her chemise.

"What are you doing?" His voice crackled with strain.

"Getting ready for bed." She smiled a wicked smile at him. She was still drunk, no matter how much she didn't want to admit it. The vacancy in her gaze gave her away.

But then, all rational thought left his tiny little brain. The chemise slid down her body and landed in a heap on the floor. Her pert, puffy nipples were the same color as her lips. He didn't know which he wanted to kiss more. When she wore nothing but her stockings, she shoved his coat from his shoulders. And he let her. Like an idiot, he let her disrobe him. First, it was his waistcoat and his cravat. Then his shirt came over the top of his head. At any time, he could have stopped her. But he didn't.

She smiled softly as she ran her fingertips though the dusting of hair on his chest. Then her fingers trailed down his stomach, and she began to work the fastenings of his trousers. When she shoved them down, he stepped out of them and let her pull his boots off.

He'd had just enough to drink that her tug on his boots nearly toppled him. Her skin glowed in the low light of the room, and he reached out, grabbed her hips, and pulled her to him. "You're certain you're not foxed?"

She nodded and stepped onto her tiptoes, pressing her lips to his. He expected her lips to be hesitant, untried. But her tongue slipped past his teeth to tangle with his. He growled low in his throat and drew her naked body against his raging hardness. She gasped and stiffened. But she didn't stop the torturous assault on his lips. She was nearly as out of breath as he was when he finally lifted his head. But he only lifted it long enough to bend and take the tip of her breast into his mouth. She tasted sweet and hot, her hard nipple pebbling against his tongue.

A sound left her throat, breaking the shroud of silence in the room.

"Have you ever done this before?" he asked.

"Done what?" she asked as she sat down on the edge of the bed and scurried like a crab to the center. He crawled up after her, settling between her legs.

"This," he said, rocking his hardness against her softness.

She merely laughed and arched her hips toward him.

She wasn't an innocent. Thank God. He shoved forward, and it wasn't until a moment later when she cried out that he realized the big mistake he'd just made. He was foxed. She was foxed. And he'd just taken her innocence. He stilled inside her.

"So, I lied," she said, her breath hard against his ear, where she held tightly to his shoulders. Her arms trembled. Her whole body trembled. Her sheath trembled around his manhood.

Too late to turn back now.

Five

LORD PHINEAS FROZE ATOP HER AND CLAIRE HELD tightly to his shoulders. How the devil had she gotten into this predicament? One minute, she'd just wanted to get him out of his clothes so she could get her dust, and the next, she'd given her innocence to a human. *To one of them.* He wasn't even of her world.

"Don't move," he said, his lips tickling her forehead as he spoke. He pressed a kiss there, quite unexpectedly.

"How could I?" she breathed. "You're inside me."

"Yes, I am," he groaned, as he looked down at her from above. "I'm your first?" he asked.

"Not very clever are you?" she quipped. She tried to make a sound like a mocking laugh, but it came out more as a sob. A tear leaked from the corner of her eye. She hated that sign of weakness. And she hated it more when he moved to kiss it away.

"Why did you do this?" he asked. He was still hard as stone inside her, but the pain was easing a bit. She wiggled her hips beneath him. "Don't do that," he warned.

Perhaps if she kissed him, he wouldn't notice how

uncomfortably sober she suddenly was. She lifted her lips to his.

His lips were tender. He sipped at her lower lip like it was made of nectar. All the pain of his taking her innocence was suddenly gone, and he was hot and hard inside her. It didn't matter that he wasn't of her world. She'd never see him again after this night. "Be gentle with me," she whispered against his lips.

"In order to be any gentler, I'd have to be a damn eunuch."

She gasped as he pulled back, like he was going to withdraw. Claire wrapped her legs around his hips to hold him in place.

"Let me go, Claire," he warned.

"Not yet," she whispered. "Be still."

Claire hooked her feet behind his back, even though that simple gesture couldn't possibly hold him. He could get free any time he wanted. "What do you want?" he muttered.

Claire tugged with her feet against his buttocks, and he slid marginally deeper inside her. A groan left his throat as his arms began to tremble.

"Make it stop hurting," she said. "All of it." She wasn't sure if she referred to the parents she suddenly had but didn't want. He probably thought she meant the pain of losing her innocence. But she didn't mean that at all. Another tear slipped out of the corner of her eye.

Finn's head bent and he nuzzled his lips atop the rise of her breast, turning his head so that his cheek brushed the aching point of her nipple. Her nipple strained to reach him, hard and painful, neglected and wanting. She arched her back toward him. He took her nipple reverently between his lips, suckling her tender skin softly.

She stifled a sob of pleasure and moved her hands from his shoulders to sift through his hair. "Claire," he whispered.

"What?" she whispered back as his wicked, whiskey-scented breaths brushed her chest.

"Why?" he grunted as he shifted his hips ever so slightly between her thighs. His way was slickened by her own desire, and she ached for him to move.

"Don't worry. I won't fall in love with you," she said, as she pulled his bottom with her heels, making him move inside her.

The next move was his as he retreated. "I don't love you, either." His lips tugged a little harder at her breasts as he surged inside her, at once desperately soft and punishingly slow.

"I can never love you. It's forbidden."

"Thank God," he groaned as he hit some spot inside her that she didn't know existed. "You might not love me, but you will love what I can do for you."

"Prove it," she whispered. But he was already inching his hand down her body, sifting through her nether curls where he tugged lightly. His hand moved into her wetness and stroked across the heat of her as he filled her again.

An animalistic cry left her throat, as he groaned and pushed farther inside her, increasing his pace as his fingers lifted her higher and higher.

"What are you doing to me?" she whispered against his lips, her words broken and battered almost as much as she was.

"I'm not falling in love with you." His wretched, hot fingers stroked her higher and higher, as that part of him that filled her stroked her fire. Hotter and higher, hotter and higher she climbed, consequences be damned.

"Never," she repeated. He buried his face in the crook of her neck as his movement inside her became a torturous push and retreat. So pleasurable that it was nearly painful, her body promising to ignite and break into a million pieces.

"Come for me," he coaxed gently.

That was all it took to throw her over that impossible precipice. Pleasure swamped her as she clung to him. His fingers deftly and aptly toyed with her, wringing every last bit of pleasure from her body. And it was only when the pleasure met the point of pain that he began to tremble.

His hand slid down to her bottom, tipping her toward him, and he grew fuller inside her, bigger than she could have imagined. But somehow it felt right. She wasn't sure why or how, but she held him close as he shuddered, his pulsing inside her slow and sweetly painful, sending her to a place she'd never been as he met her at the top of that mountain of pleasure and hurled them both over it at the same time.

❦

Robin is going to kill me, Finn thought to himself. He's going to chop my head off. Or my manhood, whichever he can get to first. Perhaps he'll do both. Finn rolled to his back, and Claire tumbled into his side. His arm went around her as she rested her head on his chest. Her breathing was as choppy as his was, but her body was lax and sated. She felt soft and comfortable in his arms. Like she belonged there.

"Don't worry," she whispered. "I still don't love you."

He tugged her closer to him, and she threw a leg over his, settling comfortably into his side. He kissed her forehead, suddenly so exhausted there was no way he could keep his eyes open. "I don't love you either."

It wasn't until hours later that Finn reached across the bed to feel for Claire. Emptiness met his grasping hands. "Damn it," he cursed as he jumped to his feet. He dashed across the room to where he'd left the clothes he'd discarded so carelessly the night before. His clothes were gone. The vial of magic dust was gone. And so was Claire. He ran a hand through his hair. She was gone. Claire was gone. The evidence of her lost innocence the night before stained the bedclothes. What they had done wasn't gone. But she was nowhere to be found.

Six

CLAIRE BRUSHED HER HAIR BACK FROM HER FACE AND regarded herself closely in the looking glass. What the devil had she done? She searched her own face, looking for some sign that there was something wrong with her. Would anyone be able to tell? Would people know just by looking at her that she was no longer an innocent? She'd never be able to show her wings again, as they would be forever stained by her misdeeds. Even worse, would the fae know she'd had relations with one of *them*?

She scrubbed her face with the palm of her hand. Why on earth had she done that? Too much drink, too much opportunity, too few wits. She knew better. Look at what had happened with her mother. She'd been cast from the land of the fae, her wings stripped, never to return. Her fae children had been taken from her, and it was her own fault that she'd not been able to mother them. Her own stupid, stupid decisions were her downfall.

Claire gazed around the chambers where she was hiding and hoped that Finn slept soundly, at least long enough for her to gather her thoughts.

A rap at the window jerked her from her reverie. She looked out into the night and saw Ronald there at the second-story window. She crossed the room and thrust the window open. He jerked back but held on tightly. At less than three feet in height, the garden gnome had a tendency to bounce when dropped from great heights, so he had no fear of falling whatsoever.

Claire looked down at her chemise and pulled the string tightly. She crossed her arms in front of her breasts and glared at Ronald. "What are you doing here?" she asked.

He smiled sympathetically at her. "A better question would be what *you've* been doing here."

Heat crept up Claire's face. "You won't tell, will you?" she whispered, her voice cracking.

"Gather your thoughts and your things. The dawn wind awaits. As does your brother." He pointed down into the yard where Marcus stood. Her brother cupped his hand around his mouth and called softly to her. "You're needed at home, Claire."

"Give me a moment to dress," she said, holding up a single finger.

"Where's Lord Phineas?" Marcus called back.

"I imagine he's in his own bedchamber sleeping." She didn't look Marcus in the face. And the garden gnome made a noise in his throat. "Shut it," she snapped. Ronald simply shook his head at her.

"What's done in the dark always comes to the light," he said softly. His look was so sympathetic that it twisted Claire's gut.

"Why is the wind swirling tonight?" Claire asked, as she stepped behind a screen and began to don her clothes.

"Special circumstances," Ronald said.

The wind carried the fae back and forth from the land of the fae one night a month, on the night of the moonful. Tonight wasn't even near the full moon, so circumstances must be special indeed. "What has happened?"

"Dress, and Marcus will inform you." The gnome never held anything back. Claire's heart began to drum within her breast. She dressed as quickly as she could and then stepped softly toward the door. She opened it slowly, wincing slightly when the door squeaked. She tiptoed down the stairs, only stopping to put her slippers on at the door.

The wind was already swirling when she opened the front door and stepped out into the snow. Marcus held out a hand to her.

"What's wrong?" Claire asked. It was rare for the Trusted Few to allow the wind to swirl on a night like this.

"Grandfather has died," Marcus said. He inhaled deeply through his nose and exhaled out through his mouth to calm himself. "Your presence is required at home."

Claire laid a hand on her chest. If she didn't, it might just stop beating. Her grandparents had raised her and her brother and sister.

The wind began to swirl in earnest.

"Prepare yourself, because Lord and Lady Ramsdale are in the land of the fae, as well as Sophia's duke and his daughter."

Humans never entered the land of the fae. "It's forbidden," she bit out.

"So is falling in love with a human. But apparently, people do it anyway."

Just as Claire stepped aboard the moving wind, ready to be swept away to the land of the fae, the light flared to life in the bedchamber where she'd been with Finn. She looked at Marcus and said, "Idiots, the lot of them. I could never, ever fall in love with a human."

"There are worse things than falling in love," the garden gnome said quietly.

Claire chose to keep her retort to herself. Just as she would keep what had happened that night to herself. Forever.

Her mother tsked at her, and Claire made her face into a horridly mocking scowl.

"Your face could freeze like that," her mother warned.

Lady Anne, the six-year-old daughter of the Duke of Robinsworth, giggled into her cupped hand.

Lord Ramsdale—Claire's father whom she'd never laid eyes on until three months ago—dropped down beside her in the grass and nudged her shoulder with his. "Why such a long face?" he asked quietly. His voice sounded almost like he cared. He hadn't cared for twenty-seven years. Why on earth should he start now? Just because Sophia, her sister, had brought their mother and father to the land of the fae? Just because she'd forced them to remember they had children not of their world? It was too little too late.

It simply wasn't done. A faerie that had been cast out of the fae and her human husband had no business being in the land of the fae. Nor did Ashley Trimble, the Duke of Robinsworth, and his daughter, Lady Anne, neither of whom was the least bit magical.

Lord Ramsdale, who Claire once more reminded herself was her father, nudged her with his shoulder again. "Are you planning to talk to me?" he asked. He leaned back on one elbow and regarded her warily.

Lord Ramsdale made a motion with his eyes toward his wife, and she took Lady Anne's hand and led her farther down the stream, supposedly so he and Claire could have a private talk. She didn't want a private talk. She wanted life to go back to normal. She wanted to go on a mission. She wanted the humans cast from the land of the fae. She wanted all thoughts of Lord Phineas Trimble out of her head. She wanted her boxes back in their appropriate places. She could see clearly where each should sit. She bit her lower lip between her teeth and didn't respond.

Claire had refused to use magic as long as the humans were in the land of the fae. She'd even gone so far as to have Marcus lock her dust up in the family safe. It just wasn't proper for humans to be in her land. And she wouldn't use magic or go on any missions until they left.

"Ignoring us won't make us go away, you know?" her father chided.

"One can hope," Claire shot back.

He grimaced and lay back with a huff. Claire almost felt bad for him. But only for a moment. It wasn't her duty to make him feel good about the way events had taken place. She'd never asked to be born, after all. They'd done that all on their own. Then her parents had let their fae children be taken back to the land of the fae to be raised by grandparents and led to believe they had no parents at all. Twenty-seven years with no parents. She certainly didn't need any at this point.

"What can we do to make it easier for you?" he asked quietly.

"Leave."

He frowned. "We just arrived."

They'd been there since winter, and now it was spring.

Her father picked a handful of daisies and began to make a chain of them, looping one together with the next until he'd made a short circle of them. He held it out to her with one arched brow.

She shook her head. The last thing she wanted from him was a chain of daisies. She wasn't a little girl anymore. She was a lady. A faerie. And he was not of her world.

"I'd do just about anything for you," he said quietly.

"I don't want anything from you." Her eyes stung with unshed tears, but she refused to let them fall. She wouldn't let her parents make her weak, not under any circumstances. He must have sensed her distress because he grunted and got to his feet.

"When you're ready to talk, we'll be here," he said, and then he called out to Lady Ramsdale for her to wait.

"That's most unfortunate," she called to his retreating back.

He turned back to look at Claire for a moment. "I'm not certain if you get your bullheadedness from me or your mother," he remarked. He looked much too pleased at the thought.

How the devil could he think she'd gotten anything from either one of them? Neither of them had raised her. They hadn't been involved in the rearing of their fae children. None of them—Claire, Sophia, or Marcus—had the benefit of parents at any point during their young lives. Yet Sophia and Marcus had opened their arms to their parents. Claire couldn't. She just couldn't.

"You shouldn't be here," she called to his retreating back. He raised a hand and waved at her without even looking back. Blast him. He had the ear of the Trusted Few, the governing body of their land. Why her people had welcomed him with open arms, Claire didn't understand.

She needed to escape the land of the fae, if for no other reason than to get away from her parents. To avoid their wounded looks. To avoid the need in their eyes. But to do so, she'd have to bribe the fish who guarded the portal to the land of the fae. And the only thing the fish, or fallen fae who were sentenced to guard the portal, coveted more than their freedom was men's clothing. She had none to spare. Claire got to her feet and started toward home. With the absence of magic, she had very little left to occupy her. So, she went to the library to find a book to read.

She turned the pages of *Claudine* but didn't feel herself falling headfirst into the pages. Not at all. She placed the book back on the shelf. What was a faerie to do when there was nothing to occupy oneself? No magic to perform? No dust to settle. Nothing to do. She yawned into her cupped hand.

Margaret, the family's house faerie, barreled around the corner, almost knocking her over. "Where are you off to in such a hurry?" Claire asked.

"Your grandmother has gotten it into her head that she needs to find your mother's baby blanket for Sophia."

Of course she wanted that. Sophia was expecting her first child. No one was certain if the baby would be born fae or not. They wouldn't know until they saw the pointy ears of a newborn faerie.

"Have you seen it?" Margaret asked.

"Seen what?" Claire shook her head, trying to shake the lethargy from herself like a dog shakes water from its back. She'd been so tired lately.

Margaret snapped her fingers. "The blanket."

"Maybe in the attic?" Claire tried.

Margaret got a gleam in her eye. "Will you go and check for me?"

Claire heaved a sigh. "Certainly." If she must, she would go.

"Come and get me when you find it?"

On a normal day, she would just use magic to notify Margaret. But she had no magic. "Shall I shout for you?"

Margaret raised a condescending brow. "If you must."

She must. There was no other way to get things done. Not with her magic locked in the family safe. And Marcus had the only key.

Claire ducked beneath the cobwebs that criss-crossed the doorway into the attic. The spiders would be perturbed if she messed up their handiwork and would probably refuse to knit for her. Finicky little beings. She saw a trunk in the corner and lowered herself to her knees before it. She slowly opened the lid, sneezing quickly as dust tickled her nose. Claire looked inside and there lay the small quilted blanket that all the Thorne children had used in the nursery. It was threadbare and well loved, but she was certain Sophia wanted it more for sentimental reasons than anything else.

Claire pulled the blanket from the chest and shook it lightly. It would have to be laundered, she was certain, but small sparks fell from the blanket, burning like fire until they petered out before hitting the floor. Magic dust? She shook the blanket again. More sparks fell from the blanket, and a stick clattered to the floor. Claire snorted to herself. Of course, there would be faerie dust in the blanket, but not enough to do her any good.

She kicked the stick with the toe of her slipper.

But then she froze. She bent over it and stared. Claire hadn't seen the paintbrush in years. She'd gotten into so much trouble with it that her grandparents had taken it away from her, never to be returned.

As she watched the last of the small sparks die, a soft mist began to cloud the floor and swirl around her feet. Claire rustled the folds of her dress to shoo it on its way. But the movement stirred the air just enough to reveal a small painting set in the corner of the room. It was a painting of a door.

The door was no more than four inches in height. The painting looked ancient, like it had been tucked in the corner of the attic for a number of years. Yet, Claire was almost certain it hadn't been there just a moment ago.

She lowered herself to her knees and wiped away the cobwebs that covered the small painting, hoping the spiders would not be too terribly miffed with her. The door had a tiny brass knocker and a small window, but Claire couldn't get down low enough to look through it. Not in her human size. She shrank herself to her faerie height—one good for sliding under doors and through keyholes, and for completing missions—and stood before the small opening. She didn't need magic dust to grow and shrink, as that was inherent to her being fae. She'd eschewed magic, but her curiosity over the paintbrush and the painting were winning over her temper-fit.

Her short skirts fluttered around her knees, and the mist tickled her naked legs. She stood on tiptoe and looked through the tiny window. With the paintbrush in her hand, she could see the door in the painting as if it were real. But all she could see through the door's tiny window was a shadowed room with a crackling fire in the hearth. It looked fairly harmless. What danger could possibly be lurking in such an average room? She would take a quick peek into the room and then come straight back if anything nefarious lurked in the shadows.

Claire stepped back and regarded the sign over the door. "*Dulcis domus.*"

If only she'd learned to read Latin.

Curiosity won over her normal reticence. What lay on the other side of the tiny door? She hadn't stepped into a painting since she was a child. The door lacked a door handle to open it, so she carefully lifted the paintbrush and flicked the horsehair ends against her fingernail. Faerie dust sparkled in the air. The brush still had faerie dust? She touched the tip to the painting and painted a tiny door handle onto the door. She could paint just about anything with faerie dust and the magical paintbrush, no paint required.

Claire turned the tiny brass door handle and pushed to open the door. When it refused to budge, she shoved it with her shoulder. It burst open quickly, and Claire fell into the mist that blew into the open doorway. Something magical waited on the other side. It had to be waiting because magic was scarce in her world. And if she didn't leave soon, the evidence of her betrayal of her own world would soon be visible. She had no choice but to leave.

Eight

LORD PHINEAS TRIMBLE BOUNCED HIS KNEE BENEATH the wench's bottom to eject her from his lap. However, the scrawny bit o' muslin just wrapped her arms around his neck and pressed her breasts firmer against his chest. "Not tonight, love," he murmured. He unwrapped her from his person and set her to the side as he got to his feet.

"Never thought I'd see the day when you turned down a tumble," the wench remarked, looking closely at him. "You haven't replaced me with another, have you?" Her auburn brows drew together sharply.

"I could never replace you," he soothed, stroking a finger along the line of her chin. "I simply have somewhere I need to be."

"That mistress of yours is keeping tight to the reins," she remarked.

He held up his hands as though in surrender. He had no mistress, though the wench had no reason to know that. Mrs. Katherine Crawfield had let him down, not so gently, and had found another protector months ago. She'd also started a little rumor about his prowess in the bedchamber. Mrs. Crawfield had a bit of a mean streak. The rumor was spreading like wildfire in his social circle, and he wasn't surprised by the number of people who'd already heard about his lack of attention to her needs.

It wasn't his fault that the only woman he even thought about was Claire Thorne. Every time a wench touched him, he recoiled. All because she wasn't Claire. Just thinking her name made his heart quicken and his manhood get hard.

Finn called for his carriage and climbed into it alone. He wasn't used to spending so much time by himself. He usually had the Duke of Robinsworth, his brother, and his daughter, Lady Anne, to occupy his free moments. But since his brother had married Sophia Thorne in the land of the fae, they'd been gone from Finn's world and had no plans to return any time soon.

His last missive from Robin had bid him to check up on their mother, who lived at the family seat, and to take care of Robin's holdings for a time. So, Finn had moved himself into the Hall and taken up residence in his brother's house. And taken up Robin's life, it appeared. Aside from the fact that Robin was a recluse, Finn was beginning to see the attraction to staying at home where one couldn't hear the whispers. Robin's life—now that Finn was taking care of his holdings, his lands, his tenants, and his investments—left little room for dalliances or social engagements.

Finn preferred his life of leisure but was certain he would be able to get back to it soon. But what he would prefer even more was to find out what had happened to Claire Thorne. He'd spent one life-changing night with her, and when he'd woken up, she was gone. He'd traveled all the way back to London through the thickening snow, trying to find some glimpse of her, but she had vanished into thin air and was nowhere to be found. At least not in this world. He wanted to ask Robin if he knew her whereabouts, but doing so would call attention to his desire to find her. That simply would not do.

Finn let Robin's butler, Wilkins, take his coat and walking stick when he walked into the residence. "Lord Phineas," Wilkins said stoically. The man rarely cracked a smile, though he did seem more lively when Robin was in residence.

"Wilkins," Finn murmured. "Anything I need to take care of before I retire?"

Wilkins held out a note on a silver salver. Finn's name was written in Robin's bold script across the front.

"The garden gnome delivered it this afternoon," Wilkins informed him.

"How was Ronald?" Finn asked.

"He was... himself."

"Pity that."

The land of the fae employed varied creatures to do their bidding. Though the garden gnome, Ronald, hated Finn with all his being, he still carried missives to and from their land. Finn snorted. Their land. Like Robin and Anne belonged there with Sophia. He shook his head. Perhaps they did. It must be nice to belong somewhere.

Finn scrubbed at his eyes with the heels of his hands and headed for Robin's study. He would look at any pressing matters, any notes from solicitors or business associates of Robin's, and then he would slide gratefully into his empty bed.

He tore open Robin's missive and began to read.

> Dearest Finn,
>> We're planning to return soon.
>>> Best regards,
>>> Robin

Finn had always appreciated that Robin was a man of few words. Until now. He wanted details. He wanted to know everything there was to know about the land of the fae. It existed. But he didn't understand how it could be possible. And he wanted to know if Claire would be returning as well, but he didn't dare ask his brother.

Tossing the rest of the day's business to the side, Finn started up the stairs toward his bedchamber. He was too tired to do any more.

He let Robin's valet, Simmons, remove his clothing, and he slid into a silk dressing gown. The man bustled about the chamber long enough to be irritating, until Finn finally motioned for him to leave. With a quick bow, Simmons exited the chambers. Finn was quite certain Simmons didn't want to be his valet, but the man needed employment while Robin was gone. He might as well make himself useful.

Finn poured a snifter of brandy and drank it in one healthy swallow, hissing as it made a fiery trail down his throat. He poured another. He slept better when he was foxed, if he had to sleep alone. He preferred to sleep sober with a warm, and preferably damp, body wrapped around his.

The brandy began to seep into the corners of his mind, and he relaxed in an overstuffed chair. When he was sufficiently numb, he stood up, shed his dressing gown, and sat down on the edge of the bed. The thought of a warm bed-partner stirred something within him, and he momentarily considered having Wilkins arrange for a visit, but it was just as well that he went to bed. Wilkins couldn't bring him Claire Thorne, and she was the only woman he wanted.

He scrubbed at his eyes again and stared absently around the room that wasn't his. The home that wasn't his. The life that wasn't his.

Movement against the far wall caught his attention, and he strained to see into the dimness. A small door appeared. Finn blinked, adjusting his brandy-hazed brain to see more clearly. Perhaps he was already asleep; he couldn't be certain. But then the door flew open and fog rolled out in small waves, clouding the room until it was smoky and hazy. He swiped a hand in front of his face. A shimmer of lights sparked from the opening, and through it tumbled a tiny creature, no more than four inches in height.

Finn got up and bent at the waist—regretting the action immediately when the room rolled like the deck of a moving ship—and glared at what had to be a figment of his imagination. But then the little lady reached behind herself and fluffed her wing, which had gotten bent when she tumbled across the floor.

"What the devil?" he remarked to himself.

The faerie looked up, got to her feet, and placed

her hands on her hips. She shook a finger at him and words tumbled from her lips, but he couldn't hear a word of them.

"I can't hear you," he said, leaning closer.

Before his very eyes, the little faerie grew to human proportions. Fog and sparks covered some of her change, but the rest of it he saw. She grew. She grew from four inches tall to where the top of her head reached the bottom of his chin.

Her cheeks were flushed a rosy red, and she put a hand over her eyes. But with her free hand, she continued to shake her finger at him. In her fist she clutched a... paintbrush?

He heard not a word. Finn let his gaze wander from the bodice of her pink gown down to the odd little slippers she wore. He finally made his eyes move back up to her face. Her cheeks were still red and growing even redder, as were the edges of her wings. Wings. Dear God, the lady had wings. Her hair tumbled over the implements of flight, which looked like lace and ephemeral material, if that could be an apt description. Her strawberry blond hair fell in mad disarray over her shoulders and tangled around the edges of lace on her wings. He moved to disentangle her. She must have gotten mussed when she'd rolled into the room.

"My lord," she cried, when he reached out to touch her. He knew that voice. It seeped into his brain slowly. Claire Thorne.

"Miss Thorne?" he asked. He'd never seen her in faerie form. He knew she was one. But he'd never seen it. Not with all the glimmer and shine, and the wings. He couldn't stop looking at her. She looked everywhere else.

"My lord," she began again. She looked down toward his feet. And then spun to face away. She hooked his dressing gown with her finger and held it out to him. "Perhaps you should dress."

Nine

FINN TOOK HIS DRESSING GOWN FROM HER CROOKED finger and shrugged into it. "What brings you to London, Miss Thorne?" he asked casually. Like he was commenting about tea or her frock or some other nonsense, rather than the fact that she'd just appeared through a tiny door that wasn't there anymore. What he really wanted to ask was where the devil she'd been for the past four months. And why she'd vanished without talking to him about what happened between them.

"That would be none of your concern, Lord Phineas." She lifted her pert little nose higher in the air and started for the door.

"Miss Thorne, you just tumbled through a magical doorway right into my chambers." He stopped and shook his head. That sounded ridiculous even to him. "A door that has disappeared, by the way."

The lady pivoted on her heel and looked back at where the door should have been and then began to pace.

She raised a fingernail to her lips and began to

nibble as she mumbled something to herself that sounded like, "The paintbrush usually leaves a way for me to get back."

He didn't even try to interpret it. "By God, are they always that big?" He reached out to tentatively touch the fine edges of her wings, which looked like lace, but now that he was closer, he realized they were edged with fine down, and they matched the color of her skin.

She looked down at herself and rolled her eyes at him. He found that social ineptitude a little endearing, actually.

"I could ask you the same," she said, with one delicate golden brow arched at him. Her gaze roamed up and down his body, a body she'd just seen way too much of. She already knew it intimately.

"I was preparing for bed." Heat crept up his cheeks. "You look very pretty in pink."

"Thank you," she murmured. She shook out the folds of the short skirt so that it swished around her knees. Finn had never seen a more erotic sight than that of her trim little silk-clad ankles. Good God, he was losing his mind. He picked up his empty glass and stared into it.

She closed her eyes tightly and her wings disappeared. They vanished. No popping, no cracking, no smoke. They just left. He reached out to touch the place where they'd been, but she dodged his hand. "Go to bed, my lord," she said. "Tomorrow you will wake and this will all seem like a dream."

His dreams of her involved her gasping and moaning beneath him, since he hadn't been able to get the memories of her actually doing so out of his mind. His dreams would not involve her tumbling through a door into his room. He raised his foot and tapped his big toe against the wall where the door had been. "Where did it go?"

She shrugged. "I have no idea."

She looked a little put out by its absence. "How do you get back?"

"I have no idea about that, either. One minute, I was in my land without any magic. Now I'm in your land without any magic."

She shook her head and began to pace. "What does that mean, no magic?"

"It means I am as human as you are right now."

Only, she was dressed like a faerie. "You can't go back?"

She bent down and knocked on the wall where the door had been. "It appears not."

"Is that a paintbrush?"

"It appears so." She drew her bottom lip between her teeth.

"What's your plan?"

"I don't have one yet."

"You'll have to stay here."

"For the night." She nodded and looked perturbed.

"You don't have a chaperone."

She looked down at the thing that someone might mistake for a gown. Someone stupid. "Not unless she's in my pocket."

If she had a pocket hidden somewhere on that dress, he would sell his eyeteeth to find it. "You're all alone." Thoughts of the last time he'd been alone with her still made him ache.

She nodded, rocking back and forth from the balls of her feet to her heels. "I believe we already discussed that."

He was honor bound to take her in. To take care of her until one of her kind came to collect her. "Robin and your sister will be returning soon," he said. Robin might be the one to collect her.

"Thanks for the warning," she said dryly.

God, the woman made him want to chuckle. But that could be the drink.

Finn pulled the cord for a servant. "I'll have someone show you to your chambers for the time being."

"Do you plan to lock me in?"

"Do you plan to bolt?"

She shook her head. "My land is the last place I want to be right now." She held out her hands in surrender. "Not to mention that I have nowhere else to go."

"Quite true." Something was wrong. She was much too complacent.

A knock sounded on the door. "Enter," Finn bellowed.

Wilkins entered the room and stopped short. But he recovered quickly. "You summoned?"

"It appears we have a visitor."

The stoic old butler bowed to her.

"Don't you want to know how she got inside?"

"Not particularly, my lord." Wilkins tugged at his necktie and then folded his hands behind his back. "Please do let me know if there is a security breach I should take care of."

Finn doubted that Wilkins could handle her kind of

breach. Finn's eyes were trained on the pale pink skin that was exposed by her bodice. Until she began to snap her fingers in his face. He dragged a hand down his mouth in frustration.

"I'm up here, my lord," she reminded him. Thin brows that arched as much as her mouth turned down met him when he finally found the wherewithal to look up.

What was up there was as pretty as what was down there. And everywhere in between. By God, he was losing his mind. They'd be calling a coach bound for Bedlam by the end of the night. "Am I going mad, Wilkins?" Finn asked.

"If you are, my lord, I'm going with you."

⤬

Claire paced back and forth across the Aubusson rug in the chambers where they'd stashed her. "Stashed" was the only appropriate word for what they'd done. She didn't have a single thing to wear. Nor did she have any money. Or magic. The only thing she could do was shrink herself down to faerie size and then back to human size again. And apparently, she could paint. But that was all she could do. She could get everything she needed if she only had some magic. But she had none.

She looked at the tip of the paintbrush and snorted. That was the only magic she had? It was left over from more than twenty years before. It had allowed her to paint that door handle on the door, and then the door had opened like a beacon on a dark night. And she'd walked straight into it. Look where it had gotten her.

She'd paint her way out of it if she could come up with a safe destination. But she couldn't think of a single place she could go.

Her chambers were extremely fine, much finer than what she'd had at home. From the thick carpet beneath her feet to the tapestry on the wall, this place was much more extravagant than anything she'd ever had assigned to her. When she came to this world, she was usually installed as a servant and given a tiny room in a drafty corner of a manor house. The Hall, which belonged to the Duke of Robinsworth, was monstrous in size, and Claire was afraid she'd get lost in the corridors if she even attempted to bolt.

A knock sounded on the door. Claire turned just as the door slowly opened. "No, I didn't intend for you to wait for my call to enter," Claire sniped. But a kind face appeared around the door and an old woman walked into the room.

"Grams, you're supposed to wait until she calls for you to open the door. What if she were undressed?" Lord Phineas bellowed at the old woman. She held an ear funnel up to her ear, and he leaned toward it.

The lady shrugged her narrow shoulders and yelled back, "She doesn't have anything I haven't seen before, I can assure you." She shot Lord Phineas a telling glance. "And I dare say nothing you haven't seen before either."

His face flushed scarlet. He was quite handsome when he was discomfited. The corners of his mouth lifted in a grin. "See here, now," he began. But he just stopped and shook his head. He gestured to the woman. "Miss Thorne, this is my grandmother, the dowager Duchess of Robinsworth."

Claire curtsied as best she knew how. "Grams has agreed to act as your chaperone while you're here."

"I do not need a chaperone."

The dowager lifted a funnel to her ear. "Did you say mascarpone? Call for a tray. I'll share it with Miss Thorne."

"Not mascarpone, Grams!" Lord Phineas bellowed. "Chaperone. Miss Thorne needs a chaperone! For propriety's sake."

"Oh, who cares about propriety?" the dowager said, waving her hand in the air. "You could crawl in bed with her and I'd have no idea of it. Why avoid the obvious?" She glared at Claire. "Do you plan to fornicate with my grandson?"

"Oh God," Lord Phineas said as he buried his face in his hands and groaned.

Claire stifled a grin. "I have no intention of engaging in any form of fornication." Not today. Not ever again. Not with Phineas Trimble.

The old lady looked toward Lord Phineas. "There's more than one form of fornication?" she asked.

"Grams," he growled. "I will not discuss fornication with you."

"Then why did you bring it up?" She glared at her grandson.

"I didn't," he growled. Then he threw up his hands and quickly left the room.

The old lady laid down her ear funnel. "I do so love to do that to him."

"I can tell." Claire extended a hand to the old lady. "I have heard stories about you," Claire confessed.

The dowager duchess had been good friends with her own grandmother when they were younger.

"All true," the lady said. "And the stories they made up, they're true too as long as I come out smelling like roses in the end."

Claire chuckled. It was the first true laugh she'd had since Sophia and Robin had showed up in the land of the fae. It felt good to laugh. "I'll keep that in mind."

"Why are you here, my dear?" the woman asked, her voice softening.

Claire heaved a sigh. "I don't know. The door brought me here."

"What door, dear?" The lady cocked her head to the side.

The door in the painting. I went through it. The sign over the door said "Dulcis domus." But she couldn't say any of that. "I ended up in Lord Phineas's bedchamber."

"Many a lady has found herself in my grandson's bedchamber. And many who weren't ladies, too, if you understand my meaning."

Claire did. She understood it all too well. She was one of them, once upon a time.

"You're Sophia's sister?"

"Yes, Your Grace."

"A lovely girl."

"Yes, Your Grace." Everyone thought Sophia was lovely. And charming. And smart. And the Trusted Few had even allowed her to marry outside the fae. With no recriminations. No clipping of her wings for committing Unpardonable Errors. Every last one of them. It was like Sophia was charmed. "She's the new Duchess of Robinsworth."

"So, I hear."

The dowager duchess made a sucking noise with her tongue against her teeth.

"I won't stay long," Claire began.

"I don't expect you to. In fact, I suspect that you will be gone by morning."

Claire's mouth opened and closed. She didn't know what to say. She probably looked like a blasted salmon.

"Rest well, my dear. I'll have a maid sent up with something you can wear."

Clothing. If she had clothing, she could leave the Hall. The farther she could get from Phineas Thorne, the better.

"Good night, dear," the old woman said.

"Did you mention you would send someone up with some clothes?"

"Oh yes, yes. I'll send someone up."

"Thank you."

Claire would linger long enough to get dressed, get a bite to eat, and then she had to get as far from Phineas Trimble as possible. Before he figured out her secret.

❧

Finn crept quietly down the corridor toward Claire's room, determined to get some answers from her if it was the last thing he ever did. It might be, if his mother or his grandmother caught him lurking in their wing of the estate near Claire's room.

The last time he'd seen Claire, she'd looked just about as disheveled as she did tonight after rolling through the tiny door. Her hair had been down, and he'd brushed it back from her forehead as she laid her head on his shoulder. He remembered the feel of her head lying trustingly on his chest as her breaths slowed. As he'd caught his own breath. As he'd realized what they'd done.

He slowly turned the handle to her door and stepped inside. A single candle burned on the bedside table, and it cast a hazy glow about the room. Her form was outlined by the lump under the counterpane, and heat shot quickly to his groin as he wondered what she was wearing beneath that blanket.

Finn sat down gingerly on her bed and lifted a hand to her shoulder. He would gently wake her before taking her to task for disappearing the way she did. His heart thumped like mad within his chest, and his hand shook just before he nudged her awake. But the lump he thought was her wasn't her at all. Finn jerked the counterpane back and jumped to his feet.

"Damn her," he cursed. She was gone. Again.

A muffled laugh sounded behind him. He turned quickly, prepared to defend himself if he needed to do so. But it was just Miss Thorne, lounging on a chaise before the fire. She wore a white nightrail that must have come from his grandmother. Her tiny toes peeped out from beneath the hem. She wiggled them and Finn bit back a groan. "You find something amusing?" he bit out.

"The look on your face when you realized that was a lump of clothing beneath the counterpane." She laughed again. She laughed like a child being tickled, and he found the innocent sound of it to be most arousing. Everything about her stirred the fire in him, from his fiery anger to his manhood.

"Where have you been?" Finn asked sharply.

"Here and there," she teased. "A little more there than here."

"Are you all right?" he asked, fighting not to strangle her. Or kiss her.

"As right as I can be," she said with a shrug. She lifted a cup to her lips and took a swallow. When she laid it down, he picked up the cup and brought it to his nose. "It's just tea," she said with a smirk. "Though you may have some if you're that parched."

He turned the glass until the point that had the print of her lips on it faced him. Then he slowly drank. Her heart leaped within her breast. She jumped to her feet and crossed to pick up a hairbrush. She began to drag it through her golden locks.

"We can find a maid to do that for you," he said. He may as well have said, "The sky is blue," but he didn't know what to say to her. *I've missed you fiercely. I think about you constantly.* And the ultimate question, *Are you with child?*

"I quite like doing it myself, thank you." She closed her eyes and let the brush slide down the length of her hair. The brush caught on a snag, and she stopped to pull the knot out. He stepped forward and took the brush from her.

"No," she protested, covering her head with her hand to stop his good intentions. He just wanted an excuse to touch her, nothing more.

He laid a hand on her shoulder to hold her steady and began to brush her hair with the other. She acquiesced with a long sigh, but she didn't relax. He could feel her tension in the set of her shoulders. In the rigidity of her posture. "Where do you plan to go?" he asked softly, afraid to break the calmness of the moment.

"I don't know," she said, allowing her eyes to close.

"Back home?" He let the soft fall of her hair slide between his fingers.

"Can't go back there until the moonful, if then." Her shoulders began to relax a bit, and she shifted lower in the chair.

"If you'd wanted to see me, you could have just come to the front door like a normal person." A grin tugged at his lips.

"What makes you think I wanted to see you?"

"Why else would you be here?"

"Because I have nowhere else to go." She sat up straight and took the brush from his hand, laying it on the dressing table with a clatter. "My land is not a good place for me right now…"

❧

And it wouldn't be, not once her secret became known. Once people knew she'd coupled with a human.

"Everyone you know is there." His eyes appraised her in the looking glass. Too closely.

"That is my problem, you see." She got to her feet and crossed back to the fire. "I can't stay there. Not right now."

He was an amateur detective. Sophia had told her. He liked to solve riddles and puzzles, and find things out about people. Perhaps she could appeal to that side of him.

"About what happened between us," he began. He stopped for a moment to cough into his closed fist, clearing his throat.

"Must we discuss that now?" She sighed heavily. She didn't want to discuss it. She didn't want to think about it. She didn't want to deal with it.

"I think there are some things we need to say to clear the air."

"You've been in my bed," she said with as casual a shrug as she could manage. "It's really no great event."

"It was for me," he said quietly.

It was for her too. But he bedded a different woman every night. She would wager on that. "It was but a moment."

"Were there consequences of our actions? In your land?" He probably wanted to know if they'd snipped her wings. Or punished her in some other way. She was being punished, but not by the fae. She laid a hand on her stomach.

"No," she replied. "They were not aware of our indiscretion."

"Good," he said softly. "I was worried for you."

"Thank you." Her voice was no more than a breath.

"Will you be here in the morning?" he asked. He looked deeply into her eyes. As though he searched for the truth. If she told him the truth, he'd run screaming from the room. Or do something equally as foolish, like try to marry her.

"If it's all right with you."

He nodded. Nothing more. Just a nod. "I'll see you in the morning."

She nodded in return. He would see her. She would let him shelter her while she figured things out. If that was at all possible.

The door snicked softly behind him as he left the

room. Claire heaved a great sigh and looked at herself closely in the looking glass. How the devil had she gotten here to this place, to this time, in this predicament? Why had the door brought her to Phineas Thorne? And what on earth was she going to do now?

Ten

FINN ROSE WITH THE SUN THE NEXT MORNING, TOSSING the counterpane off quickly as he got to his feet. A tiny voice in his head warned if he didn't move quickly, Claire would vanish like the wind. Gone before he could get an opportunity to settle anything with her.

He dressed and let Simmons shave him quickly, then stepped out into the corridor. He adjusted his clothing, feeling for certain like a debutante at her first ball. Was his cravat tied tightly? Was the sapphire pin stuck in the center too ostentatious? Were his boots polished to a shine? How did his arse look in these breeches?

Claire would hardly care about what a fine figure he could turn out. She was probably gone, anyway. He heaved a sigh, took the stairs quickly, and went toward the breakfast room. His lungs deflated when he stepped into an empty room. He turned around and ran straight into her.

"Oof," she grunted, reaching for his shoulders to steady herself.

"Bloody hell," he grunted, his hands landing on

her shoulders as he reached for her. "Are you quite all right?" She blew a lock of hair from her eyes.

"It's not every day a lady gets hit by a battering ram. But I'm well."

Claire had a way of stripping Finn down to the bare bones. He wasn't the younger brother of the infamous Duke of Robinsworth when he was with her. He wasn't a wealthy man. He wasn't a consummate lover of women. He was that idiot who'd just run into her. "My apologies," he managed to say.

"Where were you rushing off to?" she asked, her head tilting a little to the left as her eyes narrowed at him.

I was going to look for you. "To call for more coffee."

She pointed toward the footman who stood at the ready in the breakfast room. "He couldn't manage that for you?"

"He's in charge of the sausages." The corners of her lips began to tip up. "But I assume he could manage coffee."

"Yes, my lord," the servant said, as he bustled from the room.

Claire laid a hand on his chest, and he feared his heart would jump out to greet it. "If you wanted to get me alone, you had only to ask."

"I've had you alone before," he grunted.

Her brows arched in response, but she chose to ignore his response. "Do you have plans for the day?"

Aside from dogging her every footstep? No. "Yes, I have several appointments. What did you need?"

"Nothing," she said with a shrug. She tugged at her clothing, and it was only then that he realized what she was wearing.

"Where the devil did you get that dress?" It was more like a sack than a dress. He reached out and ran the fabric through his fingers. Her skin would be chafed by the end of the day.

"I think it belonged to the housekeeper. Your grandmother didn't have anything that would fit me."

That thing she was wearing didn't fit her either. "You have nothing else to wear?"

"You saw what was in my hands when I arrived." She snapped her fingers to get his attention. "I have nothing."

"That is where you are wrong. You just happen to have me."

❧

Claire's heart tripped a beat. For a minute, an hour, for a day, she might have him. But not longer than that. "I'm not certain what you mean," she said, hating the hesitancy of her own voice.

"Clothing is the first thing we must do, because I cannot bear looking at you in that much longer. Shall we send for the modiste? Or go directly to her shop? Since you'll be in a hurry for something to wear, we probably should go to her shop to see if she has something already made." He motioned toward the door. "Shall we go?"

"Shall we have some breakfast first?" she asked instead. The idea of being in a closed carriage with him was even worse than sitting opposite him at the breakfast table. She'd have to converse with him. And breathe the same air as him. And not wonder if he was remembering what they did together. Heat crept up her face.

"Shall I have someone bring a fan, Miss Thorne?" He waved a hand, stirring the air in front of her face.

"Shall you not be quite such an arse?" she retorted.

He chuckled lightly. It was an endearing sound, really. And it made her want to laugh with him, but only for a moment. "I will endeavor not to be an arse if you will try your hardest not to erupt into flames at the mere thought of spending the day with me."

"That wasn't what happened," she began, but his smile grew, and she realized that sparring with him was too enjoyable for him. It gave him too much pleasure. "I'm famished, and I might keel over from starvation if you don't allow me to break my fast soon."

He motioned her toward the sideboard, where several covered dishes lay. He picked up a plate for her. "Shall I choose for you?" A servant lifted the lid on the first dish, and the rich smell of cooked, greasy sausage reached her nose. Her stomach revolted. She'd thought she was past this point, but such was not the case, because not only did her stomach revolt, but her head began to swim as well.

"Will you cover that, please?" she bit out, looking away as she breathed in and out through her mouth. Her mouth filled with saliva, and she pressed a hand to her lips. The plate in his hand clattered to the top of the sideboard as he dropped it and reached for her.

"What's wrong, Claire?" he asked as the servant maneuvered a chair beneath her bottom, which was fortunate, since it happened just as her knees gave way. She flopped into the chair. The nausea was passing, but not quickly enough. Finn shoved her head down between her knees and instructed her to breathe deeply. If she breathed deeply, she might smell that disgusting sausage from across the room and that would just make things worse.

His hands toyed with her hair as he held her head down. It was almost amusing, the position she was in. "You can let me up," she said, but the sound must have been hidden in her hair or her skirts or something, because he was suddenly kneeling before her, his hard gaze assessing her face as he looked into her eyes.

"What did you say?" he asked. His brows were drawn together, his eyes wary.

"I said, 'You can let me up.'" She said it louder this time, and he scrambled to help her sit up.

"I'll never make you wait before feeding you breakfast again," he declared, a sparkle lighting his eyes. "Does sausage always make you want to cast up your accounts?"

"Not typically," she admitted. But she certainly couldn't explain it, could she? "Perhaps I could just get some toast?"

He got to his feet and let a servant fill a plate for her, overflowing with toast. "Jam?" he asked.

"Just toast," she clarified. She couldn't stomach jam any better than she could sausage. And the very thought of eggs...

"Just toast," he repeated as he placed the plate laden with toast at the table and helped her into a chair.

She batted her eyes at the footman. "Could I get some tea, please?"

The man turned to retrieve a cup of tea for her. "Don't bat your pretty little lashes at my servants," Finn warned.

He thought she had pretty lashes? "I did no such thing," she denied. She had, but only because she could. She hadn't expected Finn to notice. "And they're not your servants, are they? They're Robinsworth's." That little jab was unnecessary, she knew, but she didn't like to be told what she could and could not do. Not in the least.

"Right now, they answer to me. Robin hasn't been home in months."

"Do you have any idea when he and Sophia will be returning?"

"Nothing definite."

She hoped it would be longer than a fortnight. She had at least a fortnight, maybe longer, before people would begin to notice. Before she'd have to find somewhere else to stay. Perhaps she could make some female friends by then and find a safe haven.

She picked up a piece of plain toast and nibbled delicately on the edge. She'd learned in the early days of her condition that some things would sit well with her stomach, and some would not.

The butler—she thought his name was Wilkins, but she couldn't remember for sure—appeared in the doorway, where he stood at attention until Claire elbowed Finn in the side. "What is it, Wilkins?" he said with a heavy sigh.

"I wanted to inquire as to whether or not Miss Thorne will need a maid of her own."

In other words, he wanted to know how long she would darken their doorstep. "That won't be necessary," she began.

But Finn cut her off. "Yes, please. She will need

everything one needs when one travels. It appears all her luggage was lost."

Wilkins nodded and said, "I'll begin to make arrangements."

Claire chewed her toast slowly, afraid her stomach would revolt, but when she finished the piece, she looked up at him. "Have you eaten yet?"

"I am quite afraid to. If the smell of sausage does that to you, I'll wait until later."

"Thank you," she murmured. He was the reason she was in this condition, so she supposed he could suffer somewhat, couldn't he? Without her feeling remorseful? Her stomach was feeling much better, but she still didn't think she could tolerate that smell. She pushed her plate in his direction. "Would you like some toast?"

He smiled and raised a piece of toast to his lips. His eyebrows drew together like he was wondering about her. He'd better not wonder too much. Or he would find out much more than he wanted to know.

Eleven

THE BELL OVER THE DOOR OF THE MODISTE'S SHOP tinkled as Claire walked through the door. The entryway was clean and classical with a large settee, some high-backed chairs, and damask walls. It looked… expensive. Claire suddenly realized that she had no money with which to buy new clothing.

"Finn," she breathed, turning around quickly to go out and find him, but he'd stepped into the shop behind her and she ran directly into his chest. Claire stopped for a moment to inhale the clean scent of him. He smelled like morning in the forest in her land. She took a deeper breath, her nose pressed against his chest.

"Claire?" he questioned as he took her shoulders in his hands. "What's wrong?"

Nothing was wrong. Not when he was nearby. She completely forgot her qualms about money, until the modiste bustled into the shop. "Good morning," the woman chimed.

"Good morning," Finn said. His glance toward Claire worried her for a moment, but he quickly composed himself. He bent and took the lady's hand.

"Colette," he said smoothly, drawing her knuckles to his lips. "Lovely to see you."

Colette? He knew the lady? Intimately, if the way her eyes warmed at the sight of him was any indication.

She was really quite lovely, with long, dark hair and a willowy body. But then she snapped her fingers at Claire's face and said, "The maid can wait in the back." She arched a brow and ruffled her fingers to move Claire along.

Finn's face colored. "She's not a maid."

"Oh," the woman said, a sudden irritation flashing in her green eyes. "Of course, she's not." She turned to Finn and laid a hand upon his arm. "Where did you find your new ladybird?" she asked.

She watched as Finn's back went ramrod straight. "I found this one in Lord Ramsdale's parlor. She just happens to be his daughter." That wasn't the truth, not the part about finding her in the parlor—she hadn't even seen her father's home yet—but the look on his face made it seem indisputable.

"Oh, I thought she was your new mistress," the lady breathed, laying an amused hand over her mouth.

"She's the new Duchess of Robinsworth's sister," Finn said, his voice full of hauteur.

That got the lady's attention. She swallowed so loudly that Claire could hear it. "I assumed because of her attire…"

"Her luggage was lost. Carriage accident." The man could lie with a straight face. Claire didn't know if she should be jealous of his ability or in fear of it.

"The poor dear. So, you'll need everything?" The modiste looked to Finn and he nodded.

"Everything."

The woman's eyes narrowed almost imperceptibly. "And to whom should I send the bill?"

Finn's back grew even straighter. "To her father. Who else?" He looked down at Claire. "I will leave you in very capable hands, Miss Thorne." He bowed and started for the door.

Certainly he wasn't going to leave her here. "You're not staying?"

He smiled indulgently. "I'll return for you in an hour." He arched a brow at the modiste. She shook her head and held up two fingers. "Two hours, then." He nodded again and quit the room.

The modiste rang a bell, and two women appeared from the back of the shop and led Claire toward the rear. They spoke in rapid-fire French, and she had no idea what they were talking about. But when they started to unfasten her clothes and then threw them into the fire, she got the feeling that they didn't approve of them. Not at all.

She stopped them when they got to her chemise. With the fashionable high waist of gowns, she could keep her secret for a while, but not if people started measuring her waist.

❦

Finn looked down at his watch fob again and checked the time. He'd been gone for an hour, and he wanted to return to be certain Claire was all right. But he didn't want to seem overly involved in her care and set tongues wagging.

When he'd been to the shop with Katherine, his

former mistress, he'd stayed the whole time, watching her preen over silks, lace, and other fripperies. And she'd tried on clothing for him to be certain he liked it. It didn't matter if he liked Claire's clothing. He wouldn't be helping her out of it. Or squiring her about town in it. And if he paid any undue interest, the modiste would get it into her pretty little head that they had a closer relationship than he intended to portray. Then Claire would be ruined. Ruined before she'd even stepped into society for the first time.

He supposed he could waste some time at White's for a bit. He ambled down the street and entered the establishment.

He perused the room, happy to find that most of his consorts weren't about. It was much too early in the day. Only a few older gentlemen sat about, drinking tea and looking through the *Times*.

"Lord Phineas," a voice called. Finn turned and groaned inwardly when he saw Viscount Vinceberry motioning him over. The viscount was a middle-aged man, still sharp as a tack and as randy as a bull. He was everything that Finn hated in a gentleman. "Come and join me," Vinceberry suggested.

Must he? He supposed it couldn't be avoided.

"I've a little matter I wanted to discuss with you." The last time Vinceberry had wanted to discuss something with Finn, he'd put him on a wild-goose chase looking for a man who was shagging his wife. The man didn't exist. But it had been a bit of sport trying to figure out what had happened.

"How can I be of service?" Finn asked. Very few people knew he took great pleasure in solving crimes.

And that he employed a small lot of thieftakers and spies. Unfortunately, the viscount was well aware.

"Not service, particularly," Vinceberry prevaricated. "But I thought you might want to know…"

"Pray tell," Finn drawled.

"It's about Katherine."

Finn's gut clenched. "Katherine is no longer my concern."

"Rumor has it she has taken up with Mayden."

She'd taken up with the Earl of Mayden before she'd even left Finn. Mayden was an earl. But not a kind man. "That is not news to me."

"The news, my boy, is that she was seen about town looking like he cuffed her a bit too hard on the cheek. She'd tried to cover it with powder, but it was clear as day."

"Why is this any of my business?" Finn asked. He regretted the sharpness of his tone for only a moment.

Vinceberry tugged at his cravat. "I thought you might want to know, what with the fact that she's," he stopped to clear his throat, "increasing."

So someone had gotten Katherine with child? Poor sod. "I still fail to see why this should concern me."

"You didn't know." The man sat back and pushed his lips closed tightly. He inhaled, like he was steeling himself. "You needn't claim the bastard, of course."

"Why would I—?" Finn bit of the rest of his sentence as understanding dawned. "You're implying that the bastard is mine."

If it was, Katharine would have already come to him to collect funds from him. And for him to secure a place for her to live. She knew he would come up to snuff. "I'll pay a visit to Katherine," he bit out. He got to his feet.

"Brilliant idea," the old man said. His eyes narrowed. "Take care with Mayden. He's not known for his patience. I hear he's very protective of his little dove."

Protective, aside from the times he hit her. Of course. Finn understood men like him all too well. "I'll take great care."

Finn left the shop with a purpose in mind. But he glanced down at his watch and noticed the time. He didn't have time to pay a call on Katherine right now. But he'd be certain to do so very soon. Finn stepped back into the modiste's shop, and the tinkle over the door drew Colette out to greet him. The moment she saw him, the sway in her step grew almost provocative. It was most unfortunate that she no longer tempted him.

"Is Miss Thorne ready to depart?" he asked.

"Almost," she said, as she stepped close enough to graze his arm with the side of her breast. "A lovely young lady," she said, watching his face.

"She is quite dear to her family," he said. He refused to fall into Colette's trap.

"Will you be attending Ackley's soiree tomorrow night?"

He hadn't planned to attend. But it would be the best and only way to get close enough to Katherine to find out the truth of her situation. She always attended Lord Ackley's soirees. They were known for their debauchery. Ackley had married his former mistress. She walked about in polite society but was still shunned in a lot of places. So she liked to throw parties where men could bring their mistresses and feel comfortable that no one would be the wiser. These parties usually required masks, but it was fairly easy to find out who was who after speaking with them. He knew Katherine intimately; he felt certain he could find her in a crowd.

"The soiree?" Colette pressed.

"I haven't decided yet." She looked up at him like she was waiting for an invitation. "I have invited a lady to attend with me."

Colette laughed. It was a throaty sound, more like a purr than merriment. It made his skin crawl. "Who is the lucky chit?" Colette asked. She pointed toward the back of the shop. "Certainly not Miss Thorne?"

"Certainly not," he spit out, trying to look appalled. "Her father and my brother would skin me alive for even thinking of taking an innocent to such a place. I rather like my stones just as they are."

❧

Claire stood behind the curtain and gritted her teeth so loudly she was surprised Finn couldn't hear her. But he kept talking with the lady he called Colette. And Claire listened. She'd take his stones herself if he even dared to attend a soiree with the modiste. She was awfully familiar with his person. And he seemed to be enamored of her breasts. He hadn't taken his eyes off them as they talked.

Claire pushed the curtain to the side and stepped into the entryway. "Miss Thorne," Finn said with a quick bow. "Did Colette see to your every need?"

"Not the way she wants to see to yours," Claire muttered.

"Beg your pardon?" Finn asked. His eyes twinkled, so she knew he'd heard her.

"I have a small wardrobe to send with Miss Thorne," the modiste said. "We just happened to have a customer who ordered a lot of clothes and left for the continent before she picked them up. We have been waiting for the right person to come along and claim them. We shortened the hem on this one, and we're working on the rest."

"You look lovely, Miss Thorne," he said. His eyes jumped about on her body, rather like he was watching a tennis match. Did she discomfit him? Perhaps a bit.

"Thank you," she replied. Her heart thrilled at the tiny compliment. "If you'd send the rest of the clothing to Robinsworth's address?" he asked of the modiste.

"Robinsworth's address?" The modiste looked startled. "Rumor has it that's where *you're* residing, my lord."

Finn looked down his nose at the woman. "You're certainly not implying that there's anything untoward happening at Robinsworth's?"

Claire thrilled as the modiste said, "Certainly not." She turned to Claire and curtsied. "It was an honor seeing you today, my lady."

Finn held out his arm and Claire laid her hand upon it. He led her out of the shop with a determined stride. It wasn't until they were outside that he took a deep breath. "What's your relationship with that woman?" Claire asked. She hated herself as soon as the words left her mouth. But she couldn't keep from asking.

"Define 'relationship,'" he said with an unrepentant grin.

"You've bedded her." Claire's heart thumped hard within her breast. She didn't like the thought of him with the modiste at all. Not one bit. In fact, she had an uncommon urge to stomp back into the shop and jerk the woman's hair from her head.

"That was a very long time ago." He looked a little uncomfortable as he handed her into the carriage.

"Not long enough for her." Claire harrumphed, falling back heavily against the squabs. "To what party was she referring?"

"Just a gathering." He looked out the carriage window.

"Do you plan to attend?"

He shrugged. "Perhaps."

"Why?" Her heart stuttered as she waited for his response.

"I need some information that can only be obtained at this soiree."

"So, you do plan to attend."

"Only if I can find someone to accompany me."

"I would be happy to attend with you."

"It's not that kind of soiree," he said with a harsh glance in her direction. "It's not for ladies. It's for people like Colette."

"And like you."

"And like me," he agreed. "And not for ladies like you."

Didn't he know that she could be anyone she wanted to be? She spent her life in disguise. She could be anyone she wanted and make everyone believe it. "I'm not innocent, you know." She said the words softly. And he suddenly turned to look at her. His gaze was hot enough to set fire to the carriage.

"I was there when you lost your innocence, Claire. You need not remind me."

"But you just said I couldn't attend with you because I'm not the right kind of lady."

"You're still not the right kind of lady."

"I beg to differ."

"It's a masked ball. With all sorts of debauchery. Courtesans and mistresses. And a few paid ladies."

"You mean whores?"

Finn sputtered into his closed fist. "Where did you learn such a word?"

Claire rolled her eyes at him. "You've been inside me, for goodness sakes. I'm no better than any of those ladies. Let me attend with you. Just for the sport of it. You can get your information and then we can leave."

"Don't say things like that," he ground out. His voice sounded like it had been dragged down a gravel road before it left his lips.

"That I'm no better than those ladies?"

"That too." He looked decidedly uncomfortable. "And that I've been inside you."

Claire's breath caught in her throat.

"I happen to remember it in vivid detail," he went on to say. His gaze was locked on hers. "You needn't comment on it."

"You remember…?" Her voice was a quiet whisper, but he still heard her.

His fists clenched at his sides. He inhaled deeply, steeling himself before he said, "I remember everything. The taste of your skin. The smell of your neck. The feel of your thighs wrapped around me. The little breathy sounds as you cried out. I remember it all. I remember it in great detail. So, you would do well not to speak of it again."

"Or what?" she taunted.

The carriage rolled to a stop, and a footman opened the door and lowered the step. "Or you might find yourself in a similar situation."

"Take me with you tomorrow?" she insisted. She didn't want him going to a den of iniquity alone. Or with any other woman.

"No."

She would just have to change his mind.

Twelve

FINN DRESSED WITH GREAT CARE THE NEXT NIGHT, making sure his cravat was folded to perfection, and the pin that winked from the center of it matched his eyes perfectly. He let Simmons apply scented shaving soap when he shaved off his evening stubble. He looked presentable, he assumed. He tugged at the length of his jacket. Despite the debauchery that would be present, he knew this would be a formal ball.

Simmons bent and wiped an imaginary spot from the toe of Finn's boot. He stood up and surveyed Finn with a critical eye. "I believe you are presentable, my lord," Simmons said.

He was more than presentable. Presentable was a Christmas goose. He was the blasted chandelier in the middle of the ballroom, alight with a thousand flaming candles.

Finn hated these gatherings. He would rather stay at home. If he stayed home, he could go and find Claire and entice her to talk to him. She'd been surprisingly absent all day. Finn had even gone to search her out at one point during the day, worried for her, but was informed by Wilkins that she had gone out to visit the apothecary with her new maid.

What on earth might she need from the apothecary? And with what did she purchase it?

"I gave her some of the household funds," Wilkins had informed him. "I believe His Grace would have wanted me to do so."

Finn should have thought of her need for money and given her some of her own. He had plenty to spare.

He looked once more in the looking glass, content with what he saw. He would go quickly to Ackley's ball and find Katherine, and then ask her that fateful question. The question that could change the course of his life.

He highly doubted that the child was his. But one could not be certain of such matters. The thought of having a child didn't frighten him. The thought of having a child with Katherine did.

Finn shrugged into his coat, took his walking stick and hat from Wilkins, and started for the front door. He'd called for a carriage before he came downstairs, and the staff at the Hall was nothing if not efficient. Wilkins opened the door, and Finn stepped out into the night. He turned back to look at the upstairs window. He very nearly turned around and went back inside when he saw a figure standing in the window upstairs, watching him leave. He couldn't see her face, but he had no doubt it was Claire. He tipped his hat at her, and she raised her hand and waved.

The footman opened the carriage door and Finn stepped inside. He leaned back heavily against the squabs. He didn't relish this night, not in the least.

He wasn't looking forward to the confrontation with Katherine. He wasn't even looking forward to the debauchery. He had only one woman on his mind, and she'd been on his mind for months. And now she was in his house. And he was gone. He sighed heavily.

From the darkness on the other side of the coach, a throaty laugh erupted. Finn jumped and reached for the lamp. As he did, the person on the darkened side of the carriage came to sit beside him. He looked her up and down.

"Who the devil are you?" he asked.

"I can be whoever you want me to be," she purred. She wore a black silk mask that tied behind her head. Her hair was a riot of black curls atop her head, held back by shimmering diamond hair clips.

The scent of her reached up to tickle his nose. It was the soft smell of lemons and summer. He would know that smell anywhere. In fact, it invaded his dreams most nights, wrapping around his manhood and squeezing. Much like it was doing now. "Claire?" he asked.

She laughed and tugged the mask from her face. "I thought it would take you longer." Her lips formed a pout. And he immediately wanted to kiss her.

Finn moved to tap the roof so he could call the coachman to turn around and take her back. But she reached over and covered his hand with hers, drawing it down into her lap. "Claire," he warned. "You have to go back to the Hall."

"I'll do no such thing."

❦

Claire didn't like the idea of him going to a den of iniquity. Not at all. And she was bound and determined that he would not go without her. She'd spent the entire day preparing for the ball. She'd even paid a visit to the apothecary to get tint for her hair. Her normal blond locks were now a sooty black. Her face was painted and her eyes lined lightly with kohl. She even had a tiny beauty mark on her left cheek.

She looked up at Finn, prepared to explain her actions. But his eyes were riveted to her breasts. She looked down and tugged at the bodice of her gown, trying to bring it a little higher, but it was no use. Instead, she straightened her spine and stared back at him.

"That dress is positively indecent. Where did you obtain it?"

"I paid a visit to your Colette and told her what I needed."

Finn groaned. "What possessed you to do such a thing? Are you mad? She'll tell everyone!"

"She had no idea who I was. I went after I'd tinted my hair and painted my face. She thinks I am a newcomer to town and that my name is Mrs. Abercrombie."

"And she's not my Colette," he grumbled.

"She would like to be." It was amazing the things women would say when they didn't assume you were an innocent. "She was rather envious that I had been invited to this particular ball." But that was neither here nor there. She took a deep breath and pushed on. "Tell me what tonight's mission is. So I can prepare myself."

"You will wait in the carriage, Claire. I will not

take you into Ackley's ball. There are things there that someone of your sort should never see. You'd be scarred for life."

"Public beheading?" Claire gasped, teasing him.

"More like public intercourse," he said, raising a brow at her.

Claire's heart stuttered. "You mean... two people..." She let her words trail off.

"Or three or four," he corrected. "This is not your typical soiree."

"I can overlook the public intercourse." She tapped his leg, and he scooted it away from her. "What's wrong?"

"I will not take you to this party. I'd take you home if I didn't think this would take no more than a moment." He sighed heavily and rubbed his forehead in frustration. "I just need to find someone and ask some questions." He looked down at her dress again. Then back up to her hair. "What did you put on your hair?" He pulled one of her curls until the curl straightened, and then let it slip from his fingers to curl back up at the base of her neck. Claire shivered lightly.

"Don't worry. I used a little faerie dust in my hair, so it will wash out tonight."

"You look beautiful," he said, his voice suddenly raspier than usual. "But I like your real hair color more. I miss it."

"Thank you." Her heart was beating so strongly that he could probably hear it.

The carriage began to slow. "You will remain in the carriage," he warned. She wouldn't, but she would let him go inside before he figured that out. She could be a help to him in his mission, whatever it was. He just didn't know that yet.

She nodded at him and heaved a sigh. "I will remain in the carriage. Though I'd hoped for at least a dance."

"We can dance when we get back to the Hall," he said. He pointed a finger at her and shook it. "Do not get out of the carriage."

He spoke briefly to the footmen who remained with the carriage, and one of them looked through the window into the coach, surprised to see her there. "Who is she, my lord?" one of them asked.

"Just an acquaintance of mine," he said. "Do not let her out of the coach."

"You can count on us, my lord," the footman said. Then he leaned against the door and sealed her in. She could get out. She was a faerie after all. But she couldn't shrink and fly away in this dress. Definitely not. She'd need her fae clothing for that. But she would find a way. She would not let Finn attend this party without her.

❧

Finn stepped through the entrance and stopped at the door, observing the room. From behind his mask, he could still see everything clearly, and he wasn't terribly impressed with the goings-on. This portion of the party was moderately respectable, and the part that was much less respectable was farther toward the interior.

"Lord Phineas," a cool voice said at the door.

"Good evening," he replied. He walked through the crush of people, scanning the crowd quickly. Some of his men were here. He'd seen to it himself. He felt much more at ease knowing his men were in place. He was tempted to send one of them out to watch over Claire. But she had two strapping footmen watching her. She would be fine. This wouldn't take long.

Finn strode toward the back of the manor. There would be more going on back there, and that was where he would surely find Katherine. She lived for events such as this.

He finally saw Katherine at the back of the billiards room, draped over the arm of her new protector. Finn was surprised to find that he didn't feel a single bit of jealousy. Mayden could have her. But he couldn't have a child that might possibly be Finn's.

Finn motioned toward one of his men, who stalked over toward the pair. He asked Katherine to dance. It was Lord Mayden's turn at billiards, so he let her go with no qualms. Finn's man swept Katherine onto the floor, holding her much too close, but that was probably as much Katherine's doing as his detective's. The man maneuvered her expertly around the room, toward a set of open doors on the terrace.

Finn started in that direction as soon as they crossed the threshold. He slipped out into the night, gave his man a nod, and stepped into place beside Katherine. "Finn," she said, startling a bit.

"Katherine," he said crisply. "I hope you are well."

Katherine's hand lifted toward her cheek. He could see the telltale shadows of a bruise there and another at her hairline. He took her hand in his and forced her to lift her arm. She had a ring of fingerprints on the back of her arm as well. They were well hidden by a shawl, but she couldn't hide from him. "Don't," she protested, as he let his fingers graze the marks on her arm.

"Why him, Katherine?" Finn asked. He hadn't seen her even once since the letter from her had arrived, notifying him of her choice of protectors. That he was no longer needed.

"He seemed the thing at the time," she said. Her voice cracked.

"Are you happy?" he asked. He eyed her bruises, and she flushed under his frank appraisal.

"I'm glad you're here," she said. "I needed to talk with you."

"I heard," he said with a nod. "Is it true?"

Her eyebrows pushed together. "Is what true?"

"Are you increasing? And is it mine?"

Finn heard a gasp from behind him and turned to find Claire standing outside the doorway, merely a few feet from where they stood. Claire clutched at her heart, laying her hand flat over her chest like she needed a moment to collect herself. "Blast and damn," he gritted out. "What are you doing here?"

❧

The woman dressed in blue sapphire was expecting a baby, and it was Finn's. Goodness, what a muddle. Two women expecting at the same time. Claire absently wondered how many more there were as she pushed through the crowd and back toward the front door. Finn called for her to wait. But if she waited, she would break. She would rip into a million pieces. She would shatter. And he would see her.

Already tears pricked at the backs of her lashes.

She ran through an open doorway and down a long corridor. At the end, she opened the first door she found and stumbled into the middle of someone's interlude. Heavy grunts bumped the walls and the desk upon which the thrusting was centered shifted to rub heavily against the floor. Claire spun and fled. Laughter followed in her wake.

She sighted a stairwell at the other end of the corridor and ran in that direction. When she got to the top, she hid in the curtains that lined the railing. But from behind them, she could see that the area where she stood looked down upon the ballroom. She stood still, hiding the folds of her red gown within the curtains.

She didn't think he could break her heart. He was just a man she'd spent a single night with. And not even a whole night. Merely a few hours. But she was suffering the consequences of her actions. And he had another woman who was doing the same. Damn him!

"Claire," a voice hissed from outside the curtains. She wiped her nose instead of sniffling as she truly needed to do. "Claire," he hissed again. This time, she couldn't keep from sniffling. The curtains parted and he stepped into the darkness with her. "Damn it, Claire, what are you doing here?"

"Not watching you with your paramour," she said. She crossed her arms beneath her breasts.

"Former paramour," he said quietly. "What's wrong with you?"

"Nothing," she said. Then she steeled herself. "You should have told me that you had a child on the way."

"Why the devil would I do that?" he asked. He

had a point. Why would he do that? She was nothing to him.

"That's what you came here to ask her about?" She wiped her hand beneath her nose. She hated that he got even a hint of her tears. Absolutely loathed it. And herself for getting into this situation.

"Yes, that's what I needed to ask about." He reached for her, his hand cupping her neck as he tilted her head back with his thumb. "But tell me why that bothers you."

"It doesn't."

His eyes narrowed; she could see them even in the darkness. "The truth, Claire."

She couldn't tell him about her own condition. He was already dealing with one lady who was expecting his child. The man would be bound for Bedlam if he found out about Claire. Goodness, what a mess.

"Did you think you were the only one I'd ever had relations with?" The corners of his lips tipped up ever so slightly.

"Your list of conquests is probably long and varied." She bit out through gritted teeth, "And I hate that I'm on it."

"Is that what's bothered you? That you weren't my first? Come on, Claire. I can't undo my past. Don't ask it of me because it's not fair." He groaned and touched his forehead to hers. "You weren't one of a list of women, Claire," he tried. But he sounded like an idiot.

"I was one night," she said. Her voice was not much more than a reluctant grunt.

"Did you want it to be more than that?" He looked into her eyes.

Did she? She was expecting his child. It couldn't be more, however, because he was not of her world. "I don't know," she whispered.

He tipped her face up toward his again. His lips touched hers gently. He wiped a tear from where it pooled at the corner of her eye. "Could you have feelings for me, Claire?" he whispered.

"I could never love you," she replied. She couldn't. It was forbidden.

"Let's go back to the Hall and discuss this there."

He took her hand and tugged her from behind the curtains. She jerked her hand from his grasp. "How many have there been since me, Finn?" she asked. Goodness, she didn't want to ask. But she had to.

"How many what?" His eyes narrowed at her suspiciously.

"Women, Finn. How many have there been?" She fidgeted with a loose string on her glove.

He hesitated, and then took a deep breath and said, "None, Claire. How could there be anyone else when all I can think about is you?"

Claire's heart skittered. She opened her mouth to ask him to confirm what he'd just said, but then Katherine stumbled into the area. "Finn?" she asked. The question didn't need to be answered. The woman instinctively knew that there was something between Finn and Claire. Katherine smiled softly. "It's not yours," she admitted.

Claire's heart leaped.

"Why did you tell everyone it was?"

"Because I needed to see you. I needed your help."

"You could have sent a letter," Finn said, sarcasm heavy in his voice.

"He watches my mail."

It was then that Claire noticed the bruises. She touched a hand to her own cheek. "Is that why you needed help?" Claire asked. Her heart clenched within her chest.

"I'm afraid," the woman whispered.

"Help her, Finn," Claire said without even thinking. "You can help her, can't you?"

Finn nodded, though he looked pained.

"Take her with us tonight."

"That won't be easy," he warned.

"You can't send her back to him." Claire asked the lady, "Are you truly expecting?"

She nodded, her eyes filling with tears. "But it's not Finn's. It's Mayden's."

Claire clutched Finn's arm. "Take her with us."

Finn nodded, swiping a hand down his face.

The woman held up a finger. "Can you give me a few minutes? I need to get my reticule."

"Quickly," Finn said with a nod.

The woman scurried away in the dark, and Finn laughed beneath his breath. "This cannot end well."

"You cannot let her go back to him."

"I suppose I can't. What do you propose I do with her?"

"Take her back to the Hall."

"I can't take that kind of woman to my family's ancestral home."

"We can tell people she's a friend of mine."

"Everyone knows who Katherine Crawfield is, and you do not need that kind of friend."

"Just for a night? You can figure out something else tomorrow."

Finn nodded. "We need to find something to do while she retrieves her reticule."

Thirteen

CLAIRE LOOKED DOWN OVER THE BALLROOM AND noticed that it had gone dark, aside from the light of a few flickering lamps. She walked to the rail and looked down. In the center of the room, a naked man and woman danced a waltz. "Let's go," Finn said again, as he tugged her toward the door. But her gaze was riveted. She drew her hand from his and placed them both on the rail.

Her heart was beating as fast as the hooves of a runaway team of horses. The bodice of her gown was suddenly so tight she could barely take a deep breath. She laid a hand on Finn's arm and looked up at him.

His eyes sparkled with sudden awareness. He stepped closer behind her, his length pressing along hers. His arms slid around her waist. "Do you want to watch?" he murmured in her ear. His voice was rough again, and it crawled across her skin like lace, ticklish yet firm.

"I'll probably go to hell for this, but you look so damn intrigued," he said. He ran a frustrated hand through his hair and pulled a chair from its spot beside the wall, partially hiding it behind the curtains, but positioning it so that they could see out. He sat down and patted his lap. "Sit," he said gently. He tugged her fingertips until she stood between his parted legs. Then he patted his knee again. "Sit."

"We should probably go."

"You want to watch them." He raised his eyebrows at her. "And I want to watch you watch them."

"I don't think—" she started. But he cut her off when he wrapped an arm around her middle and pulled her down.

"Don't think," he said. "Just sit."

She perched precariously on his knee, which seemed much sturdier than she'd thought. Every part of him was sturdy. He obviously didn't live the life of leisure she'd assumed. He was lithe as a cat, and his body was strong and fit.

"I wanted to talk about—" she tried again, keeping her body rigid in his lap.

"Let's discuss it later." His hand landed on her hip, drawing her more comfortably into the shelter of his embrace. When had it become shelter? She wasn't certain, but the thought was a little disturbing. She fought to remain rigid.

A bell rang down below, its insistent peal catching her ears. And Finn's too, if the way he sat up to look over the railing was any indication.

"What's going on down there?" she asked.

"Remember the live intercourse I mentioned?" he replied with a smirk.

"With actors?"

He grinned and shrugged. "Does it matter?"

He was interested now, sitting forward so that his front came up to meet her back. He sat up higher in the chair and tucked her bottom more snugly into his lap so that she was facing forward, still seated between his bent legs.

A shiver crawled up her spine as he brushed her hair to the side. "Oh, sorry," she murmured as she gathered the lot of it and drew it over her right shoulder.

"Don't be. I love it." He tucked a stray lock behind her ear.

"All these curls. I don't quite know what to do with them."

"Well, I don't love the color, but it always smells so good. Like sunshine. You're certain it will wash out?" She nodded as he leaned his head into her neck and breathed deeply. The cool movement as he inhaled had the hair on the back of her neck standing up. This time, she did shiver. "Are you cold?" he asked.

She shook her head. "Not a bit." In fact, she was a bit overly warm.

"I lose all my common sense when I look at you," he said softly by her ear. She closed her eyes for a moment to keep from swooning.

"Did you have any to begin with, my lord?" she teased.

A grin quirked the corners of his lips as he placed a soft kiss on her cheek below her mask. She smiled. She couldn't help it.

The bustle of footmen below caught his attention. They hefted a big bed into the middle of the room and then placed a barrier around it.

"That's a bed. Why are they putting a bed in the middle of the room?"

"Keep watching. You'll see. You're not offended by it, are you?" He suddenly looked concerned about the fact that he was allowing her to watch such a show. "Perhaps we should leave. Your father and my brother will murder me if they find out I brought you here."

Viewing the show would be the least of his concerns.

"You know who they are?"

"I believe so," he replied. "But they'll be masked."

"I see." She didn't know what more she could say. "Why?"

"Some people like to be watched." He shrugged his shoulders. He pointed out the seating area the footmen were setting up outside the roped enclosure around the bed. "And even more like to do the watching."

Both men and women were taking seats in the audience section. "The women, are they paid to attend?"

He shook his head. "They come because they like it. Many of them come with men. To share the experience. Still others come alone and try to find an interested party."

"They're about to begin," she said, settling into his arms a little more deeply.

❧

Finn was about to insist that they leave and go home. But her curiosity won out over his need to get her out of there. And he wouldn't give up an opportunity to have her in his arms. The lights dimmed as footmen doused the lamps around the edges of the room. Only a single bright light hung over the bed.

Footmen milled about the room below stairs, ensuring everything was in place.

He allowed his hand to stroke over her hip. She didn't even flinch away from his touch.

She looked out over the railing and said, "It's not hard for them to bare all like that?"

"Not for some." Speaking of hard, he'd been as hard as stone ever since she'd sat down in his lap. But she hadn't noticed. He adjusted her bottom for a better fit.

"I should get my own chair," she said as she started to rise. But he snaked an arm around her waist and drew her back down.

"I like holding you," he said. "Stay."

She settled back gingerly into his lap.

Two performers approached the makeshift stage. "And so it begins," she whispered. "Do you enjoy these shows?"

"I don't get overly amorous because of them, if that's what you're asking."

"Do they affect you at all?"

He didn't answer, and she let the subject drop as the man and woman on the stage began to perform. As they wove their exotic little dream before the spectators, Finn watched Claire.

"Sit back," he coaxed gently, bringing her body back to rest against him. Her head landed on his shoulder. She fit him. From top to bottom she fit him. Why had he not realized that before? It was almost like she was made to fit into his arms.

He brought one hand around her body to lie on her stomach. She moved it quickly to her hip, her eyes fixed on the stage. The players were now naked, and the man tossed the woman onto the bed. Claire giggled.

"Liked that, did you?" he couldn't help but ask.

"I like their easy camaraderie," she said quietly. "You can tell they're in love."

"How?" He was blind to it, obviously.

"By the way they look at one another," she breathed, totally enraptured by what the players were doing.

Finn and Claire were shrouded in complete darkness up on the landing. He almost wished it wasn't dark, so he could see her face.

The man on the stage took his lover's breasts in his hands and drew them to his lips. Claire's bottom twitched against Finn's lap. Was she getting aroused?

"This makes your heart beat faster," he said softly in her ear, loving the lemony scent of her.

"I supposed it does," she said, squirming a little in his arms.

"It makes my heart beat faster too." She immediately stilled. She didn't even breathe.

Finn began to move his fingers across her stomach in a slow motion that finally turned into a roaming caress that went from beneath her breasts to her hips. She sat still and watched what was on the stage.

"Claire," he said quietly, when her shallow breaths were nearly more than he could take.

"Hmmm?" she hummed back absently.

"If you were alone, would you be touching yourself?" She froze again. Barely daring to breathe. "Would you?" he coaxed.

❧

Would she? If she truly asked herself that question, she'd have to say yes. She'd never even thought of doing it before that night at his house in Bedfordshire. She hadn't known what it was all about. But in the months since, she'd touched herself. Heat crept up her face at the thought. The answer to his question was—Yes, she would hike her skirts up around her waist and sink her fingers into her warm, wet folds. She'd rub herself to completion. But she wasn't alone. Which made this damned difficult.

"Look what he's doing on the stage," Finn said. His eyes were riveted there, instead of on her. But when she glanced at the stage, she saw the male character, who she assumed was some debauched lord, nibbling and biting at his wife's breasts. She didn't know if the woman was his wife, but she liked assuming she was.

"Do you like what he's doing?" Finn asked.

Absently, she allowed her own fingertips to grace the plump skin over her bodice.

"I remember what it was like to lick your breasts. They turn cherry red when they've been suckled."

Claire's belly clinched. She was already wet. At this rate, she'd leave a huge wet spot on Finn's knee when she stood up.

"You didn't answer me. If you were alone, would you be touching yourself? Would you slide a finger below the bodice of your dress so you could tease your nipples? Would you, Claire?" She barely registered it when his hand came up to cup her breast. But she didn't shove his hand away. She liked his touch. Her breasts were more sensitive than normal, but his touch was gentle.

"Yes," she whispered, ashamed of her own response. She would be touching her nipples. She would be massaging her breasts. She would be ready to find completion.

"Tell me if I do anything you don't want," he said. Then his hand grazed the sensitive skin above her breasts. It was all Claire could do not to arch her back to thrust her breasts into his hands. To shamelessly beg him to caress her. "You'll tell me if I'm not pleasing you, won't you?" he breathed. His voice had dropped to a husky murmur for her ears alone.

His finger slipped beneath her bodice and grazed that turgid little peak that ached for him. A shameless moan left her throat.

"I would give anything right now to lower your bodice and take you in my arms. Then I'd drink you in."

She was being tortured. "Finn," she protested.

"What is it, love? Do you want to come?"

If it wasn't so dark, he would see her blush furiously at that question. But, heaven help her, she did. She did want to come.

"Do you want me to make you come, Claire?" he asked softly.

She turned her head and buried it in his neck. She couldn't say no. She couldn't say yes.

He chuckled lightly. "I'll see what I can do."

She exhaled. Finally. Thank God.

His fingers left her bodice and he laid his hand flat on her thigh. Then his fingers began to gather her skirts, bunching them up more and more near her hip. He took great care not to expose her, although at this point, she was well beyond caring. When his fingers finally encountered her skin, they lingered to play at the top of her stockings.

"What color are they?" He drew her earlobe into his mouth and suckled it gently.

"Green," she replied without even thinking.

"One day, I want to remove them from you so I can lick all the way from your toes to—" He paused. Then found the passage inside her drawers through the slit in the middle, and as his fingers parted her flesh, he finished, saying, "Here."

Claire's right hand clutched the chair arm, while her left hand clung tightly to his thigh.

"You are so wet," he murmured.

How mortifying.

"So lovely," he continued. His free hand cupped her breast, his finger stroking across her nipple through the bodice of her gown. His fingers dipped inside her, as he brought her own moisture forward and circled that little nub of pleasure he seemed to be fairly well acquainted with. "Oh, it's swollen. I bet it's thumping like mad. Just like your heart."

She nodded, her eyes still closed. She didn't even need to watch the performance on the stage. Finn was more than she could handle up on the landing. In the dark, with his fingers stroking her most private places, with him driving her senseless.

His finger dipped inside her again, drawing that slick moisture from inside her channel so he could slide his finger easily across that knot of sensation.

"Finn," she cried out.

"Are you close?" he asked in her ear.

She nodded frantically, biting her lower lip to keep from screaming.

The pressure and speed of his assault increased.

"Then do it," he growled in her ear. "Come for me. Let me feel that sweet wash of your release. Let me feel your body quake in my arms. When you come, I'm going to slide my finger inside you and dream about the day it'll be me inside you again as you flutter in release."

A breathy little sigh was all she could utter.

"Come for me, Claire. Come for me. You want to come. I know you do. Can you? Will you? Trust me, Claire. Let me pleasure you."

She pushed toward that impossible cliff but couldn't fall over.

"Claire, stop fighting it. It's just me and you. We're alone. Your breast in my hand. My fingers are sinking inside you. And you are going to find that sweet release."

"Finn," she whimpered.

"Now, Claire," he grunted in her ear. And then she did more than topple. She was flung body and soul over the cliff of pleasure. And couldn't keep from crying out her release. "Shhh…" he crooned in her ear. But he didn't stop rubbing that spot that was full of concentrated longing. He replaced his finger with his thumb and slid one digit inside her.

She came. And came. And came. And he milked every last drop from her as she settled back to earth. Her body stilled, supple and pliant as he pulled his hand from beneath her skirt, covered her legs completely, and turned her so that she lay cuddled in his arms, her head on his shoulder.

He brushed a kiss across her forehead.

"Don't worry. I still don't love you," she whispered.

"I don't love you either," he whispered back. Then

he kissed her forehead again and let her go limp in his arms. She'd try to remember in a moment why this was a bad thing. But, in that moment, she didn't care at all.

Fourteen

WHAT ROTTEN, DREADFUL, DOG-TIRED LUCK HE HAD. Finn was sitting with Claire tucked into his side in the carriage. She smelled good enough to eat, and after what they'd just done on the balcony, he wanted to nibble on her all over. His hands still smelled like her, for God's sake. Just the thought of how responsive she was made him hard as stone.

But then he looked across the carriage and saw Katherine. His former mistress looked out the coach window, worrying her fingernails as her foot tapped against the floor. The situation was enough to drive a sane man mad.

"When did this start, Katherine?" Finn asked.

She startled. "Beg your pardon?"

He touched his fingertips to the space over his own eye, indicating her bruise. "When did he start hitting you?"

"Does it matter?" She glared at him from across the coach.

"It would help to know what kind of man I'm destined to deal with."

"He won't bother you," she said. Then she went back to nibbling her fingernails.

Finn highly doubted that Mayden would *not* come for her. Finn would have to hide Katherine, and hide her well, before the man came to call. "He'll bother me like a fly bothers a horse."

That wasn't exactly true. Mayden was not the smartest man alive. And he was desperate. What he wanted more than anything was to own everything the Duke of Robinsworth had ever had his hands on, and that included Finn's property.

It was rumored that Mayden had a hand in the Duke of Robinsworth's wife's murder, but no one had ever been able to prove it. She'd been tossed from the turrets of Robin's own ancestral home, Finn's current domicile, years ago, and the duke had been vilified for it. He had become a recluse because of all the talk.

That was, until he met Sophia Thorne, of course. Robin had followed her back to her homeland, which just happened to be a magical land. The same land from which the lady beside him hailed.

Mayden had a score to settle with Robinsworth, and therefore with every friend, family member, and acquaintance of his. And it was no wonder he'd chosen Katherine to twist the knife. If Katherine thought Mayden wouldn't come for her, she was dead wrong.

Finn would have to find a safe place for her to stay until after the baby was born. God, what a muddle.

He spoke, more to himself than to the other occupants of the coach. "We need to get you up the stairs and to a bedchamber with no one noticing you."

Claire opened her mouth to speak, but Katherine said, "Of course," with an almost imperceptible nod.

"You think you're going to bring her into the Hall like she's a servant."

Finn arched a brow at Claire. Katherine *was* a hired woman. Just not the kind that Claire was referring to.

"Did you expect me to bring her in through the front door?" Finn glared at Claire. She didn't understand anything about his world, its hierarchy, or his responsibilities.

"She is not a maid."

"That's for damn sure," Finn said under his breath.

Claire punched him in the side. Hard enough to make him grunt. "What was that for?"

"For being a dolt." Claire crossed her arms beneath her breasts and glared at him.

"It's all right, Miss Thorne. I understand," Katherine said. Apparently, her fire had been quite effectively stamped out. When he'd met her, she'd been sweet and charming and not a mouse of a woman. He wasn't attracted to this Katherine at all. Which was good, because the faerie beside him drew all his attention.

What the devil was he going to do with Katherine?

❧

"You can send her to your house in Bedfordshire," Claire suggested.

"Charming place," Katherine said.

"You've been there?" Claire couldn't help but ask. Of course, Katherine had been there. She had been his mistress.

Katherine raised a brow at her. No response was necessary. "Haven't you?"

"Of course, she hasn't been there," Finn said, denying her knowledge of the place.

"Of course not," Claire muttered. "I only arrived a few days ago."

"From where is it that you hail?" Katherine asked.

"I'm sure you've never heard of it," Claire responded.

"Where have Lord and Lady Ramsdale been keeping you?"

"In the country," Finn interjected.

"Alone?"

Katherine was interested in her life story. And Claire couldn't share any of it. There was no reason to explain Claire's hair color or the fact that she was at that damn ball in the first place, since Katherine would hopefully never see Claire again. Ever.

"The new Duchess of Robinsworth, Miss Thorne, and their older brother lived with their grandparents most of the time," Finn said. He shot Claire an apologetic glance. It was hard to talk about her parents, since she didn't know them well. So, she appreciated his help. "I suppose in the morning that I could send you to Bedfordshire."

Katherine nodded. "I just need to stay out of his reach for a time." She laid a hand on her still-flat stomach. The baby couldn't possibly be Finn's. He hadn't lain with Katherine in months. "If you could help me, I would be grateful."

"I'll send word to the house tomorrow. And then you can travel in a few days."

"And stay with you until then?"

"You'll stay with Miss Thorne at the Hall. As her guest. I'll return to my house."

"Are you certain that's a good idea?" Claire asked, suddenly unsure of being saddled with Finn's former mistress.

"I'm not certain of anything," Finn said as he scrubbed a hand down his face. "I probably shouldn't leave the two of you in case Mayden comes looking for Katherine." He was damned if he did, and damned if he didn't.

The coach rumbled to a stop, and the footman lowered the step and opened the door. "I'll wait for the carriage to take me around to the back," Katherine said.

"You'll do no such thing. You heard him. You are my guest."

Katherine may have had a rough start in life, but Claire refused to let her be treated like the working class, not with that wounded look in her eye, even if she was a former mistress. She took Katherine's hand and pulled her from the carriage.

Wilkins didn't even blink when he opened the door. The man deserved a medal. "Shall I prepare for another guest?" he asked.

"Please do," Claire said before Finn could open his mouth. "Mrs. Crawfield is a friend of mine, and she will need a room close to my bedchamber."

Finn growled low in his throat.

"What on earth was that for?"

"Nothing. Absolutely nothing," Finn muttered. "I trust the two of you can settle yourselves in with no assistance from me?" He didn't wait for

an answer, but turned on his heel and went toward
the study.

Claire needed some time alone. She needed to
plan. She needed to figure out what was going to
happen next. But she had to settle Katherine in
and be certain she was all right. She couldn't let a
woman like her down. Particularly since they were
in similar situations.

Maybe there was a mission here for Claire after
all. Perhaps it was saving Katherine Crawfield from
herself. Claire hadn't been on a mission in months.
She missed the challenge.

❦

"How long have you been in love with him?"
Katherine asked as they walked slowly up the stairs.
Claire stumbled over her own foot, and Katherine
reached out to steady her.

"Beg your pardon?" Claire managed to spit out.

Katherine enunciated every word clearly as she
continued to speak. "How. Long. Have. You. Been.
In. Love. With. Finn?"

Claire forced a chuckle that she didn't even remotely
feel. "I have no idea what you're talking about."

Katherine smiled softly. "A woman knows." She
waved a breezy hand in the air. "There's definitely
something between the two of you."

There was a child, but she couldn't tell Katherine
about that. "You must be mistaken." Claire absently
fiddled with a loose string on her glove.

"I am never mistaken, not when it comes to matters
of the heart." She paused, staring at nothing. "That

is, unless it's my own heart that's involved. Then I'm a complete idiot." Her eyes filled with tears, and she waved a hand in front of her face as though to dry them before they even fell.

"Why Mayden?" Claire asked as she continued up the stairs. It was much better to talk about Katherine's love affair than her own.

"He was charming. He made me feel like he wanted me more than anything. He's very good at that. I wasn't the only one he was courting. He was priming another woman for marriage, someone wealthy." She laughed at herself. "Courting is the wrong word for what women like me do, isn't it?"

"Not really. I imagine the courtship is very similar, is it not?"

Katherine shrugged. "Perhaps." She heaved a huge sigh. "I didn't realize until after I'd given Finn the cut what a mistake I'd made. I should have stayed with Finn. He might never love me, but he did respect me. And he could afford me. That's more than I got with Mayden." She laid a hand on her belly. "I never wanted a child."

"You'll grow to love him with time." Claire was already in love with the child she carried within her.

"A child is a liability in my way of life." She looked haunted. "It's difficult to convince a man that you're irresistible with a child hanging on to your skirts."

"Isn't that what governesses and nurses are for?" Claire had pretended to be both when she was on her missions. And found that the upper class typically left their child rearing to the nannies and hired help.

"Nurses and governesses are for your class. Not

mine." She settled onto the settee in Claire's private sitting room. "I suppose I can find a good family for it."

"Do you have any family who can help you?"

She shook her head. "No one who will claim me."

Claire felt similarly. "You can go to Lord Phineas's house in Bedfordshire and retire for the rest of your time. Then make a decision."

At least Katherine would get a decision. Claire's own situation would depend on the nature of the child.

"Has he kissed you yet?" Katherine asked.

Claire sputtered. He'd done a lot more than that. And even more tonight. "Certainly not."

"Then he wants to. I can tell by the way he looks at you."

Claire had to ask. "What makes you think that?"

"He gets this hungry look on his face when he looks at you. Like he's imagining what you taste like and smell like. What you'd feel like wrapped around him."

Heat crept up Claire's cheeks.

"Pardon me," Katherine said. "I keep forgetting you're not like me. Real ladies would faint to hear such things. They do it with the lights off and their nightrails shoved up to their waists, grinding their teeth the whole while." She laughed lightly.

That wasn't what it had been like for Claire with Finn. She had questions for Katherine. But she'd seem like the worst sort of whore if she asked them, so she kept them to herself. Then curiosity got the better of her. "You don't do it with the lights off?"

Devilish delight twinkled in Katherine's eyes. "I

do whatever he wants." She kicked off her shoes and lifted her feet to the footstool. "There's no shame in taking pleasure in the bedchamber." She narrowed her eyes at Claire. "What were you doing with Finn up on the landing tonight?"

"Watching the show," Claire admitted.

"And?"

"And nothing."

"That's why Finn looked like he wanted to drag you straight to his bedchamber and keep you busy the rest of the night. He's probably irked to no end that I'm blocking the path between the two of you."

"Blocking what path?"

"You're here with me, instead of with him."

Claire wasn't going to be with him, no matter what.

A knock sounded on the door. "Enter," Claire called.

Wilkins stepped into the room and bowed. "Mrs. Crawfield's chambers have been prepared. And his lordship would like to see you in the study, miss."

"Would you show Mrs. Crawfield to her chambers?" Claire asked over her shoulder as she went to see what Finn wanted.

"He has found a way around my block, apparently," Katherine murmured to Claire as she walked by her to follow Wilkins to her chambers. Claire's heart lurched.

Fifteen

CLAIRE FOUND FINN IN THE STUDY, SPRAWLED IN A chair before the fire with a tumbler of some kind of drink in his hand. "Don't even think of it," he said as she looked at his glass. "The last time you took my drink, you know what happened." He was getting hard at the mere thought of it. He hooked a chair with his foot and drew it closer to him so that they both faced the fire, but the corners of their chairs nearly touched.

"Certainly, it's not proper to sit that close together." She said it so primly that it amused him.

A grin tugged at the corners of his lips. "Surely that doesn't apply with a man who has been inside you."

Claire gingerly perched her bottom on the edge of the chair. "You shouldn't talk of such things." Her cheeks flushed a rosy shade of pink.

"How can I not? It's all I think about." He drank the last swallow of his drink and set the cup to the side. "Would you like something?" he asked.

"You just informed me that I couldn't have anything. Did you need to tell me something? Or did you just want me to watch you drink?"

Oh, he needed something. And she was it. "I just wanted to talk to you. To find out if Katherine was settling in all right."

"She's fine. She has the room next to mine."

"A genius bit of maneuvering there." With Katherine close by, he would not go within one hundred feet of Claire's chambers.

"I don't know what you mean."

"Of course, you don't."

Claire got to her feet. "If you don't need anything, I'll see you tomorrow."

"I need something," he said quickly as she walked by his chair. He snaked an arm around her waist and tugged her into his lap. She squirmed, but only for a moment. "Settle down," he growled playfully.

She wiggled her bottom against his erection and he winced. "Let me go, Finn."

"Fine," he clipped out. He loosened his arms but didn't completely let her go. He wouldn't force her to want him. Maybe he was the only one with such fierce desires right this moment. She wasn't foxed, after all, not like the last time he'd had her. He loosened his hold on her. She could have gotten out of his arms, had she tried, but she didn't. In fact, she softened against him a bit with a heavy sigh.

"Finn," she breathed.

"Claire," he mocked.

"Why did you send for me?"

Because he couldn't go to her with Katherine in the room beside her. "I just wanted to look at you."

"You're foxed. Go to bed."

In fact, he'd only had a sip or two of brandy. He

wasn't nearly foxed. He had all his faculties completely under control. What wasn't in control was her. "If you'll go with me, I will."

He laid his head against the back of the chair and closed his eyes. She should slap him. And she still might. She wasn't some whore he could talk to like that.

The palm of her hand stroked across his beard stubble, instead. "What's bothering you?" she asked. She still hadn't gotten up from his lap, and it was all he could do not to touch her.

"I don't want Katherine to be here," he admitted.

"You still have feelings for her?"

"Not at all." And that was the truth. He'd been dismayed and disillusioned when she threw him over, but that was more about his pride than any heartfelt emotion he had for her.

"But you had feelings for her once." It wasn't a question. It was a statement, which was fine, because it wasn't an easily answered question.

"Feelings didn't come into play with Katherine." He gave Claire a tiny push to slide her down his knee a bit. He could feel every breath she took in his manhood, and if he got any harder, she would be able to drive him into the wall and spin him like the hands of a clock.

"What was in play with Katherine?" Her voice was quiet, and her green eyes looked directly into his.

"Pleasure. Katherine was about pleasure. I have needs. She met them. For a time." That sounded callow even to him.

"And how do you have them met now?"

He didn't. Finn took her hand and placed it on his

raging manhood. She indelicately squeezed the tip of it through his trousers. "God, Claire." He took her hands in his and laid them upon his chest. "You'll unman me doing that."

"I don't know what that means."

Of course, she didn't. "Do you remember what we did tonight on the overlook at the ball?"

A rosy flush crept up her cheeks again. God, she was pretty. "I remember."

"That."

"Oh. I don't know how to do that."

Finn did. It felt like he spent in his hand more often lately than he ever had. And it was all Claire's fault.

Finn sat up straighter and cupped her face in his hands. He touched his lips to hers. Claire's hands fisted in his waistcoat as she clutched him tightly. But she kissed him back. She was slightly hesitant at first, but when he touched his tongue to hers, she moaned low in her throat. "What can I do to help you?" she whispered as she sat back and looked down at the ridge of his manhood. She licked her pretty pink lips.

He was an idiot. This woman had been an innocent before he'd spoiled her. And he couldn't use her as he would a whore. But he'd never felt this consuming desire for a woman before. Never. Not once in his life. He wanted to please her. He wanted to make her happy. To hell with his needs. He needed to have her. That was all.

But if he took her tonight, she'd be no more to him than Katherine. "If your father were here, I'd go to him and ask for his permission to take you driving or for a walk in Hyde Park." He drew her down to lay her head on his chest, and she curled into him like she was meant to be there.

"My father doesn't have dominion over my life. He never has." She stiffened with her statement, but she settled when he drew his hand down her back.

"But that's the way we do things here. We gentlemen see a pretty lass, and we go and ask for her father's permission to court her."

She sat up quickly. "I believe we are a little past the courtship stage."

"So, we put the cart before the horse." He chuckled at the look of exasperation on her face.

"That is a moot point. My kind doesn't marry your kind."

"Robin and Sophia did. Your mother and father did."

"My mother and father made a mistake. And I fear that Robinsworth and Sophia did too."

"Why did your grandparents raise you?"

"When a child is born to parents, one of whom is fae and one is not, the fae children are taken back to the land of the fae to be raised there, along with any parent's memory that they existed. The memories are sealed in a box and set high upon a shelf."

"That's awful," Finn breathed. No wonder she was bitter about the situation.

"That's why fae cannot marry nonfae. It's one of the Unpardonable Errors. Losing your children is the punishment for it."

"Your parents kept the ones who were not born fae?"

"Yes, two girls and a boy. One of the girls just happens to be fae. But they kept her anyway. I don't know how. Some kind of special magic my mother discovered."

"I feel certain they wanted to keep you."

"They never should have married to begin with."

"But they did. There's no taking it back."

"Just as there's no taking back a child."

Good God. No wonder Claire was bitter about her parents. She'd been all but abandoned, in her estimation.

Finn could sit and hold her like this all night. He'd never been one for cuddling, but he enjoyed having her in his lap, pressed against his side.

But his comfort also brought to mind that if he couldn't marry her, he couldn't have her at all. All of his hopes dashed like water against the rocks at the shore. He'd had her once. He supposed once would be enough.

"I think you've underestimated your parents' love for you."

"I think you've overestimated their level of caring."

"What was it like when you first saw them?"

"It was the night you and I had been together," she said quietly, so quietly he could barely hear her. "My grandfather died that night, and they sent the wind to pick me up and take me back to the land of the fae."

"The wind?"

"It's how we travel. The wind takes us to and from our land on the night of the moonful. Otherwise, we have to pass through a portal. The portal is guarded by fish. Or fallen faeries who have been turned into fish. They sent the wind for me on a night that wasn't a moonful, since it was an emergency."

He must have looked astounded, because she laughed lightly.

"There's much you'd have to learn to understand my land."

"I'd like to visit it."

"It's forbidden."

"Yet your father and Robin are there."

"They shouldn't be."

"Perhaps love is the key to their access. I have seen your parents together. They love one another to distraction. And there's no doubt Robin and Sophia are in love."

"Love matters not. Magic will rule over love. Always." She squirmed in his lap until she was in a position where she could look up at him. "Were you disappointed to find that Katherine's child isn't yours?"

Was he? God, no. "Not at all. If it had been, I'd have done my duty, however."

❧

He'd have done his duty. That was what a child was to him. A duty. He might have to do his duty to the one she carried. How would he feel about that? Because if the child wasn't fae, she would be forced to abandon it to his care, along with her memories of it.

His blue eyes were bright, and they stared directly into hers. It was like falling into an open blue sky. Claire sat forward and touched her lips to his. He looked so vulnerable sitting there holding her in his lap. He'd asked her questions about her life and given her time to explain. He'd even offered to court her. She didn't want to be courted. She wanted this in this moment. Right now.

"Claire," he groaned against her lips. "We can't do this."

"Do what?" she whispered back at him. A grin

tugged at the corners of her lips. His tongue reached out and touched hers, and she wrapped her lips around it and sucked gently.

"Don't do that," he groaned as he leaned back, avoiding her mouth. "Claire, if you don't stop, I'll have to have you."

What harm could that do? She was already expecting. The only problem was that, while she could hide the pregnancy beneath the layers of her skirts during the day, she could hide nothing when she was naked. "So, stop," she teased. Her lips tickled the side of his jaw as she kissed her way down the side of his throat. His manhood was rock hard again beneath her bottom.

Finn threaded his hand into Claire's hair and forced her to look at him. "Don't tease, Claire," he growled.

"Who's teasing?" she asked. Her hands fumbled with the fall of his trousers. They shook slightly, and he covered her hands with his.

"Stop," he urged. But it was a weak protest. He didn't mean it. He just did it because he thought he should.

"I just want to see it." That wasn't what she wanted, but it was as good an excuse as any. She worked the fall of his trousers and he bit his lower lip between his teeth, biting back a hiss of something as she revealed him to the glow of candles in the room. He was huge, and his flesh arched up high enough to touch his stomach.

She took his turgid flesh in her grip. "God, Claire," he grunted, but he thrust against her fist.

"It's so soft," she breathed.

He chuckled, but it was a broken sound. "You call that soft?"

"No, I mean your skin. It's so soft." Her fingertips dragged across a bead of moisture that leaked from the tip and she swirled it around the purple top of his arousal. "Does this feel good?"

"If it felt any better, I'd die on the spot."

"What you did for me, can I do that for you now?"

Finn groaned, still working his lower lip between his teeth. "You shouldn't."

"Why not?"

"It's not right."

"By whose standards?"

"Mine?" he growled as her questing fingers squeezed his tumescent flesh.

"You don't sound very certain."

"Stop, Claire." He raised his hands over his head, grasping the back of the chair. She couldn't tell if he was avoiding pushing her away or clutching her to him.

She continued her sensual assault and his hips began to grind a slow rhythm, his manhood reaching up to greet her every squeeze.

"Claire, if you don't stop, I'm going to come."

This only frenzied her movements. She tightened her grip and sped her fingers, sliding up and down his manhood with his thrusts. She remembered how she'd felt when he'd whispered in her ear about coming and finding that sweet release.

"Come for me, Finn," she urged, her whisper quiet beside his ear. He shuddered and released his lip long enough to grunt. His release wasn't at all what she expected. It was a silky thread of fluid that bathed her hand in his warm essence. Finn looked directly into her eyes as he pumped into her hand, once, twice, three times, his grunts at culmination music to her ears. Finally, he stilled. He pulled her tight against his chest and held her there, his essence between them, wetting his clothing.

"Don't look down," he warned.

She giggled. "I already saw all your private places."

She laid her head on his shoulder as he pulled a handkerchief from his pocket, reached between them and cleaned her hand of his seed. He closed the fall of his trousers and pulled her back down on his chest. She breathed him in, that scent of the forest now mingled with something else. Heat? Did heat have a smell? If so, that was it.

"Thank you," he said softly.

"You're welcome," she said as she sat up. "Don't fall in love with me."

"Don't worry, I won't." She kissed him gently and left the room.

❧

Finn cleaned himself up as best he could. Simmons would eat his hat tomorrow when he saw the state of Finn's clothing. The man would be livid. And Finn didn't care. That was the best sex he'd ever had in his life, and he hadn't even been inside her.

She could unman him with a simple touch, and he couldn't help but think that, in a perfect world, he would offer for her, marry her, and they could love each other until the end of their days.

But such was not the case. He had better stay away from Claire Thorne. Now, how to manage that when he needed her almost as much as the air he breathed, that was the question.

Sixteen

FINN TROMPED DOWN THE STAIRS FOR DINNER, HIS coat pristine and his cravat tied perfectly. But his insides were a muddle. Katherine was gone. He'd seen her off that afternoon and had sent one of his men with her. And a maid to see to her needs. She was gone. And safe, and that was what mattered. The last three days had been a living hell, though. He'd had his former mistress in the house along with the woman he wanted more than anything. It was like dragging flint in a pile of rocks and waiting to see if it would spark.

But finally, it was just Finn and Claire again. And he wanted to see her. He knew he'd pledged to himself that he'd stay away from her, but he couldn't.

Over the past three days, he'd seen her only at the evening meal, and that was with Katherine joining them. He'd missed her. It was an odd notion. But he had.

Finn sauntered into the dining room and stopped cold. It was empty. "Wilkins!" Finn bellowed.

"Yes, my lord," the man said as he stepped into the room.

"Do you know where Miss Thorne is?"

Wilkins looked decidedly uncomfortable. "She is in the study with His Grace, my lord."

"His Grace?"

"The Duke of Robinsworth."

"Robin's back?" Why hadn't anyone told Finn? His brother was back from the land of the fae with his magical wife, and no one had thought Finn important enough to inform?

Wilkins lifted his nose in the air and said, "The Duke and Duchess of Robinsworth are in His Grace's study, my lord. Along with Miss Thorne."

Finn stormed down the corridor toward Robin's study, but suddenly Lady Anne rounded the corner and squealed when she saw him coming. "Uncle Finn," she cried, just before she launched herself through the air at him. He caught her, unable to keep from laughing at her antics.

"Anne," Finn scolded as he hugged her tightly and set her back on her feet. "A lady doesn't fling herself at a gentleman." He winked at her.

"Sophie flings herself at Papa all the time," the girl said, her brows drawing together. "And Lady Ramsdale even kisses Lord Ramsdale." She put her fingertips over her mouth and giggled. "Sophie's going to have a baby."

Goodness, a lot could happen in three months. He ruffled her hair with his hand. "I'm glad you're home."

She scuttled past him and he continued toward the study. He didn't stop to knock on the door but admitted himself. He startled, however, when he realized that Lord and Lady Ramsdale were present, as were Sophia, Claire, and their brother Marcus.

Ronald and another woman Finn recognized as one of their servants occupied a space at the back of the room. Claire looked like she'd rather be presented to the guillotine than her parents.

"Robin," Finn said. His brother smiled and embraced him quickly, and Finn shook hands with Lord Ramsdale and Claire's brother. He bowed toward the ladies.

"Thank you for taking care of my daughter," Lord Ramsdale said. "We hadn't intended to stay as long as we did in the land of the fae, but there was a lot that needed to be taken care of." He looked fondly upon his wife. Claire looked like being drawn and quartered would be preferable to standing next to them.

"No trouble at all," Finn managed to say. Having them there was akin to having the rug pulled out from beneath his feet. Like tottering on the deck of a rolling ship. Like having his life snatched away. Like a great, yawning canyon had just been placed in the path between him and Claire.

Lord Ramsdale's eyes narrowed at him, but he didn't say anything more.

Claire looked down at her toes. He ached for her. This was painful, he could tell. "What are you all doing here?" she asked.

"We wanted to see you," Lady Ramsdale said. "We had no idea where you'd gone. You just disappeared."

"It's a long story," Claire began.

Finn interrupted. "A story best told over dinner, perhaps?" He turned toward Claire. "I came to collect you for our outing, Miss Thorne." At her confused look, he continued as smoothly as possible. "You

promised earlier today that you would accompany me
to the art exhibit in town. Did you forget?"

Her eyes lit up. "Oh, how could I forget?" She
smacked the heel of her hand against her forehead.
"We have plans to visit the art exhibit. In town." She
laid a hand on Finn's arm. Her touch shot straight to
his heart. She was going to let him attempt to save
her from the situation. Meaning she preferred his
company to theirs.

"Art," her father said. "An art exhibit, you say?"

"Yes," Finn croaked.

"I happen to be a connoisseur of art. Perhaps we
can join you?"

"Tickets had to be purchased in advance, I'm
afraid," Finn replied. "And it's sold out. But I promise
to have her home in a few hours." He quirked a brow
at Ramsdale. "She has so been looking forward to it."

"Of course," Ramsdale clipped out. He stepped
back and Finn held his elbow out to Claire. She laid
her hand upon it and let him lead her from the room.

❧

Claire didn't take a breath until they were out of the
duke's study and standing outside the closed door.
Then she did the unthinkable and threw her arms
around Finn's neck and kissed him. Right there in the
corridor. She embraced him and laid her lips on his.

Finn laughed against her mouth as he kissed her
quickly and set her away from him. Apparently, he had
more sense than she did. "I thought you were going to
toss me over, there for a moment," he admitted.

"Thank you," she sighed. "Thank you so much."

Finn's tone softened. "You're welcome." He looked up and down the corridor. "What do you want to do for the next few hours?"

"Oh, you need not entertain me. I can take care of myself."

"That's not in question. But I did tell your parents we would be going off together. So, I think we should. Where would you like to go?"

"There's not really an art exhibit, is there?"

"Of course not."

"Oh." Claire rang her hands together. But then she noticed the painting behind them. It was a painting of a sunny room, with a lady's desk off to one side. On top of the desk rested a quill pen and several pieces of parchment. "Let's go there," she said.

"Beg your pardon?" Finn looked at her as if she was bound for Bedlam.

Claire felt for the magic paintbrush that was tucked into her garter. It was there. This should work. The question would be whether or not she could take Finn with her. She reached a hand into the painting and felt for the other side. It was there. Warm and safe. She leaned her head into the painting, much the way someone would dip their head beneath the water while swimming in the lake, and saw that the room was as pictured—quiet and serene.

Finn ran a hand through his hair as his jaw dropped. He blinked his eyes open, closed them, and then did it again. "Pick me up and put me into the painting," Claire urged. She laid a hand on his shoulder and he lifted her in his arms.

"There has to be an explanation for this. I am not

going to stuff you into a painting." He held her there, suspended in the air.

"It's all right. You can go with me." She nibbled her lower lip. "Or at least I think you can." She pointed toward the painting with her toe, which sank into the painting ever so slightly before he jerked her back.

Footsteps sounded at the other end of the corridor. "Please hurry. Someone is coming."

He stood there like a dolt, holding her in the air. So, she clambered out of his arms and jumped head first into the painting.

⟡

Finn stood there in the corridor, wondering what the devil he'd just witnessed. But then a slim hand reached through the painting and motioned him forward. He took it in his grip and tried to pull her back through. But she held firm. She released his hand, shook her finger at him, and motioned him with a crooked finger again. She held her hand still in the air, and he took it reverently. Any sort of trouble could befall her in there. He had to go with her to be sure she was safe, didn't he? He counted to three and leaped into the painting to join her.

Finn had a little experience climbing out of windows from his more debauched days, but the oak floor he landed on was much harder than the ground. He rolled into his shoulder and onto his back. Claire stood looking down at him with her hands on her hips.

"Hello," she said with a tiny wave.

Seventeen

CLAIRE LOOKED DOWN AT HIM. HE DESERVED ACCO-lades for being open-minded enough to dive into a painting, particularly since he hadn't even known magic existed until a few months ago, and he'd had very little exposure to it.

He didn't make any attempt to get up from the floor. He just lay there and gazed up at her. "Would you like a hand?" she asked.

"No," he grunted, rolling his shoulder. "I think I'll just lie here for a bit. Don't mind me. I just fell through a magical portal into a painting." He shrugged and twisted his mouth in a most amusing fashion. "Happens to me every day. I should be used to it by now."

Claire sank down on her haunches and looked at him. "I couldn't think of any other place to go."

"A carriage ride wouldn't have been enough for you? A trip to the park?" He grimaced again. "No, you would only settle for diving head first into some-one's library." He sat up on his elbows and looked around. "What is this place?"

Claire looked around. She wasn't entirely sure. "Some lady's sitting room, maybe?"

"How did we get here?" He lumbered slowly to his feet, dusting himself off as he stood up.

"We jumped," she replied. "Don't you remember?" She reached for him. "You didn't hit your head when you fell, did you?" She riffled her fingers through his hair. "Never mind," she said, as she stepped back. "Nothing could harm that hard head. I need not have worried."

"Very amusing," he said, but a grin formed on his lips. "Can we go back?"

"I don't want to go back yet," Claire said. "Let's wait until my parents are gone."

"Is this a house?" Finn asked. He walked toward the walls, but when he touched one, his hand sunk as though into mist. "That's a bit odd."

"This whole situation is odd."

"So, the room isn't part of a house?" He touched the mist again and then pulled his hand back."

"No, it's just a room with furniture. No real barriers. If you walk out of it, you end up nowhere." She sat down on the settee and kicked her shoes off, then pulled her legs up beneath her skirts. "This must be a figment of someone's imagination. If it were a real place, we could walk around it just as we could any other place." He looked askance at her. "In other words, we can walk into places that are real and be in the real place, via the painting. But if the place isn't real, it's just…" She held her hands out to the sides. "Like this. Do you remember the night I tumbled into your room? I went there through a painting."

"You had a painting of my chambers?"

She still didn't understand that part. Not completely. "No. Just a painting of a door. It just happened to be your chambers on the other side."

"How do we get back?"

"The magic always gives me a frame to climb back through." The only time it hadn't was the night she'd tumbled into his room. She pointed to the painting on the wall. It was a painting of the corridor they'd come from. Nothing more.

"How does it work?" He looked closely at the painting, but when he touched his hand to it, it was firm.

"It only works for me," Claire said. "I don't understand why it works. But it does. When I was four, my grandparents put a paintbrush in my hand, and as long as I had that paintbrush and some magic dust, I could go into any painting I chose. They took the paintbrush from me after I went away for a sennight. I'd launched myself into a kitchen I'd painted, and it was filled with food and drink. I knew they'd be angry at me after I'd been gone a day, so I stayed a while. When I finally came home, they took the paintbrush from me and hid it."

"And you have said paintbrush now?" He looked from one hand to the other.

Claire patted her thigh. "Tucked in my garter." She laughed at the bemused look on his face. She had to give him credit, though. Not many men would have jumped through a portal with her.

"Does it work for anyone who holds the paintbrush?"

"No. Only me. Sophia and Marcus tried it again and again, and they couldn't go anywhere."

"Pity for them."

"They were always envious." She laughed lightly at the thought.

"I wouldn't have thought you were so precocious. You seem much more reserved than Sophia." He quirked a brow at her. "Or are you?"

"I think I proved on the night I met you that I wasn't as reserved as you might think." Heat crept up her cheeks at the reminder.

"You're pretty when you blush," he said softly as he sat down beside her on the settee. "So, what do you want to do while we're here?"

Claire yawned into her cupped hand. "Take a nap?" She laughed at his stricken look. But she was tired. She'd never needed as much sleep as she did right now. "Want to go to bed with me?" she asked.

❧

Finn's gut clenched at her choice of words. "Go to bed with you?" he said with a laugh. But then his voice dropped to a silky slide. "I think I already did that."

She blushed even more profusely. "A gentleman wouldn't mention such things."

He chuckled. "I think we have already proven that I'm no gentleman."

"What are you, exactly?" she asked as she scooted him over to the end of the settee. She lay down and put her head on his thigh. She looked up quickly. "You don't mind, do you?"

"My lap is at your disposal," he said with a flourish of his hands. She gently laid her head on his lap, and he started to run his fingers through her hair. He hit one of her pins and she flinched. He tugged it gently from her coiffure. Then he proceeded to tug them all from her hair, one by one, until her strawberry blond tresses fell over his lap in waves. "So pretty," he breathed.

She rubbed her cheek on his thigh, rooting farther into him for comfort. She sighed heavily and the heat of her breath sank through the knee of his trousers. He ignored the heavy pounding that was starting in his manhood. If she didn't look up, she wouldn't even notice it. He stroked his fingers down the length of her hair. She settled against him. "Tell me about you, Finn. What are you, aside from the duke's brother?"

She let him stroke her scalp and caress the side of her face, smiling softly as he did so. So, his little kitten liked to be petted. Evidently, she liked it a lot. He'd originally thought she was prickly, but she wasn't. She was soft as cotton but with sharp teeth and claws when she needed them.

"I am nothing, aside from the duke's brother." It pained him to say that, but it was true. He had no calling. No purpose in life, aside from his amateur detective work and the crimes he solved. He didn't even solve very many of them himself anymore, not since he'd started managing Robin's holdings. He paid his men to do it. "I like to learn things about people. I can find a needle in a haystack." He jostled her shoulder when she softened against him.

She snorted. "Sorry," she said. "I told you I was tired."

"Am I boring you?" He stroked down the length of her hair again and she purred. He felt the vibration of her throat in his leg, and heat shot straight to his groin.

An erection he could ignore had just turned into one he couldn't. He adjusted it, pushing it to the side away from her head.

"Are you comfortable?" She started to sit up, but he turned her head away from him.

"More comfortable than I think I've ever been," he admitted.

"Tell me about the crimes you've solved," she urged, and yawned again.

So, Finn told her all about himself, and he kept talking long after she'd fallen asleep because he was afraid that he would wake her if he stopped. He didn't want to give up this moment for anything.

❧

Claire woke to the soft rumble of… What was that noise? She moved, and the pillow beneath her moved too. Claire lifted her head to find Finn looking at her. "You snore," she said. He'd somehow rearranged their bodies while she slept so that he was stretched along the length of the settee with her draped on top of him.

"You make a fabulous blanket," he said, his voice raspy from sleep. He didn't make a move to change positions, so she laid her head on his chest again.

"You make a nice pillow," she said against his waistcoat. There was a small wet spot beneath her mouth. Apparently, she'd drooled on him. How mortifying. She moved to sit up, but he put his arms around her. "Don't move. I like holding you."

"Do you know what time it is?" she asked.

"No clue, but if you'd like to reach in my

pocket and get my watch fob, we can check." He yawned loudly.

"It can wait." She didn't want to move. She wanted to stay wrapped in his arms forever. But she couldn't. He wasn't of her world. And there could be no future for them.

One of his legs rested along the back of the settee and the other dangled toward the floor. Claire was nestled between his thighs, and she wiggled to get more comfortable.

"Be still," he warned.

A hard lump pressed into her belly and she suppressed a grin as she realized what it was. She'd held him in her hand last night, and he'd spent himself all over her fingers. The thought of doing it again was maddening. She liked pleasing him. And he obviously liked being pleased. She moved to the side to slide a hand down his leg.

"Careful down there," he grumbled.

"I'll be very careful," she whispered as she leaned up and touched her lips to his. He sipped at her lips softly, and she touched her tongue to his.

"Claire," he growled. "Don't play games with me." He lifted her hand from where she'd gripped him through his trousers and pushed her head back down to lie on his chest. "Just let me hold you for a bit, will you?"

But Claire just hitched herself higher, until the vee of her thighs was directly over his manhood.

"Claire," he groaned. He threaded his hands into her hair and forced her to look up at him. "Don't start something you don't want to finish. I've been

Eighteen

"MARRY ME, CLAIRE," HE SAID, PULLING BACK FROM her lips in tiny increments, saying one word at a time. She didn't even hear him until he repeated it more clearly. "Marry me, Claire?" he asked.

She stilled on top of him. "You know I can't," she said, and then she sat up with her elbows on his chest, looking down at him. She looked like a rumpled angel, lying there with her cheeks all rosy and her hair all a mess. The print from the buttons of his waistcoat was etched onto her cheek. His heart squeezed in his chest. *Is this what love felt like?* If so, he liked it. He wanted to wake up to her looking like this every day for the rest of his life.

"Why can't you?" he asked.

"Because it's forbidden."

"Yet others have done it." He jostled her shoulder. "You can't use that excuse. Give me a better reason."

"The children," she finally said, sitting up and moving off him. "It's because of the children, all right?" She suddenly sounded peevish.

"I don't understand." Thoughts roiled in his head

like a boiling cauldron, yet he couldn't make sense of any of them. "Why would children be a problem? Your kind and my kind can procreate. That has been proven. Look at you. Look at your brother and sister."

"And look at what happened to us. I wouldn't wish that on my worst enemy. It's not an easy life, Finn, not knowing where you came from. It's damn hard."

He reached over and pulled her back into his arms. She went, but not willingly, until at last she softened against him. "Can we table this discussion and go back to it later?" he asked.

"I will not change my mind."

"I think I liked it more when you were asleep," he said, as he pulled her head back down to his chest. "Go back to sleep, and then let's wake up and do this all over again with a different outcome."

"What kind of outcome did you have in mind?"

"The kind where you scream my name and swear you can see God."

She chuckled against his chest. It was a lovely sound, really. Like the bells of St. Andrews. She didn't do it often, but when she did, the effect was jarring. "I could make you happy, Claire," he said softly.

"I have no doubt that you could, Finn." She stilled against him, until suddenly he flipped their positions. She seemed surprised to find herself beneath him. "Goodness, Finn, that was fast."

"I do everything fast, apparently. Think back to that first night." He kissed her softly as he settled between her thighs, pushing her knees apart with his legs in her skirts. He rocked against the center of her, and she arched to meet him, a moan leaving her lips to tickle the air between them. "Does that feel nice?" he asked as he adjusted to rock a little harder against her. Her mouth fell open and she nodded.

"Just imagine how it would feel if I was inside you again," he said, punctuating his words with short licks across her lips.

"Remind me," she urged.

But he did something he'd never done before. He stood up and moved away from her. "We had better get back. People will be looking for you." He adjusted his clothing.

"Now?" she squeaked. She sat up, her face flaming. He wasn't certain if it was desire or anger he saw there, but he'd be willing to bet on anger.

Finn pulled his watch fob from his pocket. "We have been gone for four hours. That's long enough to have seen all the paintings at the exhibition that didn't exist. We should go back."

She was stewing. He could tell. And a tiny part of him was immensely comforted by the fact that he could make her so angry by not giving in to her physical demands and demanding an emotional response instead.

He was still hard for her. But he wouldn't give on this point. He picked up the pins that he'd taken from her hair from the side table and called her to him. "Turn around. I'll try to make do with your hair."

"It's fine the way it is."

"It's fine as it is if we don't bump into anyone until you get to your chambers. But if someone sees you looking like that, they'll think I just tumbled you."

Her face flamed again. "Then I can assure them that

you didn't, can't I?" She shot him a look of exasperation that made him chuckle. "I'm glad you find this amusing."

If he didn't laugh, he didn't know what emotion he might be forced to deal with.

Finn lifted Claire in his arms and pushed her feet through the portal, but he didn't let go of her hand when he set her down. She was just angry enough to leave him there, stuck in that room. With her gripping his hand tightly, he climbed over the edge of the painting as if it were a windowsill. It was much easier than going through the painting headfirst.

When he got to the other side, Claire still glared at him. But then a voice barked from the other end of the corridor. "What the devil have you been doing, Finn?"

❧

Claire peeped around Finn's shoulder to find Sophia and the duke glaring at them. The duke's face was alight with anger, and Sophia laid a hand on his arm to calm him. It didn't work. He turned on his heel and bellowed back over his shoulder, "I'll see you in my study, Finn. Now!" He didn't look back. He just kept walking.

Finn groaned low in his throat, then leaned forward and pressed a kiss to Claire's forehead. "Don't worry. His bark is worse than his bite."

"Do you want me to go with you?"

He laughed. It was a loud sound and it bounced around the corridor. He was so amused that she couldn't help but smile along with him. "No need." Then he whispered. "Go fix your hair."

He pressed her hairpins into her hand and turned. He bowed to Sophia and followed the duke toward his study.

But then Claire was left with Sophia. "Claire…" she began.

Claire held up a hand to stop her. "Don't *Claire* me, Sophia. You are not my mother."

"No, I'm your sister, and I'm your friend." Claire turned to walk away but Sophia followed her. "Talk to me, Claire. If you won't talk to me, talk to Mother."

Mother. Claire snorted. Some mother she was. She'd allowed Claire to be taken back to the land of the fae.

"I know how you feel about her. I felt the same for a time. But then I got to know them. You should give them a chance."

No chance in hell.

Sophia rushed on. "They tried to keep us. To keep all of us. They left a token within each of us."

Finally, Claire looked up at her. Sophia rushed on to explain. "My love of music. It was a gift to me so that I could recognize the song of a loved one. They didn't realize that Ashley would be in love with me and that I would recognize his song as easily as theirs, but they did try."

"That's ridiculous."

Sophia looked at the painting they'd just stepped through. "The painting. Our father is an artist. It's his favorite pastime. You think you can step into paintings when no one else on earth, or any other realm, can do so *just because*? No. It's a gift from them. Marcus has one, too, although I don't know what it is yet."

"Sophia, I don't want to discuss this right now." She feigned a yawn. She needed some time alone. Some time to think.

"When will you be ready to discuss it? And to discuss what you were doing with Lord Phineas?" Sophia tapped her slippered foot against the floor.

"Nothing happened with Lord Phineas." Not this time, at least. "He just went along with me to keep me safe."

An unconvincing grunt was Sophia's only response.

"Where are Lord and Lady Ramsdale?"

"Mother and Father went back to Ramsdale House."

"Good." She knew she sounded like a petulant child, but she couldn't help it.

"We'll see them on Friday. They're throwing a ball to launch us into society."

"I don't care to be launched."

"They're acknowledging us as their legitimate children to the *ton*."

Why would they do such a thing?

"It was their idea. They wouldn't take no for an answer."

Of course they wouldn't. They suddenly wanted their fae children in their lives, when they hadn't wanted them for such a very long time. Well, too little too late.

❧

Robin paced back and forth in front of the fire in his study, and Finn feared his brother would wear a groove in the rug if he didn't stop soon. "How could you?" Robin spit out.

"How could I what?" Finn snapped. "Be specific, Robin. Very specific, so I'll know if I have good reason to hit you when you say the wrong thing."

Robin took a deep breath. "What were you doing with Claire?" he asked.

Finn yawned into his hand. "Taking a nap, if you must know."

Robin's jaw fell open. "A nap? Is that what's you're calling it now?"

Finn got to his feet. "When that's what it was, yes. A nap." He balled up his fist. If Robin said what Finn expected him to say, the duke would be missing several teeth before the night was through.

"A nap," Finn repeated.

"A nap," Robin said, nodding his head. "You're certain that's all it was."

"Quite certain." He still had the ache in his stones because it hadn't been more than a nap.

"Then why did she look as though she'd just been tumbled?" Robin flinched when Finn charged him. He held up a hand to stall his younger brother. "Perhaps a nap is that pleasant for her," he rushed to say.

"It was quite pleasant," Finn agreed, letting his fist fall back to his side.

"You're serious, aren't you?" Robin asked, his mouth falling open as Finn nodded. "Well, bloody hell."

"I'm in love with her," Finn blurted out.

Robin's mouth snapped shut. "Is that so?"

"Yes." Finn scrubbed at his forehead. "I don't know how it happened, but I am. There. Are you happy?"

"Ecstatic," Robin said glibly.

"I knew I liked her a lot." Liked being inside her a lot. Like spending time with her a lot. Liked looking at her. Liked her sharp tongue. "Then she took me into that blasted painting and fell asleep with her head in my lap. I took the pins out of her hair and held her while she slept." Finn began to pace. "Well, I slept a little, but it was difficult." He stopped in front of Robin. "I want to marry her."

"And?" Robin said. His mouth lifted in a grin. "What's the problem?"

"She said no." Finn began to pace again.

"Oh, it must run in the family. Sophia did the same thing. Why do you think I had to go to the land of the fae to bring her back home? Hardheaded woman."

"Claire is too."

"Claire, is it?"

"Yes, it's Claire."

"So, you're already on a first-name basis?"

"She usually calls me a dolt, honestly."

Robin threw his head back and laughed. Loudly. "It'll all turn out for the best." He clapped Finn on the shoulder.

"How so? She declined my proposal."

"We need to make a plan."

A plan. Yes, that was what they needed. A plan.

Nineteen

BLAST AND DAMN. SHE SHOULD HAVE KNOWN HE would be there. That he would come to this event. Finn was across the ballroom from her, tucked neatly behind some potted palms with a yellow-haired nymph of a woman he'd just danced with. Did he prefer blondes? Claire picked up a curl from her shoulder and lifted it to look at it more closely. Perhaps he did like the fair-haired.

Claire wished she'd worn a different color of gown. The nymph was stunning in pink. Claire should have worn a pale green dress to match her eyes, instead of white. Something with a swooping neckline that showed more of her décolletage than she'd ever shown before. She glanced down at her almost-virginal gown and grimaced. She couldn't compete with the women of Finn's acquaintance. Why did this matter? There could be no future between them, no matter what.

"Hullo, Claire," a low voice said by her ear. Claire steadied herself. The sound of his voice skimmed over her skin and made her bite back a shiver. Would he always affect her like that? She hoped not. He'd been scarce since the night they'd stepped back through the painting. It had been a sennight since she'd been this close to him. Since she'd looked into his sky-blue eyes.

"Lord Phineas," she said. She acknowledged his presence with a small nod in his direction. "What brings you out from behind the potted palms?"

She'd wanted to march across the room, grab the chit by her hair, and fling her outside of Finn's reach. A lazy grin quirked at the corner of his mouth. "The palms don't hold as much interest for me as you do, darling."

Her heart tripped a beat. *Darling*. An endearment from this Phineas Trimble was as commonplace as the light skirt he'd been talking with behind the palms. "You can put your silver tongue away, my lord. It's not enough to get my attention." Not tonight. Not when all of her family was in attendance.

He leaned down close to her ear and said softly, "If I got my silver tongue anywhere near you, I promise I'd have your complete and undivided attention." His breath teased the shell of her ear and a shiver crept up her spine. He chuckled lightly at her response.

"Did you enjoy your time with the chit behind the foliage? Did you learn anything about her? Aside from whether or not her breasts fit your hands?" Claire heaved a sigh.

"Are you jealous, Claire?" He made a *tsking* sound with his tongue.

Was she? Dreadfully and completely. Yes.

"Jealous?" She forced a laugh from her lips, although it was the last thing she felt like doing. "I have had you in my bed, my lord. It's not an event I have any desire to repeat."

Finn's lips pressed together tightly. "Shhh. It wouldn't do for anyone to find that out. You're supposed to be Ramsdale's very wealthy, very innocent, very complacent daughter." He shrugged and cocked his head to the side. "The wealthy part is true, at least."

She was Ramsdale's daughter, though this was the first time she'd been in their home, and she'd met their other children for the first time on this night. They had two daughters and a son. The reception had been somewhat lukewarm by the boy, but the daughters had been overjoyed at getting two new sisters and a brother.

"You are lovely tonight." He said it quickly and quietly, as he nodded to an acquaintance and kissed the hand of a lovely lady who had the audacity to lay one upon his arm in passing.

Claire held back a snort. "I bet you say that to all the ladies."

"I don't ask all the ladies to marry me, though." Claire's belly dropped toward her toes.

He waited for her response during the pregnant pause. "I could just announce to one and all the nature of our relationship." He bobbed his head from side to side, like he was weighing his options. "I wouldn't even have to announce that I have been inside you." He leaned close and chuckled at her flinch. "I could just ask you to dance two or three times. Or touch your arm inappropriately. Or drag you out into the garden for a nice, long walk."

"Try it and see what happens." She ground her

teeth together so hard that he could probably hear them. But a tiny little part of her thrilled at the idea of having her will in this matter taken away. Then she could just be free to enjoy courtship and marriage. Until the baby arrived, that is.

"Don't tempt me," he warned.

❧

The little sprite had done nothing but tempt him since the day he'd met her. She smelled like a meadow in summer mixed with the sweetest lemonade. The scent of her reached up to tickle his nose as the pulse at the base of her throat began to jump. Finn already knew that she was a sight to behold when she was in a temper. Or in the throes of passion. He had a feeling he wouldn't see the latter again anytime soon. But a man could hope, couldn't he?

Finn held out his hand to her as a waltz began to play. "Come and dance with me."

"Why should I? A blink ago, you were behind the potted palms with Miss Horse Teeth."

"Miss Horse Teeth?" Was she really jealous?

"She could eat corn through a picket fence."

He pasted a grin on his face. "You should dance with me because people are beginning to stare." He took her gloved hand in his and dragged her onto the dance floor. "You do know how to dance, don't you?" he asked. Her face flushed slightly. "Don't worry. Just let me lead."

She nodded tightly as he raised her hand to his side and placed one of his hands on her waist. She flinched at the intimate crawl of his fingertips as he readied himself and nudged the hand at her waist a bit higher.

That was odd, he thought. He shook the thought of how good she felt in his arms from his mind. Lusting after Claire Thorne was not in his best interest. Making her fall in love with him was. He forced himself to concentrate and took a step.

Miss Thorne took one at the same time, but it was the wrong one, and she trod upon his toes. He winced and steadied her in his arms. "I said, 'Let me lead,'" he warned with a quirk of his brow. She nodded quickly, her face flooding with color. "Can you give up control for a moment? Just for one simple little dance?"

She nodded again and he took a step. This time, she followed and stepped back. He began to lead her in the steps of the waltz, her hand quivering in his. Her uncertainty was almost enough to tug at a man's heartstrings. But he couldn't think about his heartstrings, not tonight.

Her strawberry blond hair hung in wisps around her slender neck, the majority artfully arranged in an upswept style that looked destined to tumble. God, he could just imagine pulling the pins from her hair and letting it fall across his body while she rode him. Such thoughts would get him nowhere, aside from on Robin's bad side. Claire Thorne was to be protected, and from the moment she'd tumbled into his bedchamber, she'd been on his mind.

"You're doing well," he encouraged. "Breathe."

"I am breathing."

Finn knew of every breath she took, because her breasts grazed his chest with the intimacy of the waltz.

Her skirts swished around his legs, and he felt her every movement in his… entire body.

"Who is that man there in the corner?" Claire asked. "The one with the brunette on his arm."

Finn held back an oath. "That's the Earl of Mayden." Robin would not be happy that the earl was there. Not at all. It must have been an oversight on the guest list for him to have been invited.

"He's the one you think killed Robinsworth's wife?"

"I don't think it," Finn clarified. "I know it. I have never been more certain of anything in my life."

"What would it take to prove it?" Claire asked.

"A confession, probably. Anything else would be circumstantial. Only the late duchess knows what really happened. And the truth went to the grave along with her."

"Is there anything he loves? Something you could hold over his head? His mother? A relative?"

God, he liked the way she thought. She was brilliant. But Finn had exhausted that avenue of thought. The earl had no one he cared about more than himself. "No."

"What are his wants and desires?"

"Money, money, and money. And revenge against our family."

"What does he have against you? What makes him covet what you have?"

"He's a greedy man," Finn murmured, more to himself than to her.

The waltz stopped finally, and Finn couldn't think of any other reason to keep her with him. Not without ruining her with his attention. He delivered her back to her family, which waited on the skirts of the room. "Miss Thorne," he said with a bow. "Thank you for the dance." Then he turned and strode into the crowd.

It wasn't until moments later that he realized she was dancing again. And she was in the arms of the Earl of Mayden.

Twenty

"Miss Thorne, your father should have warned the guests in his invitation that you are so beautiful. I find that you quite take my breath away," the Earl of Mayden said. She looked into his eyes, and in them she saw… nothing. There was nothing inside this man. Claire was certain of it.

"You flatter me, my lord," Claire said, looking over the earl's shoulder. Finn stalked the edge of the room and suddenly took a lass's hand and pulled her onto the dance floor. Claire lined up facing the earl for a reel, and Finn took a place three spaces down the line from Mayden.

The music began, and Claire and the earl circled one another, and then moved apart. Claire was glad when he moved to the next lady, because he made the hair on the back of her neck stand up. She gave the next man a wide smile, and he stammered as he went around her. They separated again, and Finn wasn't any closer to her. Suddenly, the man across from her yelped as Finn grabbed him by the collar and jerked him over to switch places.

"What the devil do you think you're doing?" Finn hissed as he circled around her.

"Dancing, my lord." She smiled at him. "Have we met?" she asked with what she knew was an impudent grin.

"Don't play with that man, Claire," he warned.

Claire had no intention of playing with the earl. She intended to expose him. To ease some of Finn's burden, if she could. He deserved a life free of men who wanted to do him harm. She could want to do him harm all day long, but no one else could hurt him, blast it all.

The line moved again and Claire found herself across from the earl again. "You dance divinely, my lord," she said. "I'm afraid I feel a bit like a bumpkin out here on the dance floor. We don't have this dance where I'm from."

"Where might that be?" the earl asked, his tone amiable. But the tone didn't match his eyes.

"I'm sure you've never heard of it."

"Fortune smiled on your father, that he was able to claim you at last."

Claire tripped over her foot. She laughed lightly as she righted herself. "I'm sure you're mistaken, my lord. My father has always claimed me. He just chose to let me rusticate in the country instead of in town. At my own behest, of course."

The earl's eyes narrowed. "Your father didn't know you existed until a few months ago. Then he went away with your mother and came home with three children no one remembers her birthing." He chuckled, but it wasn't a mirthful sound. Not at all like Finn's laugh.

"What do you want, Mayden?" Claire asked. Sometimes it was best to take a direct route.

He lifted a brow at Claire. "I want everything the Duke of Robinsworth stole from me."

"I would have thought you paid him back when you took his wife's life."

The hand that held hers tightened painfully. Tears came to Claire's eyes, but she blinked them back and refused to let him know he'd hurt her. He squeezed harder. Claire stopped dancing and stepped closer to him. "It's a pity that you haven't earned back any of the things you lost, isn't it?" she asked sweetly, like she spoke of the weather.

Mayden's lips pulled back from his teeth. It was time to change partners again. Mayden stayed in place, however, and didn't stop dancing. "Tell Finn I want Katherine back," he grated out. "Or I might just have to take you up to the turrets and see if you can fly."

Oh, she could fly. And sting. And do all sorts of things he couldn't even imagine. "Tell him yourself," Claire bit out. "After you catch your breath."

"Beg your pardon?" he asked.

"I think you'll suddenly find yourself unable to breathe, my lord." She rested one hand on each of his shoulders, stepped up on tiptoe, and whispered in his ear. "Right *now*," she said, just as she raised her knee between his legs and hit him directly in the groin.

Mayden doubled over and fell to the floor. The quartet stopped playing. The dancers stopped dancing. Finn rushed forward. Claire stepped on Mayden's hand as she walked past him, grinding her heel into his fingers as he lay there on the parquet floor. He squealed like a scalded baby.

"Beg your pardon," Claire said. "I'm so clumsy." She leaned down next to him and said softly so only he could hear. "Don't ever threaten me again, or I'll feed your stones to you on a silver spoon." She motioned at two of the footmen, who stood in shock at the edge of the room. "The earl needs some help getting off the dance floor. I think he must have eaten some bad prawns. He had a most horrible stomach cramp."

Claire bustled away from Mayden as the footmen hefted him to his feet.

⁓

Finn watched the entire tableau and wanted to grin like a fool when Claire kneed Mayden in the groin. But what she did was risky, and he didn't like her putting herself in a situation like that. She should have cut a wide berth around Mayden. He wouldn't take kindly to this slight, not now that his pride was wounded. He would retaliate. And he would do so with vicious glee.

Finn took Claire's hand and laid it upon his arm. She winced as he did so, however, and fear leaped directly to his heart. "What's wrong with your hand?"

"The good earl has a viselike grip, for one so scrawny," Claire said. Her hand must hurt like the devil, because she had tears shimmering in her eyes.

"Would you care for a turn in the garden, Miss Thorne?" Finn asked.

"That would be delightful." He walked her toward the double doors at the back of the room, but stopped at the buffet and broke a piece off the ice sculpture in the center of the table.

He wrapped it in his handkerchief and held it tightly in one hand as he tried to walk casually toward the dark path he knew he'd find in the garden. He needed to be sure Claire's hand wasn't broken. And he needed to hold her, to assure himself she was all right.

If there had been any doubt in Finn's mind that he loved this lady, he'd dispensed with it the moment she'd been in danger. He would have killed for her. He might still kill for her. He would kill Mayden without blinking if the earl dared to lay a hand on her again.

Finally, the cool night air embraced them and Finn relaxed a little. He pulled her down the path until he found a bench and motioned for her to sit. He took her hand in his, wincing when she did at the pain of his touch. He placed the ice-filled handkerchief in her palm. "Can you close your fist?" he asked, flexing his own to show her what he wanted to confirm.

She opened and closed it slowly. Her hand wasn't broken, but it was already bruising, and for that, Finn wanted to rip Mayden's head off his shoulders and shove it up his arse. "What the devil were you thinking?"

"I wasn't," Claire admitted. "He asked me to dance, and the rules of this world state that if I decline him, I have to decline everyone for the rest of the night." She stuck out her bottom lip a little. Was she pouting? "I wanted to get to dance with you again, at least once."

"So, you weren't trying to get information out of Mayden?" His heart slowed a bit.

"Well, that was an unexpected benefit." She grimaced

as he poked at her hand and maneuvered her fingers. She pushed the ice back at him. "It's cold," she complained.

"Use it," he ordered.

She arched a brow at him and smiled. "I think I like you when you're being all masterful."

She hadn't seen masterful. He'd spank her bare bottom if she dared to ever go near Mayden again.

Her good hand stroked down the side of his cheek. "You can stop worrying. I'm fine."

"What did Mayden say to you?" Finn looked at her there in the dark. Good God, she was pretty. She took his breath away.

"He told me he wants Katherine back. And made some threats." She winced as she laid her hurt hand in her lap. He ached for her and would have taken her pain inside himself if he were able.

"What kind of threats?" His heart started to flutter wildly again. He wouldn't let anything happen to her. Ever.

"Something about tossing me from the turrets at the Hall to see if I can fly." She giggled. "Little does he know that I really can."

"I'll kill him," Finn grunted as he jumped to his feet and started toward the door.

"Don't leave me," Claire cried.

"What is it? Your hand?"

"No, I just need you."

If anyone had told him that love would hurt so much, he'd never have believed it. But Finn felt as if his soul had been laid bare to her. He sat down beside her on the bench again.

❧

Claire had never seen him so handsome as with thoughts of her reflected in his eyes. In a different time and a different place, she could love him. She could love him with all her heart.

"Is your hand any better?"

She tested her grip. "A little, I think." If she were in the land of the fae, she would take advantage of the healing waters there. But she would have to deal with the pain, since the waters couldn't travel from one world to another.

"I should kill him for that alone," Finn growled.

"I can think of so many more reasons to kill him." Claire tried not to laugh, but suddenly, she found the situation hilarious.

"Are you all right?" Finn asked. "You're not delirious, are you?"

If she was, it was because of him, not because of the Earl of Mayden. "I'm perfectly fine, aside from a little bit of pain in my hand. Stop fretting."

Just then, a bug buzzed by her ear. She swatted at it. It bounced off her hand and then landed on the bodice of her dress. "Finn," she warned.

"What?"

She pointed toward the bug, which was as big as Finn's watch fob. "There's a bug on me."

Finn's eyes met hers, and they were full of amusement. "It's just a little, tiny bug," he chided. "It won't eat much."

"Finn," she warned. Claire had a healthy respect for bugs, but bugs did not like faeries. They resided with mutual respect most days, but this one was crossing the line by actually landing on her person.

"Hold on, I'll get it." Finn took aim with his fingers the way one might with a billiard cue, preparing to thump it away. But right when Finn flicked it, it jumped. Claire heaved a sigh of relief. At least it was gone.

Then buzzing began in her hair. "Claire," Finn warned, reaching for her hair. "Be still," he warned. But Claire was already flipping over, trying to shake the beast out of her curls. "Claire, stop," he cajoled. "If you'll be still, I'll get it."

But Claire couldn't be still. A creature with at least six legs was burrowing in her hair, and it wasn't happy at all with its location, if the amount of noise it was making was any indication.

Pins from Claire's hair flew in every direction as she tried to dislodge the beast. Finally, Finn riffled through her hair long enough to get his fingers on it. "I have it," he said. "Now be still so I can untangle it." He chuckled. "Who would have thought you could knock the Earl of Mayden to his knees but an insect could get you this worked up." He began to untangle the bug, strand by strand of hair.

Finally, he said, "I got it. It's free."

But then something hard and heavy as a coin hit her breast. "See, it's out of your hair," he said. But now it was in her décolletage. It slipped and slithered and writhed its way between her breasts, looking for shelter. Claire screamed. She couldn't help it. She screamed.

"Would you be quiet, Claire?" Finn hissed. "Someone will call the watch."

Claire jumped up and down, hoping she could shake the bug from the top of her dress, but she could actually see its body moving beneath her clothing. "Get it, Finn," she cried.

Finn reached a hand into her bodice. "Pardon me, I'm not trying to cup your breast," he grunted as his fingers did just that. He lifted her left breast with one hand while the other grabbed for the bug. He growled and tugged at her gown, pulling it lower so he could get his hand farther inside.

"Finn, please," she urged. The bug was going lower and lower, and it would be in her drawers if it traveled much farther.

"I got it," he finally said. He held it up in one hand and gloated, while his other hand was still stuffed inside her bodice, cupping her breast. "See, Claire, I got it. Nothing to worry about."

A gasp rang out behind them on the garden path. Finn closed his eyes tightly and turned her so that her body was shielded by his. "Tell me that's not your father," he moaned.

Claire looked over his shoulder. "It's my father," she whispered. "And the duke. And Marcus." She thumped the bug from his outstretched fingers. The creature could go burn in hell for all she cared, their unspoken treaty be damned.

"What's going on out here?" Claire's father asked. "Claire, are you all right?"

"Lord Phineas was just helping me retrieve a bug that was bound to do me harm."

❦

If Claire could have seen what she looked like in that moment, she would have been mortified. She looked like she'd been well and truly tumbled. Her hair was a riot of curls, and her pins lay scattered on the path around them. Her cheeks were rosy as a newborn baby.

And his hand was still cupping her breast. "Bloody hell," he grunted. "This isn't what it looks like, my lord," Finn called over his shoulder. "She had a bug down her dress, and I helped to fish it out."

"I'll have a word with you in my study, Lord Phineas," Claire's father said.

Finn looked down at his hand, which still held Claire's breast. He let it go and jerked her bodice back up. Her mother and sister came forward and shooed her down the opposite end of the garden path.

Finn fell into step behind Lord Ramsdale. He should be damn happy no one had punched him yet. But there was still time. Finn ran back to Claire and kissed her forehead quickly. "I'll take care of everything," he assured her. He would. But would she be happy with the way he did it?

෴

Robin accompanied them to Lord Ramsdale's study, and for that Finn was grateful. Both Marcus and his lordship looked like they were just waiting to get him to a quiet place so they could beat him to a bloody pulp.

When the door was finally shut, Lord Ramsdale glared at him.

Finn steeled his jaw. "Did you want to hit me, Lord Ramsdale?" he asked. "I deserve it."

But Ramsdale just dropped down behind his desk and scrubbed his face with his hands. "What is it with you Trimbles? I just got my daughters back, and now you want to take them from me."

"I want to marry her," Finn blurted out.

"Of course, you do," Lord Ramsdale affirmed with a nod. "But you know that she won't do it." He heaved a sigh. "So, now I have a deflowered daughter in the eyes of the *ton*."

She'd been deflowered all right, but it was months ago.

"Truly, I was just getting the bug."

"Do you want the readings of the banns or a special license?" Ramsdale asked with a heavy sigh. The man looked defeated.

"Do you think she'll marry me?"

Ramsdale snorted. "I don't think she'll have a choice. Banns or special license?"

"Banns," Finn said quickly. His heart was beating so quickly in his chest that he feared it might jump from between his ribs and land in the middle of the rug.

"Banns, it is." Ramsdale pointed a finger at Finn. "You'll stay away from my daughter for the three weeks prior to the wedding."

"But—" Finn started.

But Ramsdale talked over him. "Three weeks. That's all I ask. Let me have her for three weeks and then you can have her for a lifetime." The man's voice was guttural with emotion, and Finn's heart hurt for him.

"Yes, Lord Ramsdale," he said. "Three weeks."

"You already love her, don't you?" Ramsdale asked.

Finn tripped over his own tongue. His answer came out more as a croak. So, he cleared his throat. "With all my heart," he finally admitted.

"Good. They can be stubborn, the fae. Stick with it. It'll be worth it in the end."

Stick with it. Finn would stick with it. He would stick with her. But would she hate him for putting her in this mess? It was too late to worry about that now, wasn't it?

Twenty-One

CLAIRE AMBLED THROUGH THE GARDEN AT RAMSDALE House, where she'd been sent following the ball debacle, and picked a flower from the side of the path. She tucked it behind her ear and kept walking.

"Your mother used to do the same thing, you know?" a voice called. Claire looked up to find her father strolling toward her. "You look a lot like her, but I think you got more of the blond from me, rather than the strawberry from her."

Claire looked up at him. He'd been trying for days to talk to her. He'd tried in the land of the fae, but she'd sent him packing. She'd even run away to escape talking to him. But she couldn't run away now. She would have to face the challenge. She'd never backed down from a challenge before. Why was this one so difficult? Maybe because it was the first time her heart had ever been involved.

"How are you?" he asked.

She shrugged and ambled farther down the walk. He fell into step beside her. "You can run, but you can't hide." She glared at him and he continued. "Well, yes, you could. But it won't do you any good. You have to marry him."

"It was just a bug," Claire complained.

"I know. But it didn't look like just a bug."

And it hadn't been just a bug several months ago. But it was just a bug that night. It didn't matter.

"Claire," he said gently, before he tipped her chin up gently. "If you tell me you'll be miserable with him, I'll cancel the banns and we'll deal with society."

"You'd give me a choice?" she asked. She twirled the stem of a flower in her fingers, trying to fight the feeling of falling. Like a bird in flight that had suddenly lost its wings.

"I'll give you a choice." He pointed a finger at her. "But give it careful thought. Something tells me the man is deeply in love with you. You could do much worse than a love match."

"What's the something that tells you that?" Claire asked. This was the most words she'd ever shared with her father in succession.

"He told me that. Why do you think I plan to give him your hand?" She must have looked perplexed, because he raised his brows at her. "What's wrong?"

"He told you what?" Surely he hadn't told her father that he loved her. That would be ludicrous.

"I asked him if he loves you, and he answered in the affirmative."

"Why would he do that?" Claire whispered. But a little piece of her thrilled at the idea.

"Because he does?" He heaved a sigh. "Claire, know this—it's not easy for a human man to accept magic. He has accepted it and is aware of it, and he's aware of the world from whence you came. And he loves you on top of all that. You couldn't ask for more."

"Was it hard for you to accept Mother?" Claire sat down on a garden bench, and he dropped down beside her. He leaned forward and put his elbows on his knees.

"It was difficult. What was even more difficult was watching what your mother went through. She lost her wings. She lost her homeland. She lost all her family."

"She gave up her children," Claire whispered. She laid a hand on her belly. The very thought nearly broke her in pieces.

"She never *gave up* a bloody thing," her father snapped. "We never gave up any of our children. They were taken from us. That's a completely different situation. Completely." His face reddened with anger.

"It was a choice you made," Claire went on. "You knew the consequences. If you had fae children, you'd lose them. And you bet on love anyway."

"Your mother tried everything to keep you. Sophia's love for music—that was so she could find your mother later in life. Your love for painting—who do you think hid the magic paintbrush in your bedding after you were born? And that little painting of the door. *Dulcis domus* was written over it. *Sweet home*."

He jabbed a finger at Claire again. "You were our heart's desire. We thought with the paintbrush and the painting, you could walk right into our lives. The fae took our memories when they took you, but we left a way for you to get back to us, believing we would know you, no matter what."

What? Wait just a minute. That was what the words over the door said? Sweet home? Her father had painted it and given her a magical paintbrush that would lead her back to them.

Tears pricked at the backs of Claire's lashes. "You did try."

Lord Ramsdale—no, her father—got to his feet and pulled her up, hugging her tightly against him. "We tried. We failed. But it finally did work. You're here now. And so are we. There's still time. Don't waste so much energy hating us, Claire."

Claire inhaled, a deep cleansing breath. She needed a moment to process this. "Could I have a moment, please?" she asked. "I need to think." She scrubbed at her forehead.

"Come and find me when you're ready to talk?"

Claire nodded and he left.

Claire needed to put the facts together. She needed to compile all this information into tidy little boxes and stack them on her shelves. She needed to understand.

She'd walked through the door of that painting just because it was there and she needed to get away. She hadn't seen the magical paintbrush in years, and it had been an escape. What was baffling was that the sign over the door read, "Sweet home," particularly since it had led her to Finn.

He was her heart's desire? No. Couldn't be. She barely knew him at that point, even though she already carried his child. He couldn't possibly be her heart's desire. He was just a man—and a human man at that.

Could it be that her parents had lived in a completely

different world than the one she was in now? With the changes in the land of the fae, perhaps there could be a future for humans who married fae and produced offspring that didn't include having those offspring taken away. Could it be that simple? It couldn't possibly be, not with everything her parents had gone through, but she had to look at Sophia and the duke. They had a child on the way and they were not afraid of losing it, not in the least.

She laid a hand on her belly, which was just beginning to round with the new life growing inside her. Since the beginning of this journey when she'd found out about the baby, she'd assumed she would have to relinquish a human child to Finn's care, but maybe that wasn't the case. Maybe she could be free to love this child, no matter what its nature. Maybe, maybe, maybe, maybe, maybe not.

Claire wouldn't get her hopes up. But the very thought of Finn loving her made her heart soar all the way to the clouds and back. Hope bloomed within her chest, swelling inside her, and threatened to rack her small frame. She relished the feeling of utter relief. What if it wasn't true?

Goodness, there was so much to think about. Did it all come down to faith? Did it all come down to the Unpardonable Errors? Maybe the Unpardonable Errors needed to be rewritten. Maybe that would relieve her of this feeling of rocking on open sea with nothing more than a plank of wood beneath her.

The door to her heart's desire. What was her bloody heart's desire? She didn't have a clue. But then she laid a hand on her stomach again and felt for the new life that grew there. Could this child have everything she didn't? Could this child have two loving parents? Could this child move from one world to the other? Who knew?

The biggest question to be answered was: Could Claire accept that this was going to be her new life? She didn't care about her own happiness. But her child's happiness mattered more than the next breath she would take.

Ronald suddenly emerged on the garden path. The gnome had a way of insinuating himself into family matters. He'd been with the family for a very long time. And though he often vexed her, she gazed at him fondly. He was the only one who knew about her night with Finn. And he hadn't told anyone. "Ronald." She acknowledged him with a nod of her head, and he stepped out of the foliage.

"Miss Thorne," he said with a bow. "I trust you are well."

Claire rolled her eyes at him. "You know very well how I am at all times, Ronald. Don't ask me questions you already know the answers to." She brushed down a lock of hair on the top of his head. It had a tendency to stand up straight and always had. He smiled at her. "You heard the exchange with my father."

"Your father, now, is he?" Ronald grinned.

Claire sighed heavily. "I suppose he is."

"How is the babe you carry?" Ronald asked softly.

Claire placed a hand to her stomach. "How did you know about that?"

"Do you remember that I told you what's done in the dark will always come to the light?" He nodded toward her belly. "I think your light is going to shine on you whether you want it to or not."

Claire sat down and toyed with the leaves of a nearby bush. "Tell me what to do, Ronald."

"Have you told him yet?"

"No."

"Why not?"

"I don't know how."

"Why don't you try this: 'My dear husband-to-be, I have a surprise for you.'"

Claire laughed. "How do you think he'd take it?"

"How do *you* think he'd take it?" He glared at her.

"Do you think he'll be angry?" She chewed on her lower lip.

"The man's in love with you, Claire. You could stand on your head in the middle of crowded ballroom and sing 'One Fae Night,' and he'd probably join you." Ronald gazed up at her. "Don't let what happened with your parents affect your future. Your grandfather put the wheels of change in motion before he died because he wanted to unite the two worlds. Don't let his efforts be in vain."

"How'd you get to be so smart, Ronald?" Claire asked. Ronald was full of pride, and his chest puffed up even more when he received compliments.

"When you've lived a few hundred years, you learn a few things."

"Why didn't you ever marry, Ronald?" Claire asked.

"What makes you think I didn't?"

Ronald disappeared into the foliage as quickly as he'd arrived. Ronald, married? It couldn't be. She'd always seen him as solitary. Perhaps she was wrong.

Claire walked back to the house and asked a house-maid if she knew where she could find her father. Forming a relationship with him was as good a place to start as any.

"I believe you'll find him in his paint studio, my lady. He goes there most afternoons."

The maid pointed her toward where her father was located in the big manor house, and Claire went to find it. She stood in the doorway and knocked softly. "Father?" she said.

He smiled. "Did you need something?"

"Not really. I just wanted to see what you're painting."

He turned the easel toward her and showed her a family portrait he was working on. "It's not done yet. But it'll look like this when I'm done." He held out a sketch drawing. It was Lord and Lady Ramsdale, *her mother and father*, she had to remind herself, and all their children. "I thought we might hang it in the grand salon."

Claire sniffled.

"Do you want to help me mix some paints for it?"

Claire nodded. If she tried to speak right now, she would break. Into a million pieces. But he seemed to recognize that and pushed a mortar and pestle into her hands, instead of talking with her. He ran a hand down the back of her head, and they began to mix paints.

Twenty-Two

CLAIRE LOOKED UP FROM THE BOOK SHE WAS READING when a knock sounded on the door. Her mother stood there in the corridor. And her younger sister Hannah and her even younger sister Rose. Rose was the sister who was fae and had lived in a human world with no magic her whole life. Her parents had found a way to keep one of their fae children. Hannah was human.

"Can we take a moment of your time?" her mother asked.

Claire laid her book to the side and moved her feet to the floor to free up the other end of the settee. "Of course."

Claire hadn't spent much time with her sisters, not in the days since she'd come to live at Ramsdale House. They were constantly about, but their governess and nurses kept them reined in well and didn't let them bother the guests. Claire could assume she wasn't a guest anymore. She was a daughter of the household, just like they were, for goodness sake.

Her mother motioned toward Rose. "Rose was just wondering if you might consider giving her lessons on the basics of faerie dust. She's got a lot of catching up to do."

Claire shook her head. She still didn't have any dust. But then her mother held out a shimmering vial of magic, and Claire took it in her hand. "Where did this come from?"

"Marcus sent Ronald back to the land of the fae to retrieve it." Rose held a vial in her hand as well.

"Be careful with that," Claire warned.

Hannah giggled. "She's been walking on eggshells all day."

Claire turned to her mother. "Why didn't you give her the lessons?"

"I can give her some, but it has been many years since I used mine. I'm afraid I'm a little out of practice."

Magic was as essential to Claire as her right arm. She couldn't imagine getting "out of practice." But she couldn't imagine being banished from the fae, either. It was still a possibility, so she had better not think too highly of herself. "What would you like to know how to do?"

"Can you really read people's thoughts?"

Claire nodded. "You can, but be careful with that one. You might find out things you don't want to know. The truth can be painful at times. Only use it on your missions, and never on your family."

"Can you show me?"

"It only works on humans." She motioned Hannah forward. "Hannah, will you permit me to show everyone what's in your thoughts?"

Hannah nodded and nearly danced in place at the thought of it. Claire poured some faerie dust into her hand and closed her eyes. She said one single word. "Truth." Then she gave a great heaving blow and blew the dust into the air above Hannah's head. Flickering specks of magic began to take shape, like actors on a stage, except they were glimmery clouds of living, breathing dust. Apparently, Hannah was prone to thinking about biscuits and milk. And she often snuck to the kitchens in the middle of the night to get some.

"Hannah," her mother warned.

"Sorry," the girl muttered, but she was all smiles. "That's some wonderful magic."

"Can I try it?" Rose asked.

"We already know Hannah is thinking about raiding the kitchen," Claire said with a laugh. She ruffled the girl's hair, and Hannah beamed under her attention. "We need a human."

"Could you use me?" a voice called from the doorway.

"Finn," Claire said as she jumped to her feet. Her heart leaped as she walked over to him. "I wasn't expecting you."

"I know. I just stopped by to talk with your father. I heard you from the foyer and wanted to see you."

Claire's heart did that pitter-patter thing that was so common when he was around. Would she ever grow accustomed to him? To his presence in her life? Probably not. "I'm glad you're here," she said truthfully.

"Did you want to test your magic on me, Rose?" He sat down on the edge of a chair and tugged one of Hannah's curls.

"That's probably not a good idea," Claire's mother said nervously. She sent Claire a pointed glance. "Whatever has been in your thoughts most recently is what will display. Or it could be some deeply buried truth."

He held his hands out to the side. "I have nothing to hide." He nudged Rose's knee with his. She quickly pulled the stopper on the bottle of shimmer and dumped a small amount into her hand. Claire reached for her arm to stop her. "The magic is yours. The dust is just the catalyst that takes the magic from you to the object. Do you understand?"

Claire's mother said, "What she's trying to tell you is that you need to think long and hard about what you want before you blow the dust into the air. Only by having a clearly defined objective in your head can you be successful. So, clear everything else from your mind, and you can give it a try." She nodded in encouragement.

Rose closed her eyes tightly and cleared every thought from her head. Then she concentrated on what she wanted, which was the truth. Then with a great exhale, she blew the dust into the air.

The cloud of magic suspended there in the air, not taking shape. But then Rose remembered and said, "Truth!"

The dust began to take shape.

Claire watched it closely, trying to figure out what the shapes were doing. There was a scene of Finn and Claire dancing in a ballroom. And then it morphed into a scene of Finn and Claire in a carriage, riding through the park. Then the scene changed into something else entirely. There was a bed in the middle of the room, and Finn and Claire stood next to it.

Claire's mother jumped to her feet and swiped her hand through the air. The magic dispensed like clouds on a rainy day. Finn wore a bemused expression. "Sorry," he murmured.

Heat crept up Claire's face.

Her mother said, "His lordship must be thinking about how they'll decorate the bedchamber in their new house."

Finn grinned unrepentantly. "Most assuredly. I do like the color blue."

"Why did you stop it?" Rose asked. "I had just done it right for the first time."

"Darling, his lordship has a meeting with your father. He doesn't want to keep him waiting. You can practice on him again another time."

⌒

Finn highly doubted that she would let her daughters anywhere near him with magic dust again. He bit back a grin and tried to appear regal and calm as Lady Ramsdale ushered the girls from the room. Then laughter burst from his chest like water over a dam. "Oh, I'm so sorry," he laughed. "I thought I could maintain my thoughts, but the longer I looked at you, the more they wandered. Then all I could think about was getting you back into my bed."

He crossed the room quickly and jerked Claire to him. "I've missed you," he said as he kissed her lips gently, his hands bracketing her face. She laid her hands on his chest, and when he would have pulled back, she jerked him back to her.

"I have missed you too," she whispered against his lips. Heat shot straight to his groin.

"How much longer until you're mine?" he asked as he licked across her lips. He loved the way she melted for him.

"Not much longer."

"We could race for Gretna Green tonight and be married by tomorrow," he suggested.

She smiled. "My father wants to place me into your safekeeping."

"Speaking of which," Finn said as he pulled his watch fob from his pocket and looked at the time, "I'm going to be late meeting your father. I have to go."

He kissed her quickly and then turned to leave. At the last minute, he turned back. "When we're done, will you take a drive with me?"

"Where?" Her eyes sparkled.

He shrugged. "I don't care."

"I could use some new ribbons," she said. Heat crept up her cheeks and he grinned.

"Ribbons, it is, then." He rushed back and kissed her again. "I'll see you in a bit."

"Bye," she said with a tiny wave.

She was happy to see him, and that made Finn's heart sing. He nearly skipped as he walked toward her father's study. He brushed his sweaty palms down the thighs of his trousers. The note he'd received said they were to discuss the marriage settlement. Finn didn't particularly want nor need a marriage settlement. But he supposed this was a rite of passage. Something a father must do for his daughter.

"Lord Phineas," the viscount said as he got to his feet and shook Finn's hand. "How are you?"

"Well as can be, I imagine. How are you?"

"Everything is right in my world, for the first time ever," the viscount admitted. "My daughters are home, and my oldest son is ready to take my title someday."

"How is your younger son adjusting to that?" The younger son had been groomed for the title as well as the life of a lord, but Marcus, as the true oldest son, would now inherit both.

"Oh, that's a story for another day," Ramsdale said with a groan. "I asked you here to talk about marriage settlements."

Finn nodded. Not to accept any gift Ramsdale offered him would be rude, but he truly was wealthy in his own right. He held successful lands with prosperous tenants, and he had invested at Robin's insistence in various other opportunities and had done well with them all.

Ramsdale passed a sheath of papers to Finn. "Here you'll find information about the funds I'm placing in trust for my grandchildren—and for my daughter in the event that something untoward happens to you."

"Yes, sir," Finn said. "I'm sure that whatever you have decided will be beneficial." He wanted to bite his tongue over his choice of words.

Ramsdale leaned back and scrubbed his chin, regarding Finn warily. "The only thing that worries me is your occupation."

He knew about his occupation? "What part of it worries you?"

"You place yourself in danger on a regular basis. When you have children, you'll want to assign the more dangerous cases to your hires, won't you?"

Finn hadn't given it much thought. "I suppose I could."

"Give it some thought. I want my daughter to be happy for a lifetime, just like her mother and me."

"I'll give it a lot of thought."

"Can I give you a suggestion?"

Could Finn stop him? He doubted it. "Of course."

"Give her room to fly."

Give her room to fly? What the devil did that mean?

But the viscount was already getting to his feet and reaching out to shake Finn's hand. When Finn took it, Ramsdale gripped it fiercely, until Finn was forced to look at the man. The raw and naked emotion on his face was startling. "Listen to me carefully, Finn."

Finn nodded. The viscount didn't let go of his hand.

"If you ever hurt my daughter, I'll hunt you down and shoot you."

Finn gulped. "I understand."

"Have a lovely day," Ramsdale said as he sat back down and began to shift through his papers.

Finn hesitated for a moment. But then he jumped in. "Would it be all right with you if I took Miss Thorne for an outing?"

"What sort of outing?" Her father's brows drew together.

"She said she would like to buy some new hair ribbons."

Ramsdale looked back down at his papers and said absently, "Take Margaret with you."

Finn's heart dropped. "Margaret?"

"Her maid. Claire's a lady. It wouldn't do for her to be seen without a chaperone."

Finn wanted to groan but held it in. "I agree

completely. Thank you for your time." He turned and left Ramsdale's office as quickly as he could, before the man changed his mind and sent the cavalry with them, instead.

Twenty-Three

FINN LOOKED ABSOLUTELY MISERABLE IN THE COACH, with Margaret seated across from them. His thigh pressed hard against Claire's, like with that simple action, he could tell her how very much he wanted to touch her. Margaret cleared her throat and he nearly jumped out of his skin. But he did move his leg away from Claire's.

"Where would you like to go today, Miss Thorne?" he asked. He looked over at her and smiled. His smile really was quite stunning, and she hoped that after she'd looked at it for ten or fifteen years, it would still make her heart race the way it did now.

He wanted her; she could tell. It was as plain as the nose on his face.

"Ribbons," Claire reminded him. "We were going to buy some ribbons."

"Oh yes, ribbons. Now I remember." He narrowed his eyes at her. "How many ribbons must a lady own in order to be satisfied with her ribbon purchases?"

Claire forced herself not to grin. "It really depends on how the lady will be using the ribbons."

"Particularly, what ways are there?"

"Hats, dresses, shoes. We might wear them in our hair. Then there are our underthings."

Margaret cleared her throat again.

"Margaret," Claire scolded. "You really should do something for that cough."

Margaret cut her eyes at Claire. "Oh, you're right. I'll be certain to tell your father about it."

Finn snorted. Goodness, he was handsome. His sandy blond hair had been disturbed by the wind, and he had a fine shadow on his face. He looked rather... rugged.

"I'd give just about anything to know what's on your mind," he murmured close to Claire's ear.

"I was thinking of how handsome you are, if you must know." Heat crept up her cheeks at his stark look of need, which nearly brimmed from his eyes.

"You think I'm handsome?" he asked softly.

"Dashing. Deliberately devilish. Those dimples make you look much more innocent than you are, I'm afraid. A regular wolf in sheep's clothing."

The carriage rolled to a stop. Finn stepped out and moved to hand Claire out of the carriage. Margaret went to follow. "Wait here, please, Margaret. We'll only be a moment."

Margaret harrumphed. "I sincerely doubt your father would be happy with my doing that."

"My father isn't here."

Margaret raised her nose into the air. "Exactly."

Claire rolled her eyes as Margaret descended from the coach. She waited for them to take a few steps, and then she followed them into the small storefront.

Claire jumped when Finn's fingers reached down

to tangle with hers briefly. She looked up at him, and the twinkle in his eye took her completely by surprise.

Margaret ambled away from them and pretended to be perusing some fabric, while Finn asked the proprietress for ribbons. "Where might I find enough ribbons to keep my bride happy?"

Claire leaned close to his arm and whispered. "I don't really need any ribbons."

He whispered very dramatically back down to her, "Oh no, my Miss Thorne, you need enough ribbons that I could dress you in them." His eyes darkened a bit, as a flush rose across his cheeks. "Never mind," he murmured. He stepped away from her.

But Claire followed him doggedly. "I just wanted to spend some time alone with you."

⤳

Her statement hit him directly in the groin. Finn barely withheld a feral growl. It wouldn't do to disgrace them both here in the store. Not with Margaret looking on and every other lady in town also shopping there, it appeared.

Finn wanted to be alone with Claire more than he needed his next breath. "I want to kiss you," he whispered. Then he winked at her and walked away. He had to walk away. If he didn't, he'd have no choice but to make good on his taunt.

She was going to marry him. That much had been determined. For some reason, the thought didn't make him want to run away, not the way thoughts of marriage normally did. In fact, he wanted to run toward her. He just didn't want to do it right now.

Finn held up a length of pink silk to show her.

She wrinkled her nose and shook her head.

He held up a length of green silk. She nodded and smiled at him. God, her smile could almost knock him to his knees.

Could he wait two more weeks to kiss her? He supposed he didn't have a choice. At Ramsdale House, her family pretty much had her under lock and key.

"Pardon me, my lord," a voice said by his left shoulder. He turned quickly and had to force himself not to step back. "She told me to give you this, my lord," the boy said.

"Who?" Finn took the missive in his hand and opened it quickly. When he looked up, the lad was gone. Finn ran to the exit, but the boy was faster than he looked.

Finn looked back down at the note.

> Lord Phineas,
>   The special item you ordered for Mrs. Abercrombie has arrived. Shall I send it to you, or do you wish to retrieve it yourself?
>   Best regards,
>   Colette

Finn hadn't ordered a special item for Mrs. Abercrombie. Claire hadn't dressed as her since the day they'd gone to the ball, not that he knew of.

She wouldn't have gone out as Mrs. Abercrombie on her own, would she? She had better not.

"What's wrong?" Claire asked as she stepped up behind him.

"How is Mrs. Abercrombie doing, Claire?"

Clair faltered for no more than a moment. "The last I heard, she was touring the continent."

He pressed the letter into her hand. "What do you know of a special item I might have ordered for her?"

She took it from him and read it quickly. Then shrugged. "I have no idea what that's about."

But a lady standing near them and looking at the ribbons as well said, "Did you say Mrs. Abercrombie? Lovely lady. She's not touring the continent. She was at the Asterlys' house party not two days ago."

The lady turned to walk away.

"Remind me who Mrs. Abercrombie is, darling," Finn said smoothly to Claire. He made certain he was loud enough for the other lady to hear. "For the life of me, I can't place that name."

He waited a fraction of a second for the lady to take the bait. "Oh, she's a lovely woman. Very exotic. Hair that's black as night. She's a widow twice over." So, the story of Mrs. Abercrombie was already circulating and being embellished. Good.

"Oh, I do remember," Finn said. "Lovely woman."

The lady finally did walk away, and Finn's head was spinning like a top. She turned back.

"She'll be at Lord Gelson's dinner tonight. Are you going?"

"Of course," Finn said smoothly. He had to find out who this Mrs. Abercrombie was. And if she had any relation to the person Claire had pretended to be.

"Can you choose your ribbons while I go on a quick errand?"

Claire's brows drew together sharply. "Where are you going?"

He leaned down close to her ear so only she could hear him. "I have a feeling Colette needs to see me about Mrs. Abercrombie." He arched a brow at her.

"Take me with you."

"Claire," he protested. He couldn't put her in harm's way. "I'll tell you everything she says in a few minutes. I promise." He bent quickly and kissed her on the cheek. Then he left to visit the modiste.

Colette looked up when he entered the shop, a rueful grin across her face. "Lord Phineas," she said with a nod. "I expected for you to take longer to come and see me."

"What do you want, Colette?" he bit out.

"Your young lady, the one you had with you the other day?" she asked, her head tilted to the side coquettishly. "She's enjoying her time as Mrs. Abercrombie?"

So she did know. That didn't surprise him. "What do you want, Colette?"

"I want to attend some of the functions Mrs. Abercrombie might be invited to attend." She shrugged. She looked up at him from beneath heavy-lidded lashes.

Several years prior, Colette had helped him with a difficult case, as she was able to pretend to be his paramour. At the time, he'd been intimate with her, so the ruse was easy. She was very good at subterfuge, he had to admit.

"I would bet you've already been Mrs. Abercrombie at least once, if the reports about town are any indication."

She had the good grace to look chagrined. "I could keep an eye on Mayden for you." What harm could it do? Claire would never be Mrs. Abercrombie again. Never. "You'll report back to me what you find out?"

Colette batted her lashes at him. Once upon a time, that might have been attractive. Now it was just annoying. "Of course."

"Do as you will," he said and then he strode back out the door.

He collected Claire at the store, paid for the ribbons she didn't need, and promised to tell her everything the next time they could be alone.

Twenty-Four

CLAIRE APPRAISED HERSELF CLOSELY IN THE LOOKING glass. This time, she'd tinted her hair a perfectly hideous shade of red. She perched a pair of jeweled spectacles on her nose and pursed her lips. She could do this. She was certain she could.

It had taken all afternoon to get the tint for her hair from the apothecary, and then applying it had taken even longer. It wasn't an easy task to do by one's self. But she had finally accomplished it, and she barely recognized herself in the mirror.

Claire had asked some of the staff about Lord Gelson's soiree because the staff in a household knew everything about such events, and they knew everything there was to know about every other house in town as well. Lord Gelson and his wife were a nice, middle-aged couple who had had a bit of a debauched past. But then they'd married, had a few children, raised them, and gone the way of respectability.

Except for the masked ball they threw once a month. Claire retrieved her black mask from where she'd hidden it in her wardrobe and stuffed it into her reticule.

Claire's hair was tied in a knot at the nape of her neck, and it hung over her left shoulder. Finn would murder her if he caught her in this gown. It was one she'd ordered for Mrs. Abercrombie. Claire couldn't be Mrs. Abercrombie any more, particularly now that Colette had assumed the name. But she could pass herself off as someone else, couldn't she? She tugged at her bodice. Her breasts were pushed up high, like they were set upon a shelf for display. Colette had assured Claire that she was stunning in the dress, but Claire wasn't so sure.

She plumped the pillows stuffed beneath her counterpane and stepped back, satisfied with herself. She crept to the door and opened it slowly. It was late, and her parents often retired early and then rose with the sun.

Claire tiptoed down the corridor toward the servants' stairs. She would go out the side door and catch a hackney, and hopefully no one would be the wiser.

It seemed almost a bit too quiet as she ran down the stairs and cautiously pushed the door open. Cool night air washed across her skin as she walked purposefully toward the street. She'd had a footman call for a hackney, supposedly for Marcus, a half hour before that. Hopefully, one would be waiting.

Claire sighed, anticipation sizzling across her skin. She loved this life. Pretending to be someone she wasn't.

Claire was certain Finn would be going to Lord Gelson's so that he could intercept Colette and find out what she had learned so far. No one had to know he also had some of his investigators in place at the party to keep an eye on Mayden.

She gave the driver instructions and slipped into the

waiting hack. It wasn't until someone reached out and grabbed her arm in a forceful grip that she had even the slightest bit of trepidation.

❧

Finn knew it. He'd known she would try this. "Miss Thorne," he said, his voice frosty even to him, as he sat down next to her. "Where do you think you're going?"

"Sir, I do not know who you think I am, but I must insist that you exit my carriage."

Finn had to look at her very closely to assure himself that it was, indeed, Miss Thorne who sat opposite him. Some little piece of him wasn't entirely certain, but he would bet his life that it was her behind all that ghastly red hair and those spectacles. He leaned close and sniffed her neck.

"You smell like Miss Thorne," he said softly. She shivered. He very tenderly touched his lips to the place where her neck met her shoulder and suckled. "You taste like Miss Thorne."

"What does Miss Thorne taste like, sir?" she asked.

"Heaven," he murmured against her skin. "She tastes like heaven. And she tastes like she's mine." Finn pulled the spectacles from their perch on her nose. "Where did you get these?"

"I don't recall," she said with a shrug. She folded like a house of cards under his piercing stare. "I borrowed them from one of the maids, if you must know."

Finn had never seen a maid with jeweled spectacles, so that was probably a lie. He chose to overlook it. Finn heaved a sigh. "You do know that I'm not going to let you go to Lord Gelson's, don't you?"

She tilted her head and regarded him somberly. "You do know that I didn't ask for your permission, don't you?"

"Damn it, Claire. You have to stop these missions of yours."

She snorted. It was quite an endearing sound, really. "I'll never stop my missions. I'm a faerie, for goodness sake. If you take away my missions, you might as well take my wings."

Finn lifted a lock of her hair to his nose. She still smelled like summer. Would he ever tire of that scent? He hoped not. "Will this wash out?"

"It'll be gone by tomorrow." She patted his knee. "Don't fret."

He finally looked down at what she was wearing. She wore an emerald-green gown, trimmed with a wide gold ribbon beneath her breasts. Breasts that made him fear they were about to tumble out of her gown. Would be such a bad thing? Definitely not.

"I'm taking you back home," Finn said.

"I want to go to Lord Gelson's. We don't have to stay long. I just want to see how well Colette pretends to be me pretending to be Mrs. Abercrombie. What I don't understand is why Colette wanted to be Mrs. Abercrombie in the first place," Claire said.

"Colette has wanted entrée into that part of society for quite some time. I assume she met Mrs. Abercrombie, or you, as it were, and decided that since Mrs. Abercrombie was going to be 'leaving town,' she could step into her shoes for a night or two."

"The gall of that woman," Claire bit out.

"It's actually quite fortuitous," Finn said.

"How so?"

"She's in the line of danger instead of you." Finn reached up to rap on the roof and get the driver's attention.

Claire stopped him with a hand on his arm. He looked down at her. She was a vision, even if her face was heavily powdered and her hair a hideous color. He ran one finger along her eyebrow. "You dyed those too?" he asked.

"Whatever it takes."

"Can you be anyone? Anywhere?"

She mulled it over for a moment. "Typically, yes."

"What's the real you?" he blurted out.

She laughed. "You know the real me."

"Do I?"

She looked directly into his eyes. "Yes. You do."

⤛⤜

He didn't. He didn't know anything about her. He knew of her world, but nothing about what made it work. He didn't know she carried his child. He didn't know that she was quite happy that she had to marry him. Of all the men she could have been stuck with, she supposed he was the best.

"You worry me, Claire. What was your plan tonight?"

"My plan was to introduce myself to Mrs. Abercrombie and learn what I could."

"Alone?"

"Yes."

He shook his head. Would she always vex him so? The pulse beating at the base of her throat was the only sign that she was even the smallest bit nervous.

Would he ever know her feelings? Would he ever truly trust that she was what she was supposed to be in his head?

The carriage rolled to a stop and Finn leaned to look out the window. "What the devil is going on out there?" he murmured to himself. There was a long line of coaches outside Lord Gelson's home where they'd come to a stop. But something was wrong. Guests walked to and fro on the lawn, rather than in the house. And someone had called the watch. Finn slipped his mask from his pocket and moved to get out of the coach. "Something is wrong. I don't know what it is. But the watch wouldn't be here for no reason." He pointed a finger at her. "Do not get out of the coach."

Claire pursed her lips and didn't respond to him.

"I mean it, Claire."

She looked out the opposite window and ignored him.

Finn walked slowly into the small crowd milling about on the lawn, wandering about like he'd been with the guests the whole time, until he saw one of his men. "What's going on?" he asked as he pulled the man to the side.

His man talked out of the corner of his mouth. "There has been a murder."

The hair on the back of Finn's neck stood up. "Who?"

"A widow. I'm not certain of her name yet."

Finn's heart stopped for a moment. "A widow, you say?"

"Yes, she was found in one of the playrooms. Some-one had slit her throat."

"I see." Finn's heart was still beating like the hooves

of a runaway horse. "Find out everything you can, and come see me first thing in the morning."

"Yes, my lord," the man said.

Finn walked quickly back to the carriage and opened the door. As he climbed in, nothing but empty space embraced him. "Damn her," he muttered. If she didn't get herself killed all by herself, he was tempted to wring her pretty little neck.

Twenty-Five

CLAIRE'S TEETH CHATTERED, SHE WAS SO NERVOUS, AS she slunk through the shadows of Lord Gelson's manor house. She put on her black half mask and let herself in the first unattended door she could find.

Voices reached her ears and she froze, plastering herself against the wall. But they continued down the corridor that crossed the one she traveled, and Claire followed them at a discreet distance.

Claire had never been inside this particular house, but she could easily assume that she wasn't in the servants' corridor. The rug was too well made. And the paneling on the walls was polished to a shine.

"You there," a voice called out. Claire froze, but then she plastered a pleasant but not overly friendly smile on her face and turned to face the man.

"*Oui?*" she asked. "Pardon me, but I do not speak English," she said in French, her accent heavy as snow on a rooftop. The man stopped and looked at her closely. Claire didn't speak French, aside from this one statement. She hoped he wouldn't try to ask her anything else.

He spoke to her like she was a half-wit. A deaf one at that. He pointed down the corridor and said. "You. Have. To. Go. Outside. With. The. Others. Do you understand?"

"*Oui*, I understand," Claire said again in halted English. She pointed toward the way she'd come in.

He pointed in the opposite direction. "Go. That. Way." The door to the room behind him opened and two men walked out. One shook his head. "Have the coroner come for the body," he said to the man with whom Claire had been talking.

"Yes, sir," the man said.

Body? Did he say body?

"That way," he said again, pointing.

"*Oui*, I understand." She gave him a smile so sultry that he blushed a bit. Then she turned and sauntered down the corridor in the direction he'd pointed. When she reached the end, she stopped and waited. The man kept going, perhaps to check the rear doors of the house. It didn't matter. He was leaving. And she needed to get in that room, if only for a moment.

Claire waited until his footsteps receded. Then she ducked into the room and closed the door soundly behind her.

The room was awash in lamplight, which made the situation even starker than it would have been otherwise. Claire skidded quickly to a halt as she saw the large puddle of blood that covered the floor. Nausea rose within her.

Claire swallowed and tried to breathe through the feeling that she needed to cast up her accounts. She might not be used to scenes like this, but she could tolerate it for a moment. Claire stepped around the puddle and sank down on her haunches. She looked over the body, which seemed vaguely familiar. She tugged the mask from her face, and her heart jumped into her throat when she saw who it was. Colette lay there, her mouth slack and open, her skin pasty white. Her brown eyes were wide open, and she was, above all else, dead.

Footsteps sounded in the corridor, and Claire jumped to her feet. She rushed across the room, slid behind the heavy curtains at the window, and stood completely still.

"Claire," a voice hissed. The door clicked open and then closed. "Claire," the voice whispered heavily.

Claire peeped out from behind the curtain. "Finn?"

"What am I going to do with you?" he ground out. He waved at her there in the dark. "Come on. Let's go before you get caught."

"The body. It's Colette."

Finn froze. "Colette," he repeated. He didn't look terribly surprised.

"Colette. She's dead."

❦

Colette might have been dead, but Mrs. Abercrombie was the one who'd attended the party, and she was the one who lay in a puddle of blood on the floor. "Let's discuss this in the coach," Finn said. His voice was quick and brusque, and he didn't sound nearly as charming as he normally was. He pulled her out into the corridor and began to rush her down the hall. But voices reached their ears. Two men, if he heard the voices correctly. Finn opened a random door in the corridor and dragged Claire into it.

But he didn't stop there. He pushed her farther into the room and lifted her to perch on top of the desk in the corner. Then he pulled her skirts up, parted her thighs, stepped between them, and looked into her eyes. "Trust me," he said.

She nodded as he quickly tousled her hair and pulled her bodice lower, until a pretty pink nipple popped free.

Claire reached to pull it back up, but he cupped her breast with his hand and she froze. He looked down at her, almost forgetting his purpose as he took her nipple into his mouth. He slid her bottom closer to the edge of the desk. The footsteps in the corridor were getting closer. Finn sucked on the nipple and she cried out. "Perfect, Claire. Do that again when the door opens."

"I don't understand," she murmured, leaning back on her hands at his insistence. It raised her breast higher in the air, and he wanted to lavish it with all the attention it deserved. But there wasn't time. He had to make whomever was about to walk in the room believe there was sexual congress going on.

As the door opened, Finn began to grunt loudly and thrust between her legs. He kept himself between her and whoever was coming in the room, yet he still didn't want them to see any part of Claire's body. So, he tugged her bodice up a little.

A pleasurable noise left Claire's lips as she wrapped her legs around his waist and held him tightly. He continued to thrust between her legs. He was still firmly inside his trousers, though he wanted badly to be out of them. "Close the bloody door," he grunted, just as Claire started to make little whimpery noises in her throat. God, she was good.

"You can't be in here," a voice called.

"Just a minute," he grunted out. Damn but it was hard to feign the motions of sex with Claire wrapped around him, making those noises beneath him.

"Out!" the man bellowed.

Finn made a great show of pulling back from Claire, pulling her legs from about his waist, and righting her clothing. "Let's go finish this elsewhere, love," he said, his voice slow like that of a drunkard.

Claire made a twittering little laugh. "Yes, my lord," she said.

Finn slid her bottom off the desk and helped her to stand. "Good job," he whispered in her ear.

He could almost see her smile in the dark room.

"Out that way," the man directed, and Finn stumbled trying to get out of the room.

"Thank you for your hospitality," Finn said, slurring his words on purpose.

Claire propped him on her shoulder, pretending to hold him up.

"Don't leave the premises," the man warned to their backs as they walked toward the front door.

"Yes, sir," Claire called back, all sweetness and light. "We'll be waiting outside."

But as soon as they were out of eyesight, Finn led her out one of the back corridors and into the dark night.

Twenty-Six

CLAIRE DIDN'T BEGIN TO SHAKE UNTIL THEY WERE A good way from Lord Gelson's house. The hack had given up and left them, which wasn't a bad thing since the officials would have detained a carriage if they saw it leaving the scene of the crime. But Finn was shrewd. He led her through the garden and around the house, then back out to the street so that no one noticed they were leaving.

Claire's teeth chattered and she hugged her arms around herself. "Finn," she began softly.

"What?" He glanced left and right, constantly checking to be sure no one was following them. He was distracted by his vigilance.

"That was meant for me, wasn't it?" she asked. He looked down at her briefly, his eyes skittering across her face.

"Probably," he replied. He took her upper arm in his grip and hurried her along. "Let's get a hack," Finn suggested.

It was late at night, but there at the street corner sat a shabby carriage pulled by an old bay mare. Finn handed Claire in and gave the driver an address.

As Claire got into the coach, she settled against the squabs and tightened her arms about herself even more. She'd never seen a dead body before. At least not one that was meant to be her. Her teeth chattered so loudly that her jaw hurt with the rhythm.

Finn shrugged out of his coat and dropped it around her shoulders, pulling it closed as he pulled her into his lap and held her tightly. "Shhh," he crooned. Claire settled her face into the crook of his neck and breathed in his scent. "It's going to be all right," he soothed, his hand rubbing up and down her back.

She nodded into his neck, but her body wouldn't comply with her wishes that it stop shivering. "I don't usually get like this in stressful situations."

"I know," he agreed. "You're as stalwart as the day is long. It's all right. I promise."

"She looked surprised," Claire murmured past her chattering teeth.

"Yes, she did," Finn agreed. "Though I suppose that could be any number of emotions, and we'll assume the worst since we already know she was murdered."

Claire took his face in her hands and made him look at her. "He killed her because he thought she was me."

"Yes." Finn took her hands in his and chafed them gently between his own. She wasn't terribly cold. She just couldn't stop the blasted shaking. "He killed her because he thought she was you. He wanted you. He wanted to hurt you, because you are mine."

She was his, and she'd never really appreciated that fact, had she? But she had his complete attention in that moment.

He went on to say forcefully, "But you are safe. You're in the carriage with me, and Mayden is nowhere nearby."

"Where are we going?"

"My house."

"Why?"

"Because I need to be sure you're all right."

"I'm fine," she said, but she still trembled.

"You're not fine."

"You can take me back to Ramsdale House."

"No."

His tone brooked no argument. None whatsoever.

The hackney stopped and the driver hopped down to open the door. Finn stepped out and swept Claire up in his arms when she would have stepped out on shaky legs. She instinctively wrapped her arms around his neck and held on tightly.

His footman opened the door and stepped quickly to the side when Finn nearly barreled him over. "Good evening, my lord," the man said.

"Bring a hot bath up to my chambers," Finn barked.

"Yes, my lord," the man said as he scuttled away.

"It's late. You should let them go to bed."

"It's late. You should let me do what I want." He looked down at her, his blue eyes flashing. "Will life with you always be a challenge?" he asked, although she doubted he wanted an answer to the question.

"Probably," she said. She was what she was. She doubted that would change.

His house was a small set of rooms, but it was immaculately clean and the furniture was big and bulky. She didn't see much of it, however, as he whisked her down the corridor and into his chambers.

He set her down on the edge of the bed and bent to tug her slippers from her feet. The he slid behind her on the bed and started to unfasten her dress.

His hands were tender but efficient as he stripped her down to nothing but her chemise. In the adjoining room, Claire could hear water splashing into a bath. "Is that for me?" she asked.

"Yes. It will help you relax, I hope. And might even stop the shivering."

She nodded and let him push her chemise up over her knees, so he could roll her stockings down. Finn kissed the inside of her knee quickly and then tugged her hands until she stood. He moved to pull down her drawers, but she stopped his hands. "I can do it," she protested.

"Feeling shy?" he asked, his lips touching her temple.

"A little." Actually, she was terrified. If Finn saw her naked now, he would know about the baby she carried. There was no hiding the faint bump that was the new life within her. He would know that she'd deceived him. That she'd purposefully kept something from him. He'd be angry. She was certain of it. "Could I have some privacy?" she asked as the footman knocked on the door to tell Finn the bath was ready.

"I don't want to leave you alone," he said, and Claire's heart tripped a beat within her chest.

"Can you talk to me through the door?"

He chuckled. "If you insist."

Claire padded across the room and slipped into his dressing room. The big tub stood tall at the side of the room. Steam rose from it in gentle waves. Claire tugged her chemise over her head, and then pushed her drawers down to the floor and stepped out of them. She lowered herself into the tub, and the warm water enveloped her better than any blanket ever could.

Claire laid her head back against the edge of the tub. The water rose to the tops of her breasts, and nothing more than her head and her knees stood out of the water.

What on earth was she going to do? If he saw her now, he would know she'd been deceiving him all along. He might hate her for it.

"Feeling better?" Finn called through the door, which he'd opened to a crack.

"Much," she assured him. Well, the shivering had stopped. "I don't know why I did that. That has never happened before."

"It's a very normal reaction."

"Has it ever happened to you?"

"In varying stages, yes. There are a lot of emotions that accompany death, particularly when one is relieved it's not one's own life that was lost."

◦◦◦

Finn leaned his head on the doorjamb. It could have been her. It could have been Claire. If he hadn't been there to catch her getting into that carriage, she would have gone to that masked ball, and Mayden could have killed her. The fear of losing her settled in his gut and rolled around like a cat in a sack.

"Finn," Claire called. "Do you have a housemaid who could help me wash this tint from my hair?"

Not at this time of the night. "I'll come and do it,"

he replied as he pushed the door open and walked into
the room.

Good God, she was pretty sitting here, her hair
curling with the steam of her bath. She'd pulled all
the pins from it and draped it over the lip of the tub.
She sat forward as he approached, and drew her knees
closer to her chest. "Finn!" she cried. "You shouldn't
be in here."

"Oh, I promise not to look." He was lying. But he
didn't feel even the least bit of remorse about it. He
planned to look his fill. He planned to take in every
dip and curve of her body. He wasn't sending her
home this night. Not a chance in hell.

She'd nearly died, for God's sake. He'd nearly
lost her.

Finn divested himself of his coat and waistcoat, and
he jerked free his cravat and tugged it off his neck.
He rolled up his shirtsleeves and dropped to one knee
beside her. Her skin was rosy and pink, her cheeks
flushed with the heat of the bath. Tiny tendrils of hair
had begun to spiral at her forehead and around her
ears. He would be glad when that dreadful tint was
gone and her strawberry blond hair would be back.

Finn picked up a pail and put it beneath the fall of
her hair. Then he picked up a rinse bucket and leaned
over her. "Ready?" he asked.

She nodded, not looking him in the eye as she
leaned back. She kept her eyes closed, and as she lay
back, her breasts rose above the water. But he wasn't
here to ogle her body. He was here to wash her hair.

Finn slowly and carefully wet her hair with the
rinse water and then soaped her tresses gently. "I

don't think it's all going to come out," he warned. He massaged her scalp, letting his fingernails gently abrade her skin. She made a sound of contentment as he rinsed the soap from her hair. He hadn't realized how very long it was when it was wet. When it was dry, it was springy and curly, and looked luxuriously perfect.

"Feeling better?" he asked as he sat down next to the bath and laid his arm along the side. She sat forward again, hiding the shadow of her breasts behind her knees.

"Better," she said. "Thank you."

Her teeth were no longer chattering, and most of that god-awful red was out of her hair.

And she was naked.

Gloriously naked.

Sinfully naked.

And Finn was aroused beyond bearing. "Would you like some help with your bath?" he asked and waggled his eyebrows at her.

She laughed lightly. "I think I can finish the rest on my own. Can you give me a little privacy?"

"Must I?" Finn didn't mean to beg. But he wasn't above it either.

"I just need a moment," she said.

Finn left a stack of towels within her reach and hung his dressing gown over the back of the door.

"Thank you," she called to his retreating back.

❦

Claire had no idea what the right thing to do was. She needed to tell him about the baby. She would have to if he wanted to be intimate with her that night. And if the bulge behind the fall of his trousers was any indication, that was what he had in mind.

What should she do? Should she ask him to take her home? Should she ask him to sit and then tell him? He might be so surprised he'd fall over and crack his head on the floor. He might have an apoplexy. He might hate her forever.

Claire washed quickly and climbed from the tub. She wrung the water from her hair, and then flipped her hair over, wrapped it in a towel, and righted herself. She blotted herself dry with a second towel and slipped into his dressing gown.

When Claire walked back into his bedchamber, she found him reclining on a chaise longue before the fire. He called her over with a quick motion of his hand. He looked up at her from beneath heavy-lidded lashes. "I must confess that my plans were innocent when I brought you here."

"And now?" she asked as she sat down on the edge of the chaise. He shifted to the side to give her room.

"My plans are no longer innocent." His voice sounded like it had been dragged down a gravel drive. "Come here," he said as he spread his thighs and pulled her between them, and then pulled the towel from her hair, combing it gently with his fingertips before he drew her forward to lie on his chest.

"I'm going to get you all wet," she warned.

Finn sat forward and jerked his shirt over his head, and then pulled her forward. "I want to hold you," he said, his voice raw and full of emotion. He kissed her forehead gently. "I could have lost you tonight."

Claire's soul hummed as he held her against him.

"Don't ever put yourself in danger like that again, do you hear me?"

She heard him, but she couldn't possibly comply with his wishes. Not in this matter.

Claire was naked beneath his dressing gown, and she'd never been more aware of her skin than she was at that moment. Goose flesh rose on her arms and chest, and her nipples were hard points against the soft fabric of his dressing gown. Finn tipped her face up and touched his lips softly to hers.

"I wish I could marry you tonight," he murmured as his tongue teased her lips open, just before he dipped inside. Claire met the greedy thrusts of his tongue, and he moaned low in his throat. He leaned back and looked down at her, emotion brimming in his eyes. "If anything ever happened to you, I don't know what I'd do."

Claire scooted up onto her knees and laid her upper body against his naked chest. With her hands on his shoulders, she lifted herself until she was nose to nose with him. "Ouch," Finn said, as her knee brushed the rigid curve of his manhood behind his trousers.

"Sorry," she said, pulling back a little.

Finn adjusted her body, pulling his legs together as he spread her thighs over his lap, setting one knee on each side of him. His robe was still closed about her waist, but Claire looked down to find that it gaped open at the top, and spread widely at the bottom, pulling tight across her hips. Finn sat forward and growled, just before he reached into the vee at the neck of the robe and pushed it wide around her breasts. He stared down at them for a moment, his

mouth open wide, then he nudged her higher and
brought her left breast to his lips.

Claire's breath caught when he gently tongued the
rigid peak, and she squirmed to get closer to him. The
ridge of his manhood pressed against her aching cleft.
Claire spread her legs wider and snuggled down closer
to him.

"Just a minute," he warned as he reached between
them and unbuttoned the fall of his trousers. He pulled
the turgid length of himself free and then tugged her
knees forward, pulling her tighter against him. "God,
Claire, you're going to unman me."

Finn's hands gripped her naked bottom tightly,
kneading the tender flesh, as he brought her forward
to slide back and forth along his length. Claire could
see the tip of his erection as it shimmered in the fire-
light, moving back and forth, but not sliding inside.
"Please, Finn," she murmured against his lips.

Claire reached between them and took his erection in her fist. She pointed him toward the core of
her, the part that wept with want for him. "Claire,"
he moaned.

Claire wasn't certain what to do.

Finn sucked her earlobe between his lips and
suckled it gently. His fingertips slid up to the pointy
tip of her ear and back down. "Put me inside you,"
he said, his voice low by her ear. Where his voice was
broken before, it was volcanic now. It was full of heat
and want. "Put me inside you, Claire."

Finn bent his head and took her nipple into his
mouth again as his other hand strummed at the other
breast. Claire's slit wept with need, and his manhood

was shiny wet with his strokes against her cleft. But this was not enough. She ached. She needed him.

"Take me inside, Claire," he ground out.

Claire took him in her fist again and pulled his manhood away from his body, aiming it toward that pulse that pounded so loudly inside her. "I don't know what to do," she admitted. She chuckled, a weak sound, and laid her forehead against his naked chest.

Finn took himself in one hand and raised her bottom a little with the other. His hardness pressed at her softness and the tip of him slid inside. Claire stilled as he filled her just that much. He didn't advance. He stayed still as a statue, with just the crown of his manhood inside her.

Then he pulled her forward and down all at the same time, filling her in one solid stroke. Claire cried out. He filled her completely and totally. Claire looked down between them and saw through the slit in the dressing gown that he was indeed buried to the hilt inside her. "Mine," he said.

"Yes," she breathed. Then she rocked forward. She wasn't sure if it was the right thing to do. Not at all. But the noise that left his lips told her it was good.

He was hard as iron inside her, and his hands firmly gripped her buttocks, rocking her back and forth. He pulled her hard onto himself, and Claire thrilled when he began to push her back and pull her forward and down until she was riding his manhood. His rhythm grew more forceful, and Claire took up some of it with her knees and her hands on his shoulders. When she was moving freely on him, he pulled one hand away from her bottom and touched the place between her thighs that he'd rubbed so well and so forcefully before, the place that had made her shatter and break into a million pieces.

He strummed his finger across that aching little bundle of nerves, and Claire's legs began to shake as tension built within her. It was like water pushing at a dam. With enough force, the dam would break. And so would she.

"Does that feel good, Claire?" he asked. His voice in her ear made her sheath clench around him and he groaned loudly, biting his lower lip between his teeth. His face was a mask of emotion. His jaw clenched so tightly that a muscle ticked in his cheek. "Claire," he groaned.

"Finn," Claire cried as his fingers and his manhood pumping inside her pushed her toward that precipice.

"Claire," he ground out. "I need to come. I'm going to come so deep inside you. I like the way you wrap around me and squeeze me. And I want to feel you squeeze my manhood when you come. I want to feel the ripples of sensation as you reach the peak with me."

His fingers pushed harder against that special place as she continued to ride him. Claire lost her breath as he continued to talk to her. To tell her how much he liked her riding him, how much he liked having her on top of him. How much he liked having her be in control of how fast or slow he took her. "I am yours to do with as you will. But I need for you to come, Claire."

Claire cried out as the waves of sensation crashed over her. She stilled on top of him and rocked with the waves of her release, and he grunted beneath her and began to pulse within her. His release was a hot wash of fluid, almost as powerful as hers. She pulsed around his manhood, and he grunted and groaned as he said dirty things in her ear. She didn't know what many of them meant, but he said them with such power and force as he emptied his seed inside her that she continued to pulse. Her culmination wasn't complete. It was ongoing. And when he'd finally wrung all the pleasure from her and stilled beneath her, the warm wash of his spending leaked between then.

"Don't move, Claire," he said. "I'll get something to clean us up. I'm afraid you're a mess."

Heat crept up her cheeks, but she really didn't care. She'd just rode his manhood until they'd both found that sweet release. She'd just taken him. All of him. And he'd given all of himself back to her. He reached for the towel he'd pulled from her hair and brought it down between them.

"Be still, Claire," he warned as he slipped out of her. "Claire, are you having your menses?" he asked.

"What?"

"You're bleeding, Claire," he warned. He kissed her forehead. "Don't worry. I don't mind. But it would have been good to know." He chuckled.

Claire looked down between them and her heart leaped into her throat. She was bleeding. Her blood bathed his manhood, mixed with his seed. "Oh God, Finn," she cried. She scuttled back from him, placing a hand over her belly where their child lay. "Something is wrong, Finn," she cried. Tears pricked at the backs of her lashes. "Something is wrong. Call for a physician. Do it now!"

"I don't think it's as bad as all that, Claire," he said.

"Now, Finn," she screamed. "Call for a physician. Now!"

"Claire," he warned. He got to his feet and approached her. But she didn't let him touch her. He didn't let her get away, however, and pulled her into him. "Don't fret."

A sob shook her frame.

"Claire, what is it?"

"I need a physician. Now."

"All right," he said.

❦

Something was wrong. Claire was frantic. She sobbed against his chest, her tears wetting the front of his shirt as her body heaved with sobs.

"I'll call for the physician. Do you want me to call anyone else?"

"My mother," she said. "I need my mother."

"All right," he said, and he ran from the room to get a servant. He would send for the physician and send for her mother, and then he would find out what the devil was wrong with her. She was frantic for a reason. He just didn't know what it was.

Twenty-Seven

CLAIRE WAS TUCKED BENEATH THE COUNTERPANE ON Finn's bed when her mother arrived. She'd managed to stop the frantic sobbing. And she didn't appreciate the whimpers her crying had left behind. Finn stood across the room and looked down at her. He'd donned a clean shirt and tucked it into his breeches, but he didn't come any closer. Every time he tried, Claire cried even more. Finally, the door opened and her mother stepped through. Her auburn hair hung loose around her shoulders, and she wore a day dress that was buttoned wrong.

"Claire," she said as she walked into the room.

But Claire felt a sob rise within her again. Her mother quickly searched the room until she found Finn. "Could you give us a moment?" her mother asked.

"I want to know what's wrong."

"So do I, but I have a feeling she'll be more likely to tell me if you leave the room."

"I'm going to marry her. I'm not going anywhere. Talk of menses and natural functions will not frighten me."

Finn went and sat in a chair in the corner as Claire's mother approached the bed. She sat down and pulled Claire into her arms. "What's wrong, Claire?" she asked.

There was blood on the towel by the bed. "Did he hurt you?" Claire's mother asked.

"I'm bleeding," Claire sobbed.

Her mother struggled not to laugh. "Honey, that's what happens when it's the first time. It's all right."

"It's not all right," Claire wailed. Then she leaned forward and whispered to her mother. "This wasn't my first time. My first time was several months ago, and I'm with child."

Her mother's mouth fell open, and remorse didn't begin to describe what Claire felt.

"Did you call for the physician?" her mother barked at Finn.

"Yes, he's on the way," Finn replied. He sat forward in the chair and placed his elbows on his knees. "What's wrong?"

Claire's mother tucked her in more tightly behind the counterpane. She crooned to her as she stroked the side of her face. "Everything will be fine. You'll see."

The physician came in and shooed everyone from the room, including her mother. Claire squirmed under his gentle probing as he listened, manipulated, probed, and prodded her. He finally looked up, pulled the counterpane back up, and tucked it beneath her arms. "Everything will be fine, I think."

"It will?" Claire whispered, hope swelling within her.

"I believe so. These things are rather common at this stage."

"I've never heard anyone mention any such a thing."

"Because old wives usually don't talk of such things to young, unmarried ladies."

Heat crept up Claire's cheeks. "I see."

"Shall we bring Lord Phineas in and give him the good news?"

Claire chewed on her lower lip. "I don't know."

"Is he the father?" The man began to pack his tools and implements back inside his case.

"Of course. We're to be married."

"Yet he didn't know about the pregnancy."

"Not yet."

"I believe you're past the point of no return now."

Claire nodded. "I know.

The physician went to the door and opened it, and Finn and Claire's mother came back into the room. But this time, Finn sat down on the side of the bed to comfort her.

The physician spoke. "Congratulations, Lord Phineas," he said. "You're to be a father."

~*~

Finn choked. Like a dolt, he choked on his own spittle. The physician clapped him on the back with a laugh. "It's not as bad as all that," he said. "The babe is all right. I suggest that she stay in bed for at least a sennight, and then I'll come back to check on her to see how things are progressing."

"The bleeding wasn't just her menses?"

The man chuckled again. "She hasn't had menses in several months, my lord."

She'd gotten with child the one time they'd been together, before she'd left to go back to the land of the fae. And she'd known all this time and hadn't told him. Not a word. She'd been pregnant, his child growing inside her, and she hadn't told him.

"Thank you, sir," Finn bit out. He pulled some banknotes from his pocket and pushed them into the man's hand. "I'd appreciate your discretion in this matter."

The physician saw himself out, and Finn felt like he couldn't catch his breath. He couldn't look at her without knowing he'd done this to her, and without remembering that she'd kept it from him all this time.

"I'm going to ask you once, Claire. And then I'll never bring this matter up again." He waited and then said very quietly, so only she could hear. "It's mine, isn't it?"

She nodded, biting her lip so hard he feared she would rend it in two. "That night, I got with child." Her voice broke. "I had planned to tell you."

"When?"

"As soon as I got up the nerve."

"You have enough nerve to walk into danger, but you can't tell me something like this?"

"I'm sorry," she said, her voice a broken whisper.

Finn got up to leave the room. At the door he turned back to see Claire's mother sit down on the side of the bed and pull Claire into her arms. Claire let her, and her mother was soothing her as he left the room, closing the door tightly behind himself.

A baby. Claire was increasing. She carried his child. A smile he couldn't bite back tugged at his lips. A child. God, the idea of Claire growing big with his child… it was everything he'd ever dreamed of.

He was hurt that she hadn't told him. But he knew

now. And now he knew he couldn't wait for the reading of the banns. He would get a special license and marry her tomorrow. Her father had wanted three weeks. But this would be a six-month pregnancy, if his addition was correct. She would deliver their child no more than six months after their marriage, if it took that long. Tongues would wag.

He grinned. Let them. Let them have their fun. He would have Claire. And they would have their child. And more on the way someday.

Finn poured a whiskey and tossed it back. The door to his study opened without a knock. "Are you angry?" Lady Ramsdale asked.

"Angry?" Finn said as he set his glass down. He was giddy with excitement. He strode quickly across the room and spun Lady Ramsdale around in a quick circle. "Are you bound for Bedlam? I'm going to be a father. I couldn't be happier."

Lady Ramsdale smiled as soon as she got over the shock of being spun around. "She's afraid you're angry at her."

Anger was the last thing he felt. "I'll go talk to her. I just needed a moment."

She arched a brow at him. "And whiskey."

"Where is your husband?"

"At Ramsdale House. Asleep."

She knew. "You knew all along, didn't you?"

"I had a feeling." She went on to clarify, "Claire missed her menses for several months. Why do you think we stayed in the land of the fae so long?"

"Does your husband know?"

She shook her head. "No."

"Do we have to tell him?"

She grinned. "I would suggest after the wedding."

"Great idea." He looked at her closely. She really was a lovely woman. And Claire did favor her. "Thank you for coming. You're the only one she wanted."

Her eyes welled with tears. "Thank you for telling me that." Emotion choked her. "I'll see myself out."

Finn walked slowly back up the stairs. He opened the door to his bedchamber to find Claire had dozed off. Her face was blotchy and streaked with tears. He took off his clothes and slid beneath the counterpane with her. She stirred as he rolled her toward him. "Finn?" she asked, her voice groggy with sleep. And tears.

He pulled the counterpane lower and unbelted his dressing gown, which she still wore. In the low light of the room, he could see her looking down at him, as he looked at her no-longer-flat stomach. It was ever so slightly rounded. He ran his fingers over her flesh, which teemed with the life they'd created.

"I'm sorry," she whispered.

He bent and placed his lips to her belly. Then moved up and kissed her lips just as softly. "I'm not," he said.

Claire began to cry, softly this time, not the great wrenching sobs of the moments before. Finn rolled her to the side and pulled her back against him, until she fit him like two spoons in a drawer. He placed a hand on her belly, his son or daughter, and said, "Sleep, Claire."

"You're not angry at me?" she asked, her voice raw with emotion.

"Sleep, Claire." He buried his face in her hair and breathed her in.

Twenty-Eight

Finn paced back and forth in front of his brother's home, unsure of how to proceed. He'd never felt so out of sorts in all his life, and he'd been in some precarious situations before. In his head, he had three problems.

One—It was obvious that Mayden had set his sights on Claire. Mayden had known Claire played the part of Mrs. Abercrombie. Finn's guess was that Colette herself had told him. They were acquaintances from way back, which was one of the many reasons Finn had stopped sleeping with her when he did. Then Colette had decided to impersonate Claire impersonating Mrs. Abercrombie, much to her misfortune. He'd used Colette as a warning to Finn. But the threat was still real.

Two—He needed to marry Claire sooner rather than later. Her father wouldn't appreciate that. He would probably be spitting mad. But Finn didn't want to wait two more weeks for the reading of the banns.

Three—He needed to confess that Claire was increasing and that it was his child. He wouldn't have anyone assume anything else. He just couldn't. He had to let everyone know that the baby was his, even if it would be a six-month pregnancy.

A voice rang out from the shrubbery. "Are you going to pace outside all day or knock on the door?" Ronald, the garden gnome, was in the bushes.

"Sod off, Ronald," Finn grumbled.

Ronald stepped out of the foliage and grinned. "You're all out of sorts. Anything the matter?"

"None of your concern," Finn murmured.

"She's my concern," the gnome said.

"Who?" Finn asked as he paced by the small man and back.

"Claire. She's like family to me. Don't tell me she's not my concern." He straightened his back and puffed out his chest.

"Yes, yes, family," Finn murmured.

The little man smiled an almost feral smile. "Wonder what has you out of sorts. Could it be that Claire is increasing?"

Finn stumbled to a halt. Ronald stood there scratching his chin, a challenge in his eyes if Finn had ever seen one. "If you were a bigger man, I'd call you out for that."

"If you were a bigger man, she wouldn't be pregnant."

He couldn't hit the gnome. It wouldn't be a fair fight. But Finn could trip him when he wasn't looking. Or stuff him in a barrel and roll him down a hill. Those ideas wouldn't be very fair either. But the little devil would appreciate Finn's trickery after the fact.

"Shut it, Ronald," Finn said coldly. He went back to his pacing.

The little man sat down on the bottom step of the manor and rested his chin in his hands. He stopped talking and just regarded Finn with a cold eye. Finally, after a pause long enough to make Finn uncomfortable, he said, "When's the wedding?"

"Not certain yet."

"I hope it's soon."

"As do I."

Ronald slapped his knee. "That's it. That's why you're so out of sorts."

"I don't know what you're referring to."

The gnome laughed loudly. "You're afraid to tell her father. Not to mention your brother."

"That's not the case." It was the case, but he'd be sent to hell and back rather than confess it to Ronald.

"You were asked to take care of her. And not for very long. And she came out of it pregnant."

All right. So that was the problem. His honor was at stake. No matter that he was making it right. He would always be the man who'd taken advantage like an idiot and gotten her pregnant. Then didn't make right on it when he should have. But she'd left, for goodness sake. She'd taken off in the dead of night and stayed gone for more than three months. He couldn't change that fact, any more than he could change the fact that she'd be shamed in the eyes of society, all because of him.

Good God, what a muddle.

The front door opened and Wilkins stepped out. "My lord, His Grace insists that you come inside now."

Robin knew he was there?

"Can I give you some advice, my lord?" Ronald asked quietly.

"If you must."

"The damage is done. Stop acting like you'll do more good by finding a likely story to explain it all."

The gnome had a point. He was wearing himself out, not just with the pacing, but also with coming up with a good enough lie. He could tell them all the truth. And see how they thought it might be best to handle it. "Rightly so."

Finn turned to walk into Robin's house and went straight to Robin's study. The duchess was there, and she sat on the edge of Robin's desk facing him. Finn coughed into his hand, and she jumped from the edge of the desk and skirted around it, her cheeks pink and her eyes avoiding his. "Lord Phineas," she said. "Good morning."

"Yes, it is," Finn said.

"Is everything all right?"

He heaved a sigh. "It will be."

Sophia looked toward Robin, and he nodded his head at her. "I'll leave you two alone," she said.

"Thank you." Finn tugged at his cravat.

"What's the matter, Finn?" Robin asked as he sat down in the chair behind his desk.

"Claire is expecting my child," Finn blurted. God, he was an idiot. He could have done that so much more smoothly.

Robin jumped to his feet. "What?" he yelled.

"Claire is increasing and it's mine."

Robin jerked Finn from the chair he was sitting in by the lapels of his coat. "Tell me you're jesting."

"Would I make light of such a thing?" Finn asked. He pried Robin's hands from his clothing and set him back. It had been a long time since he'd tussled with his older brother, but he wasn't above it. And he might even win.

Robin looked at him and growled. He sank back into the chair he'd vacated and dropped his face in his hands. "At least you're already marrying her. In nine months, you'll have an heir to your fortune."

"It won't actually be nine months," Finn murmured.

Robin looked confused.

Finn rushed on. "Do you remember when you asked me to take care of her for you when you went to the land of the fae?"

"Yes," Robin replied slowly, stretching the word out like a hiss through his teeth.

"We both had a little too much to drink that night, and… well… we were intimate."

"You were." Robin's voice was monotone. And quiet. Much too quiet.

"Then when I woke up, she was gone." He held up a hand to thwart Robin's next complaint. "I scoured the roads between here and Bedfordshire. As she explained to me, she took the wind back to the land of the fae that night because her grandfather died." He still didn't understand that part. "Some kind of special transportation they have. They sent the wind to pick her up while I was sleeping."

"Go on."

"I looked everywhere for her, and then in one of your notes, you said that she was back in the land of the fae with her family. I couldn't tell you about her, because, well, she's your sister-in-law."

"Yes, she is."

"Then suddenly, she was here one night. She tumbled directly into my bedchamber."

"Tumbled."

"Tumbled. Right into my bedchamber."

"And?"

A grin tugged at the corners of Finn's lips. "And I was damned happy to see her."

"Happy."

Finn jumped to his feet. "Damn it, Robin, can you say something else and just stop repeating after me?"

"You don't want to hear what I have to say."

"Oh, I do."

"You took advantage of an innocent lady." Robin growled and withheld the rest of his speech.

"Those Thorne women," Finn said, "they're quite irresistible."

"Apparently."

"Don't pretend you were a saint where Sophia was concerned."

"Sophia wasn't entrusted into my care, Finn," he said. "And I was in love with her."

Finn grinned. "So am I."

Robin looked confused. "You're in love with my wife?"

"I'm not in love with Sophia, you idiot. I'm in love with Claire."

"Oh, yes, I remember you confessed that the other day."

"So, my problem is that this is most assuredly going to be a six-month birth." He did some math in his head. "And there's no doubt the child is mine. I need to protect Claire from the tongues that will wag."

"You'd have to take her out of the country to do that."

That wasn't a bad idea, actually. He could protect her from Mayden that way too.

"Her father is going to kill you. You might want to be out of the country so he won't skin you alive. Her mother might boil you in oil."

"I think that's witches who do that. Not faeries."

"Oh."

"What do faeries do?"

"No idea. But I'd wager it's hideous. And painful."

Finn shrugged. "Her mother likes me. I saw her last night. She already knew about the pregnancy. Though she suggested that we not tell Ramsdale until after the wedding."

"She already knew?"

"Yes, that's why she stayed in the land of the fae so long. To help Claire sort things out."

"I see."

"We have another problem."

"Don't tell me Marcus is pregnant too. Because that will be three Thornes expecting." Robin chuckled. It was good to hear his brother chuckle. He hadn't done it for a very long time.

"No, it's Mayden. He tried to kill Claire last night."

"*What?*"

Finn went on to tell Robin what had happened the night before. By the time he was done, Robin was the one pacing the floor.

"So, what do we do?"

"How many of Mayden's debts do you own? Enough to break him?" Robin asked.

Finn had started to buy up Mayden's debts years ago, and the ones that Finn hadn't bought, Robin had. The man owed more money than he would ever earn in ten lifetimes.

"I think it's time to call in the debts," Robin said grimly.

"Shall we pay him a visit?"

"I think it would be prudent."

"Debtor's prison would be a nice place for him to rot. I want to marry Claire. Do you think you could get a special license for me?"

"I think we should handle this with Mayden as the first priority," Robin said. "Let's get this settled, and by the time we're done, two more weeks will have passed and you can be married by banns."

Claire had to stay in bed and rest for a week anyway, per the doctor's orders.

"Her father is probably going to hit you when he finds out, even if you're married to her by then."

"I don't doubt it."

"I would do the same for Anne."

"Hell, I would do the same for Anne." Finn repeated. He would. He loved his family, and he would love this child Claire was going to have.

❧

Claire stretched wide beneath the counterpane as the sun filtered through the curtains and woke her. The sun was high in the sky, so she'd slept much longer than usual. The linens felt cool against her skin and she knew she'd been warm through the night with Finn wrapped around her. But now he was gone.

He hadn't forgiven her when he'd come to bed. He'd just pulled her into his arms and murmured softly in her hair as she'd cried into the crook of his arm. But he'd held her and soothed her, and she'd finally exhausted herself and slept.

Did his being gone mean he was still angry at her? What if he didn't want a fae child? She'd been so worried with the fear of having a human child that she hadn't even considered that he might now fear having a fae child, one that could be taken from them if the circumstances weren't just right.

He was in an impossible situation, and he had been in it since the day he'd met her. Guilt niggled at her conscience a bit as she reasoned with herself that this was all right. They would marry and they would have a child. Then they could move between the two worlds at will. She could continue to go on her missions, and he could continue to take care of his holdings, his investments, and manage his detective business.

She actually wanted to find out more about his business. As they'd lain there on the settee in the painting, he'd told her a little about his cases, but she'd fallen asleep in his lap before she'd heard much. Maybe over dinner tonight, she could ask him more questions.

Claire tossed the counterpane off and moved to get up. The physician had told her to stay in bed for at least a sennight. But certainly she could get up to use the chamber pot, couldn't she? She took care of her personal needs and washed herself using his wash basin and a pitcher of cold water someone had left.

Claire still wore his dressing gown from the night before, and she belted it more tightly around her waist.

But then she caught her reflection in the looking glass and unbelted the robe, slid it from her shoulders and let it drop to the floor. She stood in front of the full-length mirror and turned to the side. Her breasts were bigger than before. She hefted them in her hands and glared at herself.

Her stomach was slightly rounded, but it wasn't overly large and she could probably go about in society for a few more months before she had to go into seclusion.

A knock sounded at the door and Claire jumped, sliding back into Finn's dressing gown. "Come in," she called, when she was tucked back beneath the counterpane.

Sophia opened the door and stepped through it, and behind her was their mother. "Good morning," Sophia chimed. She took in Finn's bedchamber as she walked into the room. "It seems a little odd to be visiting you here."

Claire chuckled. "It's a little odd to be here."

"Well, I suppose you can't leave, since the physician told you to stay in bed for a sennight," Claire's mother chimed.

"A sennight?" Sophia asked. "Goodness whatever did you do to yourself? Did you twist your ankle? Did you hit your head? Do you have a stomach ailment?" She felt Claire's forehead with the back of her hand.

Claire grabbed for her hand. "I'm fine, really."

"Well, you can't possibly be fine if you have to stay abed for a week." Sophia regarded her skeptically.

"I'm going to call for a tray," her mother said. "Have you eaten anything yet?"

Claire yawned. "I just woke up, actually."

Her mother slipped out of the room. Sophia pulled a chair closer to the bed and hissed, "Are you all right? Lord Phineas was at the Hall when I left, and he looked like he had a difficult night."

Claire snorted. "I imagine finding out you have a child on the way is a difficult way to spend the night."

"Oh, thank goodness," Sophia said, dropping her face into her hands. "I thought you were going to pretend it wasn't so."

"How long have you known?"

"I listened outside Ashley's study, if you must know." She smiled a fearless grin. "Old habits die hard."

"So, Finn went to confess all to Robinsworth?" That could not have gone well.

Sophia nodded. "He fears for your safety, apparently. And so do I."

Footsteps sounded in the corridor and Sophia raised a finger to her lips. "Shhh. Mother is coming."

The door opened and Lady Ramsdale stepped back into the room. "I asked the servants to put together a tray." Then her shoulders slumped in defeat and she groaned. "For heaven's sake, Claire, please tell me you've told her. The suspense is killing me."

"Told her what?" Claire asked innocently.

"Told me what?" Sophia jumped to her feet. "Someone will tell me right this moment what is wrong!"

Claire's mother's mouth opened and closed like a fish. Then both girls began to laugh. Sophia rolled onto the bed and held her stomach tightly, she was laughing that hard. "I already know, Mother. It's all right."

Lady Ramsdale picked up a pillow and tossed it at them. "The two of you should be ashamed. Teasing your mother like that." Her eyes shimmered with what appeared to be delight. "Are the two of you close?" she asked as she sat down in the chair Sophia had placed beside the bed.

"I tolerate her pretty well," Claire said. "When she's not being shrewish."

"I'm never shrewish." Sophia put her hands on her hips and protested. "Now that I'm a duchess, I have to behave myself."

"Yes, Your Grace," Claire said with a laugh.

But they both froze when they realized their mother's eyes were misting with tears.

"We do like each other," Claire said quickly at the same time Sophia said, "We're great friends."

"I just can't believe I have you two back. And that I'm about to be a grandmother." She wiped a tear from her cheek.

"How did you find out? About the baby?" Sophia asked of their mother.

"I sent for her last night, when things weren't going well."

Sophia almost looked hurt for a moment. "You could have called me."

"I was afraid you would tell your husband."

Sophia sighed heavily. "I probably would have."

"But now you are relieved of keeping my secret since Finn is there unburdening himself already."

A footman entered the room with a tea tray and set it up on the bedside table.

"Will you pour?" Claire asked Sophia.

"Of course," she said as she picked up the teapot.

Claire reached for a biscuit.

"What went wrong last night?" Sophia asked, looking up from beneath lowered lashes as she poured tea. Their mother sat quietly at the bedside.

"Bleeding," was all Claire said.

"Is everything all right?" Sophia put down the teapot to glare at her.

"Fine, according to the physician." She placed a hand over her mouth to stifle a laugh. "You should have seen Finn's face. He tried to convince me it was my menses. He was so *sensible* about the whole thing."

"How long did that last?"

Claire's mother interjected. "Until she confessed. Then he looked like he'd been knocked over the head with an anvil."

"He was rather surprised." Claire heaved a sigh. "I just hope he doesn't hate me."

"I don't think that's possible," her mother said. "I went to talk to him about it last night. I wasn't leaving until I knew he was calm and reasonable." She ate the edge off a biscuit. "And he was already calm and reasonable. And giddy."

Sophia looked at her again, a sly grin crossing her lips. "So, what were you doing when the bleeding started?"

Heat crept up Claire's cheeks again. "What do you think we were doing?"

"I take it Lord Phineas knows his way around the bedchamber," Sophia asked.

"Lord Phineas knows his way around everything," Claire confessed.

Their mother wiped a tear from her cheek again.

"Are you all right?" Claire and Sophia both asked at the same time.

"Ignore me. I'm just happy to get to be here at this point in your lives." She waved a dismissive hand in the air. "That's all."

"So, what scares Lord Phineas the most? He honestly sounded like he feared for your safety. Something about Mayden?"

"The earl?" their mother asked.

"The murderer. He killed Ashley's first wife." Sophia shook her head sadly. "She wasn't a very good person, but Mayden had convinced her that she loved him. And then Mayden threw her from the turret of the castle when things didn't go his way. Ashley has always felt responsible for it."

"And last week he killed the modiste, who he just happened to believe was me. So Finn is worried for my safety." She told them that story, and they listened intently. The three of them lived for these kinds of things. At least they had that in common. Once a mission faerie, always a mission faerie.

Twenty-Nine

FINN ARRIVED HOME SO LATE THAT CLAIRE WAS dozing in the bed. He walked quietly over to the bed and looked down at her. Her strawberry blond hair was plaited over her shoulder, and her nightrail was open at her throat. He had a sudden and nearly overwhelming desire to place his lips there.

Finn bent over to tug off his boots, and then divested himself of his coat and waistcoat, but she stirred when he put his watch down because it made a soft noise.

She stretched tall, her arms over her head. Then she smiled at him. "Did you just get home?"

"Sorry I woke you," he said softly. Damn, but she was beautiful. She was sleepy eyed and looked soft as cotton. He wanted to grab her and never let her go.

"I'm not," she said with a smile as she sat up. "Where have you been?"

He pointed to a trunk he'd placed on the floor by the bed. "Your father sent you a present."

"My father knows where I am?" She looked frantic. And scared.

"Your father thinks you are spending time with Sophia and Robin this week."

She relaxed perceptibly. "Thank goodness."

He sat down on the side of the bed and looked down at her as he pulled off his cravat. "Are you worried about what your father will think?"

She shrugged, but he could tell she was bothered by it. "A little," she finally admitted.

"It can't be changed now," he said drolly.

"I wouldn't change it if I could." She looked directly into his eyes as she said it.

"You wouldn't push it back a few months? To lend it some respectability?" He watched her closely. She didn't even flinch.

"No." Her eyes narrowed. "Would you?"

"If I had it to do over again, the only thing I would do differently is that I would have tied you to me that first night. So I could have enjoyed the last few months with you."

"Have you eaten?" she asked.

He shook his head. "Not yet."

"Neither have I," she said.

"What?" He jumped to his feet. "Why haven't you eaten yet? That's not good for the baby."

She laid a hand on her belly. "The baby is fine," she said softly. "You're happy with the idea of a child?" she asked.

He leaned forward and kissed her softly. She tasted like sunshine and sleep. Like she was his. Like she was perfect. He drew back with a groan. "I couldn't be happier."

"Where have you been?" she asked again. "Why so late?"

"I was with Robin, trying to figure out what we're going to do about Mayden." He pulled his shirt out of his waistband and picked up the small trunk her father had sent. He sat it on the edge of the bed. "That's from your father."

Then he walked away to call for some food.

When he came back, Claire was poking at the box. "I feel certain there's no snake in it," he said with a laugh.

"Our kind uses boxes to hold memories." She took a deep breath, as though weighing her words. "I hate to say it, but I don't want to know what the memories felt like for them. I like the way things are right now. I want to get to know them from now forward. I don't want the past, except to say that it made me who I am."

He leaned forward and kissed her forehead. He lingered there, his lips pressed against her skin. She raised her hand to brush the stubble on his cheek, so he dipped his head quickly and scrubbed his chin in the sensitive skin of her neck. She squealed and shoved at him, laughing.

He pushed the box farther toward her. "Open it," he said.

Tentatively, she flipped the latch that held the box closed and lifted the lid. Then she smiled, and it was a smile so beautiful and so perfect that he smiled with her.

"He thought you might need something to do while you're under the weather."

"He thinks I'm sick?"

"He thinks you have a stomach ailment or something."

"I wonder if he'll be angry at Mother when he finds out the truth."

"I think he'll probably be angry at all of us." Finn chuckled. He wanted to chuckle about it now while he could. Because when Ramsdale found out Finn had impregnated his daughter, there would be hell to pay. "What did he send for you?"

"Paint. Brushes. Parchment." She reached in and retrieved jars of paint. "I helped him make some of these." She grinned.

"There are canvases too. I'll have someone bring them inside."

"He thought of everything."

"I'd say that he knows you very well for a man who just met you."

She nodded, a ridiculously charming smile on her face.

"What are you going to paint?"

He narrowed her eyes and looked at him, her eyes running up and down his body.

"Don't even think about it," he said, biting back a laugh.

"I can't paint you?"

"After the doctor says you're well, you can paint any part of me that you want." He leaned forward and kissed her quickly. To do more would be akin to suicide. Unjust and painful.

"Would you let me paint you?" She touched his throat just below the open vee of his shirt with the soft tip of a paintbrush. "I could write my name on your chest."

❧

His voice was raspy when he replied. "You already wrote your name on my heart, darling."

His words hit her like a team of runaway horses. "I told you not to fall in love with me."

His eyes narrowed. "I never did listen to instructions very well."

Her heart leaped. Finn pulled the counterpane from where she had it tucked beneath her armpits. "Finn!" she protested, laughing.

"How's my son or daughter?" He laughed as she scurried to cover herself back up. "Have you forgotten that I have seen all of you? I have no idea what you think you're hiding from me. When you're better, I plan to kiss every part of you." He began to ruck her nightrail up her thighs. "Every single bit."

Heat struck directly between her thighs. "Finn," she complained, warmth creeping up her cheeks. "You shouldn't say such things. It's not proper."

He chuckled. "Since when did you care about proper?"

"Never," she admitted. "But it sounded like the right thing to say at the time."

He tossed his head back and laughed. He threaded his hand into the hair at the back of her head and pulled her toward him. He kissed her softly, so softly it was almost painful. "God, I love you," he whispered.

"I warned you not to do that," she teased.

He sobered at her words. "I can't help it. Don't expect me to."

He needed for her to say it back. But she'd rather wait for the right time. She didn't want to say it just because he did. She loved him to distraction, but she wanted her confession about it to be spontaneous. And real.

"What did you and Robinsworth decide to do about Mayden?"

Finn sat back, his eyes suddenly mirroring how serious he was. "We're going to beat him out of the bushes, I think."

"What do you mean?"

"Between Robin and myself, we have bought up almost all of Mayden's outstanding debt. It's time to call in his markers."

"Won't that make him a little desperate?" It's what she would have done, but she still worried about what Mayden's reaction would be.

"We hope so." He looked down at her nightrail and started to push it up over her knees again. "Where were we?" he said with a laugh.

"You weren't there. You were professing your undying love for me."

"No, that distracted me for a moment. Now I want to say good night to my daughter." He pushed her nightrail up over her thighs. She pushed his hands back down as he got to the top of her thighs.

"Finn! That's indecent."

"Lady," he warned playfully, tugging against her grip. "I have seen you naked. I have seen you beneath me. I have seen you on top of me. I have seen you come at my fingertips."

Her sheath clenched.

His voice dropped down to a whisper. "And as soon as you're better, I'm going to make you come with nothing but my mouth."

"Your mouth?" she croaked.

"My mouth," he whispered back playfully.

She was so distracted that he pushed her nightrail up over her thighs, exposing her curly hairs to his gaze. He licked his lips and threw the fabric up over her belly.

She closed her eyes and refused to look at him. She was completely mortified.

"I'll come up there if it'll make you feel better," he said, coming to lie with his head next to her belly. It was better than having him *right there*. "Better?" he asked.

"Better," she said with a sigh. "There's no deterring you, is there?"

He grinned. "No."

Her stomach was slightly rounded, and he ran his fingertips over her skin softly. "My daughter is in there," he said quietly.

"Or son."

"I want a daughter first. So, I can kill any bastard who tries to sleep with her before he marries her."

"I don't think you get a choice," she reminded him. His hand was flat on her stomach, and he just let it lie there as he looked up at her.

"I'll make you happy, you know?" Finn said.

He covered his hand with hers. "You already do."

Suddenly, he shoved her nightrail up even higher, exposing her breasts. He cupped them in his hands, looking down at them reverently as he licked his lips. "Good God, they're perfect." He plumped them with his hands and suddenly said, "The first time I touched them, I don't think they fit my hands this well." He shifted, his fingers spreading to cup her more closely.

"Look, I can barely fit them in my palms." He

wasn't being silly. He was completely serious. And he was enjoying exploring her body. All of it. He leaned down and kissed her nipple. Then did the same with the other. "Call the coach bound for Bedlam. Because I might go mad waiting for you to get well."

He dropped down beside her and lay on his back, his arms thrown over his head. She rolled to face him. "You don't mind if I sleep in here with you tonight, do you?"

She laughed. "I would be offended if you didn't."

"I just want to hold you. All through the night."

"That can be arranged." She tugged her nightrail back down to her knees.

"How do you feel? All right?"

"I feel fine," she said. And she did. She felt like she could leap mountains. Like she could scale tall walls. Like she could fall in love.

Thirty

FINN WOKE TO THE GENTLE HUM OF A SONG ACROSS THE room and rolled over, shading his eyes from the sun that shot through the open curtains on the window.

The bed was empty, and Finn quickly sat up and called, "Claire?"

"I'm here," she said, smiling over her shoulder. She sat across the room, her paint jars spread over the small tea table in the corner of the room. She had a canvas leaned against the wall where she painted, and three more completed paintings were spread around the floor surrounding her. "Good morning," she said quietly.

He could wake up to this every day, he couldn't help thinking. She was wearing her nightrail, and her hair was unbound, hanging down her back. Her hands were spattered with paint, and a smear of orange marred the left side of her nose. "You're supposed to be in bed."

He rolled onto his side and laid his head in his hand, his elbow pointed toward the head of the bed.

"I'm in a chair." She grinned unrepentantly. Then she shrugged. "I wanted to paint."

"With the magic paintbrush?"

She held up the one she was using. "Just an average one," she said.

Finn wanted to get out of bed to go and look at her work, but he needed a moment to compose himself. It was morning, and she looked damned fine sitting there across from him. He was hard as a rock, and it wasn't getting any smaller. "What are you painting?"

She pointed to each one in turn. "That's the house I grew up in."

It was a manor house, much like the ones in his world. "That's in the land of the fae?"

"That world looks a lot like this one," she said. "Except we have fantastically odd things happen in my land that seem completely normal."

"Will you take me there one day?" He wanted to see where she came from more than anything.

She shook her head, a sadness overcoming her features. "I don't think so. It's forbidden. Or at least it was for a long time."

"Your father and Robin got to go." He was hurt by her refusal. And hated that he was, but so be it.

"Special circumstances, I think. I doubt they'll admit humans on a regular basis."

Finn sat up. "What if our child is fae? Wouldn't they make an exception?"

"They never have before." She went back to painting.

Finn was disturbed. Very disturbed. "But you plan to visit the land of the fae with our child, should that child happen to be fae."

She looked back over her shoulder again. "How else will he or she learn about my life and my beliefs? And magic, for that matter."

Finn tossed the counterpane to the side and got out of bed. He no longer had to worry about surprising her with his raging manhood. That had been sufficiently doused, as though with a cup of freezing cold water.

"What's wrong?" she asked.

"Nothing," he bit out.

"It's not nothing," she said, rising to her feet. "Talk to me."

"Why should I? You have the fae to talk to. And my child, for that matter, if he or she happens to have pointy ears and wings." He knew he sounded like a petulant two-year-old, but he didn't like the idea of her taking his child to the land of the fae. Or to any place where he couldn't accompany them. Not one bit. He jerked on his trousers and pulled a shirt over his head. Then he quit the room. It was either quit the room or let her see how hurt his feelings were. And that just would not do.

"Wait," Claire called to his retreating back. He didn't stop, so she jumped to her feet and followed him down the corridor. "Wait!" she called again.

Finn heard her call to him. He just didn't want to hear her. He didn't want her to try to explain away all the differences between her world and his. He didn't want her to try to justify it. It was what it was. And what it was was damn hard.

Her bare feet pounded down the corridor behind him. It was then that it sank into his brain that she wasn't even supposed to be out of bed, much less upset with him. He turned around and pointed his finger at her. "Go back to bed."

She tilted her head to look at him. "You go back to bed."

"I am not the one who has been confined to bed rest."

"I am not the one who has his short pants in a twist."

Good God, she was maddening.

"Don't walk away, Finn," she said softly. "Come and talk to me."

"I don't want to talk. It's not going to change anything."

He stalked toward her and she stood her ground, just lifting her nose higher in the air and squaring her shoulders. She did squeal, however, when he scooped her up in his arms and started for the bedchamber. "Put me down," she cried.

He lowered her gently to the bed, but she wrapped her arms around his neck and held him down there with her, until he gave up and sat on the bed beside her. "Claire," he warned, as he scrubbed a hand down his face.

"Talk to me," she said, rubbing a hand down the side of his face. She scuffed her hand against his beard stubble.

"I don't like the idea of you taking our child to the land of the fae, where I can't go."

❧

Claire could understand that. But didn't he see that she was giving up time with their child too? If the child wasn't fae, she wouldn't be able to take him or her back and forth with her to the fae.

"What if our child isn't fae?" she asked him.

"I don't care if she's fae or human, Claire."

"You're thinking about yourself," she said softly. "This affects me too."

"I don't see how. You'll be going back and forth to the fae with our child, to a place I can't go. I don't like it. I don't like it a bit. And there's nothing you can say that will change my mind."

"I have to give things up too," she reminded him.

"Like what?" he snorted.

"I can only take our child to the land of the fae if he or she is fae. Don't you see that? So, when I travel to and from there, I won't get to take any child who doesn't have pointy ears and wings, as you say. I'll have to leave that child in your care while I travel."

"How often do you plan to travel?"

She hadn't given that any thought at all. None. "I have no idea. Whenever there's a mission for me or I'm needed in the land of the fae."

"Do you still want to go on missions after the baby?" His brow furrowed.

"Did you think I would stop?"

His eyes opened wide. "I'd assumed you would."

He assumed wrong. "It's what I am."

"No, it's what you were. Now you'll be a wife and mother."

"What does that change?" She knew her voice was rising to a dangerous pitch. But it was impossible to ignore his implications. "I'm still fae."

"So, where's the compromise?"

"I don't see a compromise."

He gave her a blank look.

"Do you intend to stop with your special investigative work?"

"Why should I?" Now he looked offended.

"Because now you'll be a father and a husband, and if I can't put myself in danger, neither can you."

"That's ridiculous."

"Almost as ridiculous as you asking me to stop taking missions. Goodness, you might as well clip my wings and take my memories if you're going to do that. You'll be taking part of me. Don't you see that?"

"And I'm giving you part of me." He pounded a fist over his heart.

"It's not the same."

"Apparently, I'm not as important to you as that part of your life." He looked at her, and she could feel his pain. Was he as important to her as that part of her life? It really couldn't be compared.

"That's not the case."

He got up and stalked toward his dressing room.

"Where are you going?" Certainly, he wouldn't leave in the middle of their argument. He wouldn't do that. He couldn't do that.

"Out," he said curtly.

"Where?" She wouldn't let him shut her out. She just couldn't. Not even if he wanted to.

He sighed heavily from the other room. "I need to go and talk with Robin about Mayden. To see what the next step is."

"We haven't settled anything, though."

"Is that possible?" He looked around the corner of the door. "You're not going to pick me over magic. Ever. I should have known that." He stalked by her and out the door.

"Finn!" she called to his retreating back. Tears

pricked at her lashes. The front door slammed hard behind him, and she jumped with the force of it. He was gone. He'd left and they hadn't resolved a single thing.

⤴

Finn made his way across town to meet Robin and some of his men so they could make plans for Mayden's upheaval from society. They might not be able to prove that Mayden had killed Robin's wife, or Colette for that matter, but when they called in all of his debts, they hoped he would get scared and leave England.

Typically, Finn had all of his men over to his house for meetings like this, but he couldn't do so with Claire there. See? He was already making concessions for her in his life. Didn't she see that?

He was changing the way he lived. For her. And she didn't plan to change her life at all? Impossible.

His heart twisted in his chest at the thought of her leaving him to travel back and forth to the land of the fae. Much less taking their child or children to a land he couldn't visit. But she'd obviously picked that life over him.

He supposed he'd have to accept the cards he'd been dealt and play them as he was able. He had a woman he loved, a child on the way, would marry her in a matter of days, and he'd get to hold her in his arms every night as she fell asleep. And wake with her every morning. It wasn't such a bad life, was it?

Robin walked into the room, and his men filed in behind him. "Let's get Mayden on the run, shall we?" Robin said, smiling at him.

Finn nodded and they set about putting the wheels of justice in motion.

Thirty-One

CLAIRE SANK DOWN INTO HER BATH, THE GLOW OF candlelight the only light in the room. Finn wasn't home yet, and she refused to give up waiting for him. He'd been scarce all week, coming in after she was in bed at night and getting up before she rose in the morning. The only time he touched her was when he thought she was sleeping. He'd pull her into his arms and inhale her scent.

The first time it had happened, Claire had rolled into him, but then she'd remembered the way he'd walked out angry, and she'd pretended to be asleep. His hands had roamed over her body, teasing her to delicious wakefulness, but she'd still pretended to sleep. He'd finally given up, drawing her into the crook of his arm as he fell asleep, his breath deep and even.

The next night, he'd come home and done the same thing, but Claire had feigned sleep again. He'd finally grunted and rolled away from her, and she'd lain there crying silently into her pillow.

Tonight, she refused to pretend. She had waited all

day for him to come home. She wouldn't give up now. When she felt like she'd need toothpicks to hold her eyelids open, she'd called for a bath to keep her awake.

Claire hung her hair over the lip of the tub, determined to keep it as dry as possible, particularly since it was difficult to wash it by herself. She settled back against the tub and tried to make a plan. Finn would come in tired. He'd been gone all day, doing whatever it was he did. And she would be waiting for him.

The door to their bedchamber closed with a soft click. Then she heard his voice. "Claire?" he called out.

She didn't answer. She was feeling more than a little dejected, unwanted, and unloved. And now that he was home, she still didn't know what to say to him. *Come help me with my bath, darling?* No, that would be ridiculous.

The dressing-room door, where the big tub was kept, flew open quickly. "Claire?" Finn called.

"I'm here," Claire said quietly. She didn't make a move to cover herself.

Finn stumbled to a halt just inside the room. "Are you all right?" he asked.

"Fine," she murmured.

"Why are you up so late?" He stood there in the doorway, not bothering to move away as her fingers made patterns in the top of the bathwater.

"I was waiting for you."

He froze. "Why?"

"The doctor came today."

He was across the room in a thrice, and he settled down next to her. "What did he say?"

"He said everything is fine with the baby, Finn. Nothing to worry about anymore."

Finn softened almost perceptibly, and then he lowered himself to sit beside her on the floor by the tub.

"Where have you been?"

"Putting out fires," he said with a sigh.

"Fires?" She made a move to get out of the bath.

"Not real ones. The kind that Mayden likes to create. He's not happy about his debts being called in. And he's making a bit of noise in town."

"Is it bad?"

"I wouldn't call it bad. I'd call it a nuisance."

His finger trailed up her naked arm as he leaned toward her and placed his forehead against her nose. "I'm sorry I haven't been here for you this week."

"You were angry at me. I understand."

"Do you?" He tilted his head at her, his blue eyes dark in stillness of the room.

"Yes," she replied. "I believe I do."

"I tried to make it up to you when I came home, but you were asleep."

She hadn't been asleep. She'd been angry. "Yes." A grin tugged at her lips, even though she really wanted to pout. "What were you going to do to make it up to me?"

He kissed her lips gently, and his hand slid into the water to skim across her breast. Heat pooled at the apex of her thighs. "So beautiful," he breathed. "Are you almost finished with that bath?" he asked.

"I just got in, actually." She stretched luxuriously, enjoying the way his eyes stayed focused on her breasts as they rose and fell in the water.

"How long will you be?" he asked, his voice raspy all of a sudden.

"All night," she said quietly.

"Do you need some help?"

"With my bath? No, thank you."

"Are you certain? I could wash your back." He picked up a sponge and some soap, and dipped them in the water. "Sit forward. I'll wash your back." He picked up her hair, gathered it and rolled it, and secured it haphazardly with a pin at the top of her head. "Very pretty," he said with a laugh.

"I probably look like a deranged pixie," she said, crossing her eyes in an attempt to make him laugh.

"You look like a debauched pixie right now."

"Debauched? Me? I think not."

"If you're not already, you're about to be," he murmured as he began to soap her back. His hand was unhurried, and his face was right beside hers as his hands dipped and retreated. He soaped slowly across her shoulders and down the middle of her back, feeling each lump of her spine and swirling around the dip just above her bottom.

Finn raised one of her arms above her head and soaped down the length of it, sliding across her armpit and down into the water to rinse the sponge. He did the same with her other arm.

Claire's breasts were aching, begging to be touched. She hitched herself higher up in the tub and arched her back. But he ignored her, and soaped down her breastbone and to her stomach, where he replaced the sponge with his soapy fingers, stroking lightly where their child rested.

"I'll never get used to the feeling of having you so close to me, growing heavy with our child. It's like magic."

He lifted her leg to rest on the edge of the tub, and proceeded to wash her knee and down to her toes, slipping between each one with his fingertips, tugging lightly as he moved from one to the next. Claire giggled when he brushed across the bottom of her foot. He bent his head and took her big toe in his mouth, nibbling the sensitive tip of it lightly. "Finn!" she cried.

"Oh, that is only the first thing I plan to taste, my lady," he said with a chuckle.

His manhood pressed hard against the front of his trousers. Claire reached one hand out to touch him, but he took her hand and placed it back on the edge of the tub with a soft, "No."

"Why not?"

"It has been a week, Claire. I can't last if you start touching me now."

She lay back in the tub, making sure her breasts were out of the water. The water brushed the hard peaks of her nipples, and she squirmed her bottom against the bottom of the tub.

"Something wrong?" he asked. But his tone was teasing and light and as hot as a summer fire at the same time.

"Not a thing," she said as she reached into the tub and touched the aching peak of her left breast, just to see what he would do.

"Oh my God," Finn breathed. But his hands didn't stop his slow sensual assault. He walked around the tub and lifted her other leg to the edge, and soaped it, cleaning from her knee to her toes and back. Then he rinsed both legs, but he didn't lower them. She lay there with her legs spread indecently, and she'd never felt more beautiful.

∽

She'd never looked more beautiful. Finn was about to spend his seed inside his trousers, he wanted to come that bad. He leaned forward and ran the tip of the sponge over her nipple, and she responded by arching her back and pushing her breast harder against the sponge. He forced himself not to linger, however, and soaped around the curve of her breast and beneath it, careful not to touch her nipple again. He did the other the same way, and Claire was fidgeting with her hands by the time he was done.

She laid her head back against the tub and regarded him from beneath heavy-lidded blond lashes. His debauched pixie. God, he loved her.

Finn threw the sponge into the water and soaped his hands, then he cupped her breasts in his palms, testing the weight of them, testing their buoyancy... testing her. Claire drew her lower lip between her teeth to nibble it. Finn lingered about her breasts until her cheeks were rosy and damp.

"Finn," she warned playfully. "We should probably get out of the tub before I turn into a prune."

"We're not done yet," he whispered. He soaped his hands again and slid one down her breastbone, across her belly, and down into her curls, where he sifted lightly and tugged gently. She squirmed her bottom, pushing her mound against his hand.

"Is that where you want me?" he asked.

She nodded, still worrying that lower lip.

"Did the doctor say I could put my fingers inside you?" he asked, leaning close to her ear, and then he leaned in to kiss her as he parted her hot folds, sliding through the warmth that was her desire, rather than the warmth of the water.

"He said we could have intercourse," she said. Her cheeks pinkened even more. "I didn't ask him about fingers."

"But you did ask him about intercourse?"

"Of course, I did. I miss you."

"I'm right here," he said.

"But you haven't been here all week."

"Sorry," he breathed as he slid one finger across the pulse of her, finding it swollen and throbbing for his touch. Claire nearly left the tub, she jumped so high. But she didn't pull her legs down from where they were draped over the edges of the tub. And he could clearly see her curls and her most private places through the sudsy water in the tub. He stroked across her pulse again and then dipped a finger quickly inside of her to bring her own slickness forward, to mix it with the slide of the soap.

Claire arched her hips to meet him as he dragged a finger back and forth across her pleasure center, alternating between that place that he knew ached for him and her channel, which quivered every time he slid inside it. She grabbed on to his free hand with hers and squeezed it tightly, mimicking the motion of his fingertips and their speed.

He leaned his forehead against her temple and felt her wicked little breaths as they left her mouth, battering his evening stubble. She could unman him with a well-placed breath. Or a poorly placed breath; it mattered not the kind of breath. Just that she was there and she was his. And she was going to come on his fingers.

Finn slid two fingers inside her and rocked his thumb against the center of her as she arched to meet him. She was tight inside and gripped his fingers so well that he wanted to grab her from the tub and bend her over it, just so he could feel her quiver around him. But this moment was hard won. He had her at his mercy, and she had him at hers. With one breath, he could shatter along with her.

Her little pants were wicked markers of her pleasure, and they grew faster and faster. He sped his thumb, hooking his fingertips inside her so he could rub that squishy place inside her that might make her squirm.

"Finn," she whispered, her voice too broken to respond. "Finn," she chanted. "Finn, Finn, Finn," and then she broke. He leaned close to her face, taking in her breaths as though they were his own. Her inhale was his exhale, and her exhale was his inhale. They shared the same air, the same space, the same body. She squeezed his fingers in a viselike grip as she broke around him. Her breasts bounced in the water as she slowed, and her head came back to rest against the lip of the tub once more. Her body was lax and sated, and she was more relaxed than he'd ever seen her.

"Goodness," she breathed.

Then she curled into herself, and he wanted to wrap around her. "I missed you," he said softly. He had. He'd missed her like crazy. Holding her at night was nice, but it wasn't the same as talking to her. Not the same as sharing his life with her.

※

Claire looked up at him from the bath, not sure what to say to him. "Thank you" seemed inadequate. "I missed you too," she finally said.

"When you have the wherewithal to stand up, I want to wash up really quickly." He patted her knee and started to take his clothes off.

He pulled his shirt over his head and tossed it to the floor. Then he tugged his boots off and shucked his trousers, letting them fall to the floor as he stepped out of them.

His manhood was rigid and arched up toward his belly, purple at the tip. She reached out a hand to touch him. But he dodged her. "Do you need some help getting out?" he asked as he offered her a hand. She took it, supported fully by his firm grip and bolstered by the challenge in his eyes. She was naked. And he liked the way she looked naked, if his staff was any indication. She stepped out of the tub and let him wrap her in a towel. He stepped into the tub and took up the sponge. He arched a brow at her when she looked at his manhood. "Something wrong?"

Claire stepped toward him and sat down on the ridge of the tub. She took the sponge from him, and took up where he'd already moved it across his shoulders. She moved across his flat stomach, and he flinched as she dragged a fingernail across the ridges of his abdomen. "Careful there," he warned. Claire stood up and went around behind him, soaping the sponge as she went. She washed slowly across his back and shoulders, inspecting his shoulders the way he'd inspected the ridges of her spine.

Her hand slipped down his belly, and she dipped into the springy curls that made a path from his navel to his manhood. He groaned aloud when she brushed the sponge across the head of his staff. "Comeuppance is painful," she whispered, biting back a laugh at the look on his face.

"Don't play with me, Claire," he warned.

"Don't play with me, Claire," she mocked.

Claire dropped the sponge into the water and soaped her hand, then grabbed his manhood in a fist.

"I promise I won't just play with it," she whispered dramatically. He chuckled as he rocked forward on his heels, arching into her hands.

"I can't take much of that," he warned.

"Yes, you told me," she said with a laugh. "I just want to get you as clean as you got me."

Claire sat on the edge of the tub and looked up at him as she stroked up and down his length. His face was harsh, his teeth pulled back from his lips.

"Claire," he warned.

"You mentioned the other day that you were going to make me come with nothing but your mouth," Claire reminded him.

He groaned low in his throat. She dipped her hand in the water and washed off the soap, and then slicked all the soap off him with the sponge. He was gritting his teeth by the time she was done. And she was nearly giddy inside at the way she could make him feel.

"Are these sensitive?" she asked as she hefted the

weight of his balls in the palm of her hand. He hissed and jumped back, but she held tight to his manhood and wouldn't let him move back too far. "Are they?" she asked as she rolled them in her fingertips.

"Just a little," he breathed.

～

Claire wet her lips and blew gently on the tip of his manhood, and the slit wept with want for her. He forced himself to hold in a groan as she stuck out her pert little tongue and licked across the tip of him, tasting the seed that he'd spilled. She sat back and licked her lips. "Salty," she said with a smile.

"Aah," he groaned. Would she do it? Would she take him inside her mouth? He lifted his bent knuckle to his mouth and bit it hard. If he didn't, he'd spill down the front of her. But then she opened her mouth wide and took the tip of him inside the hot cavern of her mouth and closed her lips around him, sucking gently, testing his flesh with her teeth and tongue.

"Damn, that's lovely," he whispered. He threaded his hands through her hair and tugged her lips back a little. She looked up at him questioningly, and he motioned her back forward with a tug of her hair.

"Like this?" she asked, talking around the tip of him before she closed her mouth and began to suckle, her head bobbing up and down as she worked him.

"Stop, Claire," he warned. "If you don't stop, I'm going to come in your mouth." She hitched herself higher on the edge of the tub and took him even farther, until he could feel the back of her throat. And then he fell over the edge. He tugged at her hair to pull her back, but she held tightly, refusing to pop free. He had no choice, so with a grunt, he raised up onto his tiptoes and spilled his seed within her mouth. She swallowed, surprised, and looked up at him. "Let go if you don't want it." But her throat just worked as she took all of him.

When he was spent, he forced her mouth from around him with a gentle tug, and he reached down to wipe the corner of her mouth.

"Goodness, Claire," he said, his voice broken. "You didn't have to do that."

"I know," she chirped. Then she tossed off the towel she wore and sauntered naked into the bedchamber, and he followed her home like a little lost puppy.

Thirty-Two

THE WEDDING WAS AN INFORMAL AFFAIR. THEY'D opted to have only family at the event, which was held at Robin and Sophia's house, since theirs was the place where Claire had supposedly been staying during her recovery.

She'd actually been staying in Finn's bed, and they had barely gotten out of it since the night they'd bathed together. He'd kept her busy, and she'd returned the favor. He'd taken her fast. He'd taken her slow. He'd taken her mouth. He'd flipped her upside down on her knees, and he'd lifted her knee so far by her head that she would have sworn she could kiss her calf.

But through it all, he'd been so very conscious of her, of her needs, of the life that grew within her. He'd fed her and bathed her and let her sleep on top of him. He'd brushed her hair and rubbed her feet, and he'd said so many dirty things to her in the throes of passion that she no longer cared what he said. She had even repeated many of those words when it was her turn to take charge.

Finn hadn't seen Claire since last night, when he'd

come to the hall to drop her off. They'd made love in the carriage on the way over, and she was slightly mussed when she entered Robin and Sophia's home. Sophia had dragged her away to help her clean up, and Robin had taken Finn into the study for a drink and a stern lecture, Finn had later confessed. "You should have seen his face. He was stuck somewhere between really happy for me as a man and really irritated about his brother having relations with his sister-in-law." He'd laughed. And there was no sound sweeter to her ears than that of his laughter.

Claire let her mother and Sophia help her dress, and she turned back to look into the looking glass. "I wish Grandmother and Grandfather were here," she said. Her grandmother had opted to stay in the land of the fae for a bit as she was still grieving for her husband.

"I'm sure she'll be ready to pay you a visit before too long," Sophia said. "She just needed some time to get used to being alone, I think."

"Do you think that Finn will ever be able to go there with me, to see the land where I came from?" Claire asked wistfully.

Her mother and Sophia shot a glance at one another.

"What is it?" Claire asked.

"We have been warned that to bring a human into the land of the fae without prior approval will be grounds for the clipping of our wings." Her mother said it in one great, big breath. And then she froze, as though she was afraid of Claire's reaction.

She should be afraid. "But you were just there! Both of you, with your human husbands." She pointed a finger at Sophia, who automatically recoiled.

"And you even took your human stepdaughter for a visit! But I can't take my husband to my homeland?"

A knock sounded on the door. Finn stood there, and he looked a bit worried with his eyebrows drawn together so severely. "What's wrong?"

"Nothing," Claire snapped. "Nothing at all." She swiped a hand beneath her nose and blinked back a tear. This was supposed to be a happy day. And here she was growing angry at her family for something that was well beyond their control.

"Can I have a moment with Claire?" Finn asked. Sophia and her mother scuttled out of the room.

He closed the door behind them and leaned against it, crossing his arms over his chest. "What's wrong?" he asked.

"Nothing," she barked, as she sat down on the edge of the bed.

"Something is wrong," he said as he came to sit beside her. "Come on. Tell me. You'll feel better if you do." She leaned her head on his shoulder. How much she'd come to rely on him in such a short time!

"There's a prohibition against humans in the land of the fae. I have to have prior permission to take you there."

He shrugged. "So, ask for permission. Problem solved." He tweaked her nose playfully. "You want to go marry me now?"

"I want to marry you no matter what," she admitted. He beamed down at her.

The door opened with a soft click and her father stuck his head in the room. He eyed Finn warily. "Hello," he said.

"Hello," Claire said with a tiny wave.

"I heard there's a bride who needs to be delivered to the vicar for marriage," her father said lightly, but he narrowed his eyes at Finn. "Why are you in here?"

"I needed him," Claire said. Her heart clenched with love for Finn. "I'll always need him."

Her voice cracked on the last words and she hated it, but Finn tipped her chin up, kissed her softly, and said, "Let's go get married."

"Can I have a minute with my daughter?" her father asked suddenly.

Finn looked at her and arched his brows. She nodded at him, and he bent to kiss her forehead softly. "I'll see you at the wedding."

When the door shut behind Finn, her father came to sit down beside her on the bed. "It's not too late to back out," he said, looking at her thoughtfully.

"And let someone else end up with that wonderful man?" She snorted. "You have to be mad."

"He loves you," her father said, as he pushed a lock of hair behind her pointy ear.

"I love him too," she admitted. She nudged her father's shoulder. "Don't tell him that, or he'll think much too highly of himself."

"You'll make a great mother," he said, looking deeply into her eyes. Did he know?

"Umm," she said.

"Things happen in their own time, Claire," he said. "As they are meant to be."

Claire exhaled long and loud. "I'm so glad you already know."

He nodded thoughtfully. "So am I."

"We were going to tell you after the wedding."

"Why were you going to wait?"

She snickered. "I wanted him to look handsome for the wedding. And if you'd known about the baby, you'd have given him a black eye. Or worse."

Her father's expression clouded. "Baby?" he asked.

Claire sucked in a breath. "You didn't know?"

"Baby?" he asked again, his mouth twisting. "I'll kill him." He thrust open the door and charged from the room, pushing past the startled guests as Claire clung to the back of his coattails.

"Don't!" she cried. But her father already had Finn's shirt front in his grip.

"What did you do?" he snarled.

Finn looked over her father's shoulder and glared at Claire.

"Sorry," she murmured to him as she continued to pull at her father's coat. Truth be told, his allegiance was touching, and he felt more like a father to her than he ever had before.

Finn tried to duck when her father swung the first fist. But with the way her father had him in his grasp, it was difficult. Finn took one punch directly across the cheek before the duke grabbed her father and pulled him back.

Finn wiped his hand across his cheek, pressing at his cheekbone, as he said, "I take it she told you."

"I didn't mean to! He made it seem like he knew!" She still held on to her father's coat.

Her father raised his fist and charged toward Finn again, but this time, her mother stepped between them.

Finn said, "The first one is free. The next one might cost you."

"Not more than it already has. She's my little girl," Ramsdale bellowed.

Claire's mother patted his chest and said, "Come with me."

❦

Lady Ramsdale led her husband from the room by the tips of his fingers. It was like trying to drag a tiger by his eyeteeth, but she held fast and didn't let him jump back into the fray with Lord Phineas, though he obviously wanted to. She took him into the drawing room and closed the door behind them.

"Did you know about this?" he bellowed.

She arched a pretty auburn brow at him. "Are you yelling at me?"

He ran a hand through his hair and spun in a circle, alternately stopping to swipe at his mouth and spin again. "Sorry," he finally murmured. Then he asked much more calmly. "You knew?"

She nodded.

"How could you keep this from me?" he asked.

"She needed to tell you in her own time. I just don't think this is what she intended."

There was no use avoiding the obvious. Their little girl wasn't an innocent. But she wasn't their little girl, either. She'd grown up without them and was woman enough to fall in love, marry, and raise a family. And she would do a damn fine job with it. "She's about four months into the pregnancy."

"Four months?"

"Do you remember when we went to the land of the fae and left her in his care?"

He ran a frustrated hand through his hair. "We picked the wrong person, didn't we?"

"Everything happens for a reason, darling," she reminded him. She crossed the room to lay her hand on his chest and look up at him. "Do you remember when we fell in love?"

He covered her hand with his. "Of course, I remember."

"They fell in love too."

"But he wasn't very honorable," he murmured, finally settling down.

"I hope our children never do the math and figure out Marcus was born a mere seven months after we married."

His face colored. "That was different."

"How so?"

One of the many reasons she loved him so much was because he was like this. He loved fiercely and completely. He was protective and he could even be overbearing at times, but he had a good heart.

"Never mind," he murmured as he heaved a great sigh.

"Can we go back out without you trying to beat Lord Phineas to a bloody pulp?"

"Maybe," he said, begrudgingly.

"Stop pouting," she warned playfully. He jerked her against him and pressed his lips to hers.

"I can't believe you knew and didn't tell me."

"She called me for help. I didn't want to betray her trust and have her never call on me again." She searched his eyes. "She called for me, of all people, when she needed someone. I would have expected her to call on Sophia. But she didn't. She called on me." Tears pricked at the backs of her lashes, even though it had happened more than a sennight ago.

"Of course, she called you. You're her mother." He pressed his lips to her temple. "I imagine we should go back out there so that scoundrel can marry our daughter."

"It would be a good idea to do it before the baby is born." She bit back a laugh.

He chuckled and squeezed her hard in his arms.

Thirty-Three

CLAIRE HAD NEVER LOOKED MORE BEAUTIFUL THAN AS she stood there with her hand in his, staring up into his eyes. "Wilt thou have this Woman to thy wedded Wife, to live together after God's ordinance in the holy estate of Matrimony? Wilt thou love her, comfort her, honor and keep her in sickness and in health; and, forsaking all others, keep thee only unto her, so long as ye both shall live?"

"We had better live for a very long time," he murmured. She smiled softly and wiggled her brows to scold him. "I will," he affirmed.

She repeated similar words, her eyes filled with so much emotion that he wanted to crawl inside her and live there forever. Finn reached into his pocket and pulled out a ring. He slid it onto her fourth finger and said, "With this Ring I thee wed, with my Body I thee worship, and with all my worldly Goods I thee endow: In the Name of the Father, and of the Son, and of the Holy Ghost. Amen."

"I pronounce that they be Man and Wife together, In the Name of the Father, and of the Son, and of the Holy Ghost."

Finn bent and kissed her, although the vicar didn't seem too pleased by that.

Robin coughed into his closed fist in warning, just as Claire's father stepped toward them. Finn pulled her into his chest and hugged her hard. "She's mine now," he said playfully to her father.

"That won't keep me from kicking your—"

Claire rushed to cut him off. "Is there cake?"

"Of course, there's cake," her mother said, as the footmen brought in a cart full of tiny cake squares, little sandwiches, and tea. "Let's all take a seat, shall we?"

※

How had she gotten here? How had Claire gotten to this place where everything fit so right? She'd never even liked this world, much less the people in it. She'd believed in magic and only magic, and had eschewed anything that didn't have magical origins. Her life had been simple—she'd had her missions, her brother and sister, and her grandparents. She had her magical homeland, and it was her refuge.

All of her boxes had been neatly stacked where they belonged, until she came here and they were scattered and turned on their side. But now Finn was her refuge. He was her everything. Finn's cheek was splotchy where her father had hit him. He would certainly have a bruise there tomorrow. He touched his fingertips to it and winced, and then bent down so she could kiss it softly. Her lips lingered over his skin, warm and firm.

He'd put her boxes all back in order for her. They sat nicely upon the shelves, all stacked and tidy.

They were solid, firmly supported by her family, her friends, and her husband. Claire laid a hand on her belly and thought about how she'd felt a few short weeks ago.

She'd been desperate to escape her life, to run far, far away from everything she considered to be home. But now he was home. He winked at her. Heat crept up her cheeks.

She loved. She loved him the way she'd never loved anyone, and she couldn't wait to tell him. That night, she could just imagine climbing on top of him, fluffing her wings, and encouraging him to touch them. To learn them as he'd learned every other part of her body. She needed for him to embrace that part of her, just as she was willing to give it all up to be with him.

She would give him children and love him until the day she died. If someone told her today that she would have to give up her wings to be with him, she would do so. She couldn't wait to tell him all about it that night.

Wilkins, the butler, stepped into the room and crossed to speak to His Grace. He handed the duke a missive, sealed with a wax marker. Finn leaned over the duke's shoulder to read as he did. His face blanched.

"What's wrong?" Claire asked.

He took her hand and led her down the corridor to the duke's study. "I think we have a problem," he said as he closed the door.

"What is it?"

He held the missive out to her, and she took it with trembling fingers.

Dear Lord Phineas Trimble,
   Bedfordshire is lovely this time of year.

It wasn't signed, but it didn't need to be. Only one person could have sent it. Mayden. The Earl of Mayden had found out where Katherine was, and he'd gone there.

"Is your man still there?"

Finn nodded as he began to pace.

"Then Katherine will be fine, right?"

Finn didn't look certain, but he nodded. "Probably."

"What do you think we should do?"

"I can send more men." Finn continued to pace back and forth across the floor. "But I really wouldn't feel comfortable sending anyone else into the situation blind."

The door opened and Robin stepped into the room, followed by Sophia. "What do you want to do?"

"It's my wedding day. I want to take my wife home."

Robin just looked at him.

Claire knew that wouldn't be enough for Finn.

"I sent her there. And now he has found her."

Claire had visions in her head of Katherine being tortured. She laid a hand on her own belly. "You'll have to go to her."

Finn cupped her face in his hands and looked into her eyes. "I don't want to leave you."

"It's not as though you won't come back," she said, attempting a light laugh. He wouldn't get hurt, would he? "Maybe you should stay here," she said, instead, suddenly fearful for him. "Don't go."

"I'm afraid it can't be helped. She's under my

protection. And he's there with her. She could already be hurt."

"He wouldn't hurt his child, would he?"

"You saw her eye after the soiree. He knew full well she was increasing at that point."

"There's no end to what he will do to win," Robin said. "I'll have horses saddled and go with you."

"Must you?" Sophia asked, her voice high with worry.

"I'm afraid so. This is my battle as much as Finn's."

Finn looked at Robin. "We started this by calling in all his debts. He's probably rather desperate."

"There's no telling what he might do to her as retribution. She's innocent in all of this."

"No one has ever claimed Katherine Crawfield is innocent." Finn snorted.

Robin just rolled his eyes. "We'll have to go there. If we leave now, we can be there in a matter of hours." He tugged his watch fob from his pocket. "We can ride through the night."

Finn nodded and turned, drawing Claire into his arms. "I love you," he said. Claire opened her mouth to return the sentiment, but he laid his mouth on hers, his lips soft and coaxing, a promise of what would come when he returned home. He leaned his head close to her ear. "I will expect you to be naked and waiting in bed for me when I get back."

"I think I can do that," she murmured back.

Sophia and Robin stepped into the corner, where he kissed her quite soundly. She staggered when he let her go. "Do be careful, Ashley," she said, her voice quivering.

"I will," he said, pulling her to him once more.

Finn wrapped Claire in his arms and held her close, breathing deeply with his head buried in her hair. "I need to speak to your father," he said, and then he started in that direction. He pulled her fingertips, dragging Claire with him as he went back into the parlor. He placed Claire's hand in her father's and said, "Only until I return."

Her father nodded, pulling Claire to his side as he dropped an arm around her shoulders. "Only until you return." He pulled Sophia forward with the other arm and did the same with her. She looked up at him and smiled.

"I'll accompany you," Marcus said. Finn nodded and the three of them started for the door.

"Finn!" Claire called. He looked back at her with that smile she'd so come to love. She wanted to confess her love for him. But she really wanted to do it at a time when he wouldn't assume it was forced. "Be safe," she whispered, instead.

Then the three of them left, the door closing soundly behind them. Claire looked around the room at the remains of the wedding cake and sat down, popping a piece into her mouth. Someone had to eat it. It may as well be her. She shoved a piece at Sophia. "Eat," she said. Sophia joined her in her misery, the only one who could.

Thirty-Four

I<small>T WAS NEARLY MORNING WHEN</small> F<small>INN</small>, R<small>OBIN</small>, <small>AND</small> Marcus reached Bedfordshire. The day was still dark, but faint edges of light hovered on the horizon. Finn drew up his horse to the front of the house and stopped, tethering the horse as Robin and Marcus dismounted. He stretched and patted his horse on the side. He'd done a great job. Finn would bed him down with warm blankets and hay once he'd had a chance to find out what the devil was going on.

"Where's your man?" Robin asked.

"Probably sleeping," Finn said. He'd only sent one man, and it was impossible for him to be awake twenty-four hours a day.

"Shall we go see, gentlemen, what's going on?" Robin asked.

"We shall," Marcus breathed. He had a feral gleam in his eye that surprised Finn. He usually seemed like such a laid-back young man. So proper and responsible.

Finn and Robin entered through the front door, each of them moving off in different directions. Finn took the stairs, Robin went toward the kitchen, and

Marcus skirted around the back of the house from the outside.

Finn lit a taper on the table in the landing at the top of the stairs and lifted it high in the air. He slowly pushed open the master bedchamber door and stopped when he saw two lumps beneath the counterpane. "Please tell me Katherine didn't take him into her bed," he murmured to himself as he crossed the room.

With a jerk, he pulled the counter pane from the bed and tossed it to the floor. Katherine, with all her dark hair tumbling around her, jumped up and covered her breasts. She was completely naked. The man beside her took a little longer to react, and she had to punch him twice.

He looked around frantic. "What's wrong?" he asked.

The man was blond. It wasn't Mayden. Finn lifted the taper higher in the air. "Are you the only two here?"

"Yes, my lord," the man said, getting to his feet to pull on his pants. He scrambled like a kid caught with his hand in the biscuit jar.

"Richard?" Finn asked. He tossed the man his shirt.

"Did you find anything up here?" Robin asked from the doorway.

"I paid you to protect her, you numbskull."

"I did," he floundered. "I am."

"By sleeping with her?" Finn cried.

He turned to Katherine, who'd had the good grace to wrap herself in the counterpane. "Where's Mayden?"

"How am I supposed to know?" she cried.

"He hasn't been here?"

"Not that I know of."

Finn turned to Robin. "Did you find anything downstairs?"

"Nothing but Mrs. Ross. She threw a skillet at me." He rubbed absently at his head.

"Sorry about that," Finn murmured.

Marcus poked his head around the corner of the door. "What did you find?"

"No one is here but them. There's a young man asleep in the barn. But he said no one has been here. The only horses here apparently belong to him." He moved his chin toward Richard.

"No one has been here," Richard confirmed. "What's this about?"

"Mayden sent a note that said he was here. With Katherine."

"Over my dead body," the man grunted.

"That's probably what would have happened if he'd shown up the way I did. You were like a sitting goose, you idiot."

"Well, he's not here," the man said petulantly.

"I can see that."

"Where is he, Finn?" Katherine asked.

Marcus, Finn, and Robin all spoke at the same time. "It was a trick."

Finn flew down the stairs as though the hounds of hell were after him. Young Benny Ross met him at the bottom of the stairs. "We'll need fresh horses, Benny."

The boy just looked at him. "Now!" he bellowed.

"Yes, my lord," the boy said, ducking his head as he ran around the house and toward the stables.

Mrs. Ross pressed a wrapped bundle of meat and cheese into Finn's hand and said, "You need to eat."

"I can't." He could probably run all the way back to London and not stop, he was so scared.

"My Benny will be a few minutes with the horses, what with changing over the saddles and everything." She pressed the bundle into his hands again and gave him a cup of water. He drank the water and split the food up between the men. She pressed water into their hands too. "None of you will be good for anything if you fall over from hunger. Now eat."

"Yes, ma'am," Finn mumbled. What was taking so long?

"I'm sure Ramsdale didn't let Claire leave the hall. And he's going to stay with Sophie." Robin paced back and forth across the floor. He probably had visions of his last wife and what had happened to her with Mayden. But she hadn't been a faerie, for Christ's sake. The Thornes could take care of themselves, even without their father's protection, couldn't they?

"Everything will be just fine," Mrs. Ross said, bustling around to be sure they were all taken care of. "Miss Thorne is such a lovely lady."

"Mrs. Trimble," he corrected.

"Beg your pardon?" She looked confused.

"Claire Thorne is now Claire Trimble. We were married today."

"You don't say?" Mr. Ross said, stomping into the room. His gray hair was askew, and he had a severe limp. It was a good thing Mayden hadn't come here. With only Mr. Ross, Benny, and Richard to protect her, Katherine had been fully exposed. "Congratulations," he said, clapping Finn on the back.

Benny rushed back into the house. "Your horses

are ready, Your Grace," he said. He looked at Finn. "My lord."

Finn ran out the door and leaped onto one of the horses. He had to get back to London. He had to get back to Claire. He had to be certain she was all right. He felt sure she was with her family, anxiously waiting for his return. She had better be with her family.

❧

Claire covered a yawn and moved her chess piece. "Checkmate," she said.

Sophia knocked the remaining pieces to the tabletop. "That's two out of three. Do you want to go for three out of five?"

"I want to go to bed." Claire yawned again. She wouldn't go to bed. She'd never be able to sleep. "Set the board up again," she said, instead.

Wilkins stepped into the room and held a missive out to Sophia on a silver salver. She took it and opened it, and then her face broke into a smile. She laid a hand over her heart. "They're fine." She held the note out to her father and he read it, the faint lines around his mouth softening as he smiled.

"Thank heavens," he breathed.

Claire took it from him and read.

> *Dearest Sophia,*
>   *Mayden has been apprehended, and we will return as soon as possible. We've need of food and a brief rest.*
>
>   *Always,*
>   *Ashley*

Robinsworth must have sent a runner to inform them. That was very thoughtful of him. Claire would never have been able to sleep if she hadn't known what fate had befallen them.

"I wonder what happened when they caught him," she said. Where would they keep Mayden through the night? Surely Robinsworth would have mentioned if they were injured or not.

"We'll find out soon enough," her father said, laying a comfortable hand on the top of her head. "It's late. Your mother and I will take you to Lord Phineas's house on the way to Ramsdale House."

"Are you certain you'll be safe, Sophia?" Claire asked.

Footmen lingered in the room, pouring tea and bringing coffee and food. "There are enough men here to forge an army."

She was right. The hall was like a fortress, they had so much staff. Claire got to her feet and kissed Sophia on the cheek. "Good night."

"Good night," her sister replied as she walked them to the door.

Claire stepped out into the chilly night air and wrapped her arms around herself. She was almost giddy with relief. Finn was well. Marcus and the duke were well. They were on their way home and would probably arrive after they had a good rest and got some food.

The carriage stopped, and two of the duke's footmen walked her to the door. Finn's butler met them at the door, holding it open for her. "Good evening, my lady," he said formally. "Might I offer my felicitations on your marriage?"

Claire slapped her naked hands with her gloves. "You may. And I accept." She turned to go up the stairs, but his voice stopped her.

"Would you like a bath, my lady?" the butler asked with a smile.

"Thank you, but no," Claire breathed. She wanted to do nothing but sleep.

She took the stairs slowly, feeling as though a great weight had been lifted from her shoulders. Finn would be home soon, probably before she even woke.

Claire stepped into her room and didn't bother to call for a maid to help her undress. Finn usually did it for her, and she'd gotten used to his attention. No one else would do.

Claire took off her dress and hung it over a chair, and then kicked off her slippers. It was a bit chilly in the bedchamber; she would have to ask the staff to bolster the fire.

It wasn't until she was about to pull her chemise over her head that she saw the shadow move against the far wall. She froze. A voice came at her through the shadows of the room. "Good evening, Miss Thorne," the Earl of Mayden said.

Thirty-Five

CLAIRE WRAPPED HER ARMS AROUND HERSELF AND fought back a shiver. The man would respect her more if she had a backbone. Or did respect even matter? The man was mad. She could see it in his gray eyes. The way he couldn't focus on any one thing for any length of time. The way he scratched at his chest as if he needed to remove a barnacle. The way he fidgeted from foot to foot.

"So nice of you to make an appointment to talk," Claire said. "It's a pity my husband isn't here to welcome you." She shrugged into Finn's dressing gown, which hung on the back of their bedchamber door.

"I'm certain he'll appreciate that I paid a social visit on this the day of your wedding."

"I'm certain he will."

"Where is Lord Phineas?" Mayden asked as he perched himself on the edge of the bed. Claire would have to burn the linens when he finally removed himself.

"He should be home any moment," she said. Her heart was tripping like mad, but she refused to let the earl see how discomfited she was.

His eyes narrowed. Then he grinned. It was a diabolical display of mirth. "It'll take him quite a while to get here from Bedfordshire." He pulled out his watch fob and glanced at it. "We still have hours left to entertain one another."

He crossed the room to her, and Claire steeled herself, forcing her body to remain still rather than retreat. His arms shot out so quickly that Claire wasn't expecting it. His long, slender fingers grappled in her hair, dragging her closer, his greedy fingers pulling so harshly that she covered his hands with hers. "I don't like it when you lie to me, Claire."

He had a score to settle. This wasn't just a matter of him being angry at Robinsworth and Finn. Claire had humiliated him publicly when she'd kneed him in the groin and stomped on his hand. This was about more than just money. It was about his pride. "I'd apologize for lying to you, but you'd accuse me of lying again."

Claire flinched when he let go of her hair with one hand and raised it high to the side. Pain exploded on the side of her face, snapping her head to the left so quickly that her neck wrenched. Tears came to her eyes as she looked down at the floor. He wanted to cow her.

Her grandmother had once told her that, when you're in a bad situation, whatever you do to save yourself is all right, as long as you come out of it alive. Claire would go against her nature and bow to the mad earl. "I'm sorry I lied to you," she said.

His grip eased marginally. "That's better."

"What do you want?"

One corner of his mouth quirked up. "What do

I want?" He made a sucking noise with his teeth. "What do I want?"

"I asked you first," Claire said.

His hand in her hair tightened.

Claire rushed to say, "I asked you first because I value what you have to say."

His eyes narrowed at her.

"You're obviously a smart man. Look what you have gotten away with." His chest puffed out with pride.

"I am a clever man. One must be clever to be an earl."

"That's true. Your kind is smarter by nature than the average gentleman."

"Like Lord Phineas," he sneered. "He's a lord, but he's not titled. Therefore, not as intelligent."

Finn looked like a genius compared to this man. But that was because of the earl's madness rather than because of intelligence. Goodness, she wished Finn were there. But she was glad he wasn't. "Is there anything I can do for you, my lord? Shall I call for tea?"

He reached into the waistband of his pants and pulled out the pistol she hadn't even noticed he had. Finn would have noticed such a thing. But she'd had no idea. "If you call for anyone, Lord Phineas will come home to find nothing more than your lifeless body draped across the floor."

Claire nodded. "I understand." He seemed to calm down when she talked. So, she continued. "What was she like?"

"Who?" he asked.

"The late Duchess of Robinsworth," she clarified. She wanted to say, *The woman you threw from the tower.*

The one you killed. But that might set him off. "What was she like?"

His lips pulled back in a feral smile. "Easy. She was easy to manipulate. Easy to lie to. I could do just about anything to her, she was that lonely, and she would preen and walk around as if I'd given her the world."

"Why her?" Claire asked. The earl took his hand out of her hair and shoved her into a chair. He sat down across from her. Pulling back the hammer of the gun he held, he shook it at her.

"She was promised to me, until her family found out Robinsworth had more money. He was a duke. I was to be an earl. We were of comparable lineage. But he married her." He hit his chest with his closed fist. "She was supposed to be mine."

"You loved her?" Claire asked. He'd tossed her from the tower, but she wouldn't bring that up. Not yet.

He snorted. It was a sound with no mirth. "She was but a thing."

"I see," Claire replied.

The earl suddenly jumped to his feet. "Just what do you see? You see that she was supposed to be mine? You see that Robinsworth ruined me. That he and his brother continue to ruin me."

"I'm sorry," she said.

But he wasn't happy with her pity, if the look on his face was any indication. "I don't want to talk anymore," he snarled.

"All right."

Claire would be quiet. She would do whatever he wanted. There was a time when she would have fought him without a thought. But now she wouldn't.

She had a life growing inside her. Someone she was responsible for. Did he know about the life she carried? She certainly wasn't going to tell him.

Mayden crossed to the sideboard and opened the doors. "Does Lord Phineas have any whiskey in here?" he asked.

Oh, thank heavens. She could wait until he was foxed and then overtake him. But Finn's bottle was empty. The earl cursed.

"I could call for more."

He ground his back teeth together. "Quiet!" he barked. "You will not call for anyone."

Claire didn't say anything more. The earl scrubbed at his eyes with the heels of his hands. How long had it been since he'd slept? Too long, apparently.

"They think they can ruin me," the man mumbled as he paced. "They are wrong."

Claire didn't reply. When would Finn be back? By now, he knew the circumstances. He knew the earl wasn't in Bedfordshire. He was probably racing hell for leather to get back to her. Just as Robinsworth was racing toward Sophia. How could anyone know which of them Mayden would go to first?

"Why me?" she blurted.

"Why what?" he asked. It was almost as though Claire was jerking him from a fog.

"Why did you choose me? Why not Robinsworth's new wife?"

"The duke has too many servants about. Lord Phineas lives like he's in bachelor's quarters. It's much easier." He cackled. "But don't worry. I'll be going there next."

"Which brother do you hate more?" Claire asked.

"I hate them equally. They both contributed to my ruin." He hit himself in the chest again with his fist. "They called in my debts."

"What are you going to ask for in exchange for me?"

His eyes glimmered in the dark room. This was what madness looked like. "What makes you think you'll still be alive when he gets here?" The gleam in his eye made Claire's heart lurch. Then he raised the gun and swung it at her head. Pain exploded at her temple and darkness was all she saw.

❦

Finn burst through the doors of his home so hard that the windows rattled. "My lord," the butler said, "What is the matter?"

"Where is Miss Thorne?" he barked.

"She's still abed, my lord," the man said. "She didn't get home until very late last night."

Finn bolted up the stairs and ran into his bedchamber, stopping short when he saw Claire lying on the floor. He ran to her and rolled her onto her back. She stirred, groaning low in her throat. A knot was growing at her temple, angry and purple. "Wake up, Claire," he urged.

Finn had never been so happy to see anyone in his life as he was her. She was injured, but she was alive. He could feel her heart beating beneath the hand he laid on her chest.

"Claire," he called, jostling her a bit.

She was wrapped in his dressing gown, her nightrail peeping from where it opened. Claire blinked her green eyes open and a smile curved the corners of her lips. "You're home," she said softly. But then her eyes focused on him, and she looked over his shoulder. "Mayden," she whispered.

"I know. Where is he?" She looked so damn good that he didn't want to take his eyes off her.

"Behind you," she whispered.

Finn turned and looked over his shoulder. "Hullo, Mayden," he said.

"Lord Phineas," the man said. "I'd like for you to let go of your lovely wife and stand up. Hold your hands where I can see them."

Finn lowered her slowly to the floor, where she raised herself to her elbows and looked up. "He's mad, Finn," she warned.

The bump on her head was turning even purpler, and there was blood at her hairline, he noticed. "Not as mad as I am." He stood up and faced Mayden. "You will die for hitting my wife."

"Perhaps. But if I do, I'll take her with me."

"Try it and see what happens." Mayden's eyes were rimmed in red, and he looked like he hadn't slept in days. He was disoriented and confused. Mayden skirted around Claire to where he stood behind her. He wasn't even touching her, but Finn wanted to rip his throat out. He would, as soon as Claire was safe and out of the room.

Mayden now stood behind Claire, who was lumbering to her feet. "Move out of the way, Claire," Finn warned.

He should have known she would try something stupid. She was a faerie, after all, and thought herself invincible. But the blood at her temple proved she wasn't.

"Move out of the way, Claire," he tried again.

Mayden moved the gun, raising it slowly in the air. His hand shook with fatigue, and it would be a miracle if he actually made his shot. But Claire stood between the two men.

"Claire!" Finn snapped. He held out a hand. "Come to me."

Mayden pulled the hammer back, and Finn watched the earl's finger on the trigger. He jumped toward Claire just as fire burst from the tip of the gun. But she jumped toward Mayden, rather than coming toward her husband. Pain hit his chest, flinging him backward as the noise from the shot finally rang around the room. "Claire!" Finn cried.

His backside hit the floor hard, and the wind was knocked out of him. He could barely take a deep breath, but he held up his head long enough to see the length of his dressing gown fly through the air, directly toward Mayden. She hit the earl so hard that he fell from his feet. When he went backward, he fell into the wall, where one of her paintings rested. He didn't fall *on* the painting, however. He fell *into* it instead. Mayden disappeared into the painting, Claire's hand on his foot. He flailed, screaming until his body disappeared, and Claire let her hand sink into the painting, until he was completely gone.

She jerked her hand back and scrambled across the floor to Finn. She picked his head up and laid it in her lap. "Finn," she cried.

❧

Blood was pooling from the wound in his chest, and fear leaped to clench Claire's heart in its fist. She pulled off the dressing gown, balled it up, and pressed it to the hole in his chest.

"How bad is it?" he asked, his breath shallow.

"Not too bad," she squeaked, pressing tightly to the wound. It was awful. Blood was seeping from the wound, despite the pressure she applied. "What were you thinking, you idiot? You walked right into the room with a man holding a gun." Her words came out as great heaving sobs.

"He shot me," Finn said. He looked down, his jaw quivering.

"Yes," Claire shot back. "He shot you."

The dressing gown was soaked in his blood, drenched with his life force.

Finn clutched her hand. "I would do it again. I wouldn't change a thing."

His eyes were closing, as though it was simply too difficult to keep them open. His head lolled to the side and his eyes closed completely. Claire cried out. "Finn!" Fear clogged her lungs. She couldn't breathe.

The butler and Robinsworth burst into the room at the same time. "Finn!" the duke cried as he sank down beside his brother. "Finn," he said more quietly. He sank back on his heels when he saw the stillness of his brother's body. "No," he whispered.

But then Claire saw the painting that sat beside the bed. It was the painting of the house she grew up in, the house in the land of the fae. "Healing waters!" she cried.

"What?" Robin looked confused.

She pointed toward Finn's supine form. His heart still beat. But it was weak from the loss of blood. "There are healing waters in my land."

"What good will they do us there?" the duke gasped out. He took in the lump on her forehead. "I think you have lost your wits."

Claire pointed to the duke and the butler. "Pick him up and follow me."

Claire walked toward the painting. She would lose her wings for this, she was certain of it, but there was no other way to save him.

"Trust me," she ground out, when the duke hesitated.

He motioned to the butler and, together, they picked Finn up and followed her to the bed. She sank a hand into the painting and Robinsworth's eyes grew larger. The butler backed away, taking Finn with him.

"Stop!" the duke ordered. "Follow her," he said.

Carefully, Claire stepped into the painting, and then she held out a hand for Robinsworth to follow. He adjusted Finn so that he held his legs beneath one arm, took her hand with the other, and hoisted himself over the edge of the painting. Finn grunted as he was jostled, and more blood poured from his chest. A bubble of blood escaped his lips.

The butler balked at the last moment, afraid to step into the painting. "I order you to follow," Robinsworth said, using his most ducal you-will-obey-me voice. The man took a deep breath, closed his eyes, and leaped into the painting with them.

When they were all through, Claire looked up at the front porch of the home she'd grown up in. Her grandmother bustled down the steps. "I need healing waters," Claire yelled.

The land of the fae held healing waters for faeries who were injured on missions. It was rarely used, but it was there. Claire wasn't even sure the waters would work on a human. But she couldn't lose him. Not now. Not now that she knew she loved him. She'd never even told him.

"Where are we?" the butler asked.

"In a dream," Robinsworth said. "You'll wake up tomorrow and barely remember any of this." He carefully laid Finn's body in the grass and held his hand tightly, even though Finn was unconscious.

Claire's grandmother bustled down the steps, a vial of shimmering water in her hands. "Will it work?" Claire asked.

Her grandmother shook her head. "I'm not certain."

Claire took the bottle and hunkered down next to Finn. "Drink," she said as she poured it past his lips.

"Now we wait," her grandmother said.

∽

Finn woke to a thousand tiny anvils being pounded by mallets in his head. And someone had stuffed his mouth full of sand. He licked his tongue against the roof of his mouth and blinked his eyes open. Lying beside him was Claire, asleep. She was curled into a ball, fully clothed. Robin slept in a chair across the room. Finn looked toward the window. Night had fallen.

He lifted his head, groaning at the pain of it. "Where the devil am I?" he said.

Claire startled awake. "Finn!" she cried. She rolled

quickly toward him and pressed kisses to his face over and over and over. "I knew you wouldn't die," she whispered, tears rolling down her face.

"I wasn't as certain as you," Finn croaked out. She reached over and got him a glass of water and brought it to his lips. He drank slowly until she pulled the glass away. "Where are we?"

"Land of the fae," Robin said as he woke.

"How did we get here?"

"We came through one of Claire's paintings."

Finn looked down at his naked chest. He'd been shot in the chest. He'd bled. He'd bled so much that her body had been covered with it.

Claire wore her faerie clothing, which she'd once told him was made to shrink and grow when she did. She wasn't wearing his blood. "Am I alive?"

Claire nodded. She'd never looked happier, not in all the time he'd known her.

The butler from home stuck his head in the doorway. "Lord Phineas has awakened?" he asked.

Finn arched a brow at Claire. "We brought the butler to the land of the fae?"

"You're heavy. Robinsworth couldn't carry you all by himself." She shrugged.

"How's the land of the fae treating you?" Finn asked the butler.

"Well, my lord. Very well." He blushed furiously.

"He thinks he's in love." She rolled her eyes.

"So am I," Finn said.

Claire's heart expanded. "I love you too."

"You do?" He looked like a motherless child, looking for hope.

"I gave up my magic for you, didn't I?"

Finn sat up on his elbows, clearly startled. "What are you talking about?"

"It's forbidden to bring anyone to and from the land of the fae without permission," Robin clarified for him. "Claire was aware of it, but she brought us all anyway." He coughed into his closed fist. "She might lose her wings."

"Why would you do such a thing?" Finn cried, the motion of it making his chest hurt. He wasn't healed completely, though he was better than he'd been before.

"Because I love you more than my magic, you dolt." She punched his arm, looking guilty when he winced. "I always will."

Finn's heart swelled in his chest. But at the same time, it broke for her pain. She loved her magic. Yet she'd chosen him over it. "Will they punish you severely?"

She shrugged, taking his hand in hers and clasping it tightly. "I don't care."

"I care enough for both of us." He would never forgive himself if she lost that part of herself because of him. She'd chosen him over magic. She'd picked him for forever. She'd given up the most important thing in her life. He wanted to weep with the beauty of it. "You should have left me to a human physician so you could keep your wings."

"You were dying." She rolled her eyes again. "Don't be obtuse. I picked you, you idiot. You! I picked you. You're all I want. You're all I'll ever want."

A knock sounded at the window and Claire went to thrust it open. Ronald climbed over the sill and landed on the floor. "Can't you use a door?" Finn grumbled.

"Can't you use a window?" the gnome grumbled back. He had him there. If Finn could come and go through windows, he might be inclined to do so. "I have word from the Trusted Few."

He held the note out to her.

She read it quickly, placing a hand to her heart. She read short phrases from it aloud. "Robinsworth, as an ambassador between the two lands, has come forth with a proposition…" She paused, reading some more, looking up at Robin occasionally. "…By decree of the Trusted Few, you may keep your wings on a probationary basis…" She read some more, her brow furrowing. "…Mentor fae that would like to shift from world to world as your penance, and teach those who grew up the way your younger sister Rose did to embrace their magic…"

She stopped reading. Her eyes filled with tears. "Some penance," she said.

"Does this mean we'll have a fae household in London?"

"Apparently. Does that bother you?"

She passed him the note. At the bottom, the instructions also said, "That man you tossed into a painting must be located."

"Can't we just leave him there to rot?"

"Where did you send him?"

Claire shrugged. "I'm not certain. We can check the paintings when we get home and go look for him."

"Wherever he is, my lord, I imagine he's a bit confused," the butler said from the doorway. "Like me."

"You're in the land of the fae," Robin chided. "What do you have to be confused about?"

"I just saw a unicorn prance by, and it turned its nose up at me, Your Grace." The butler laughed.

"They hate to pull carriages. Way too high in the instep, if you ask me." Claire giggled. God, he loved that sound.

Finn reached for the lump at her temple. She had a good-sized bruise on her cheek as well. "Mayden had better hope no one ever finds him in that painting, because I will make him pay for hurting you if he ever comes back."

"I love you," Claire said, clutching his hand.

"Because I was about to die?" he asked. He was teasing, but she wasn't.

She was dead serious when she looked into his eyes. "Because I need you, love you, want you, and can't live without you." She placed his hand on her belly, which had grown even rounder.

"You told me not to fall in love with you," he reminded her.

She pressed her lips to his. "It's a good thing you're not a good listener."

Epilogue

CLAIRE'S ANKLES WERE SWOLLEN TO THE SIZE OF loaves of bread. And her back felt like someone was on the inside, wringing her spine in his hands, twisting until she writhed with the pain. At least the pain was coming and going. It had been since the night before, when Claire and Finn had made love into the wee hours of the morning.

"Sophie swears to me that making love is what brought their first child into the world," Claire said.

He pulled her to sit in front of him in front of the settee. "Then I think we should do it over and over until we bring her into the world," he growled in her ear as he massaged her shoulders.

His hands slipped down and hefted her naked breasts in his palms. "I want to see my son or daughter suckling here," he said quietly in her ear.

"Any excuse to look at my breasts," she teased, slapping at his hands. She turned in his lap and laid her head on his shoulder, her legs draped over the arm of the chair. She was completely naked and so beautiful. He almost hated for her to put clothes on at times. He loved watching her body grow, talking to her belly, and rubbing her all over when she was achy and stiff.

A kick rose against his hand, where it lightly stroked her belly. "Ouch!" she cried. "This one is going to be active," she said.

"You need something to keep you busy," he said.

She snorted. She was constantly busy with the school for faeries that she ran. She got to hand out missions and attend missions with new faeries, and they didn't have to go back and forth to the land of the fae and leave their human families for very long.

She also stayed busy helping with Finn's investigations. She could play the part of anyone he made up, and play it to perfection. He didn't ask her to do it often in her state, but at times, it was helpful to have her around.

As she'd gotten bigger, it had become more and more difficult to go into and out of paintings. So, they hadn't yet located Mayden. But they'd checked all the paintings that were not of real places, and he wasn't in any of those. If he had been, he would have been stuck there. Instead, he'd been tossed into a real place and was now fending for himself wherever he ended up. They'd find him eventually. But it hadn't happened yet.

Claire's belly tightened beneath his hand. "What was that?" he asked.

"That was your son. I believe he's ready to make an appearance in the world." She grunted and lumbered to her feet. "You had better send for the physician. And my mother."

Sophia had had her baby two weeks earlier and was

still settling into motherhood. She would visit after the baby was born, Finn was certain. Robin visited with him often and even helped with his investigations. Not to mention that Robin had left some of his land holdings in Finn's care since he'd done such a good job those three months when the duke had been gone.

Finn didn't mind the work. It kept him busy. But no matter what, he always found time for Claire. He loved her to distraction. And when he'd learned that she'd given up her magic for him, that she'd chosen him, his heart had swelled with pride and affection. She'd picked him.

Another contraction racked her small frame as she climbed into bed naked and pulled the counterpane beneath her armpits. She looked up at him. "Finn, I have a secret to tell you," she murmured. "But you have to promise not to be angry at me."

Any time she said that, the hair on the back of his neck stood up and he grew truly fearful. "What is it?"

"The physician said I've gotten awfully big during this pregnancy."

Finn was aware of every nook and cranny of her body. He knew exactly how big she'd gotten. "What of it?"

A contraction racked her frame. "He said there's a good chance we might have more than one baby."

"At one time?" he barked.

"Yes, at once," she said, the contraction easing as her face softened. "I need my mother."

Not long after that, her mother and the physician both arrived. And the physician was right. They had one little girl with pointy ears and one little boy with the same. Two fae children. The boy they named Lucius after Claire's grandfather. And the girl they named Cynthia. As she came into the world, Finn said, "She sounds like a tinkling bell."

Then she let out the biggest cry they'd ever heard. "That's no tinkling bell, my lord," the physician had said. "That's a church bell, which can be heard far and wide." But the moniker stuck. She was often called Tink or Bell when she was old enough to protest the nickname. But she was Lord Phineas's first fae child. The first of many.

Double Enchantment

by Kathryne Kennedy

Too much of a very good thing...

High society enjoys their powers based on their rank, but Lady Jasmina Karlyle's magic causes nothing but trouble. Her simple spell has gone horribly wrong, and now she has a twin running around the London social scene wreaking havoc on her reputation. When both she and her twin get intimately involved with gorgeous shape-shifting stallion Sir Sterling Thorn, Jasmina finds herself in the impossible position of being jealous of herself...

Still isn't enough...

Sterling is irresistibly drawn to Jasmina. She seems to have two completely different sides to her personality though, and the confusion is driving him mad. Is love just the other side of lust...or is what he has with Jasmina much, much more than that?

"A hugely imaginative story with terrific characters, a complex plot, and a heartwarming love story."—Star-Crossed Romance

For more Kathryne Kennedy, visit:

www.sourcebooks.com

Magic Gone Wild

by Judi Fennell

Every time she uses magic, something goes terribly wrong...

Vana wishes she hadn't dropped out of genie training. Now she's determined to get a grip on both her genie magic and her life. But the harder she tries to fix things for her intriguing new master, the more she drives him crazy...

Except there's nothing ever wrong about him...

Pro-football player Zane Harrison finally has control of the family estate and is determined to put to rest his grandfather's eccentric reputation. Until he discovers that behind all the rumors is a real, live genie who stirs feelings in him he's never known before. The more Zane tries to help Vana harness her powers, the more her madcap magic entangles his heart...

"Cleverly written, uproariously funny, with quirky, interesting characters."—RT Book Reviews, 4 Stars

"A fun and sexy world... Sometimes funny, sometimes sweet, but always engaging."—Long and Short Reviews

For more Judi Fennell, visit:

www.sourcebooks.com

Charming Blue

by Kristine Grayson

He's lived through ages with the curse of attracting women… who end up dead…

Once upon a time, he was the most handsome of princes, destined for great things. But now he's a lonely legend, hobbled by a dark history. With too many dead in his wake, Bluebeard escapes the only way he knows how—through the evil spell of alcohol. But it's a far different kind of spell that's been ruining his life for centuries.

How will she survive this killer Prince Charming?

Jodi Walters is a fixer, someone who can put magic back in order. She's the best in Hollywood at her game. But Blue has a problem she's never encountered before—and worse, she finds herself perilously attracted to him.

"A beguiling mystery is matched in power by the palpable and forbidden attraction… one of the best series installments to date."—*Publishers Weekly*

For more Kristine Grayson, visit:

www.sourcebooks.com

About the Author

As half of the Lydia Dare writing team, Tammy Falkner has cowritten ten books, including *In the Heat of the Bite*, *A Certain Wolfish Charm*, and *Wolfishly Yours*, named by *Publishers Weekly* as one of the Top 10 Best Fall Romance Books of 2012. She is a huge fan of Regency England, and her new series explores the theory that the fae can walk between the glittering world of the *ton* and their own land. The first book in the series, *A Lady and Her Magic*, garnered glowing reviews. *RT Book Reviews* called it "charming and filled with the magic of love and faith, joy and trust, family and friends. Falkner's tale whisks readers into a realm of enchantment… 4 Stars."

Tammy lives on a farm in rural North Carolina with her husband and a house full of boys, a few dogs, and a cat or five. Visit her website: www.tammyfalkner.com.